The Date Coach

Ellie Finch

The Date Coach by Ellie Finch

Published by Enfield Books, LLC. 7901 4th St N STE 300, St. Petersburg, FL 33702

ISBN: 978-1-7337057-0-7

Chapter One

While Brett What's-His-Name and his new girlfriend vomited heartfelt, emotional thank-you's at her over the edge of her desk, Meredith Hartman tried to care. Tried to have a normal emotional response. Tried to be happy for them. Tried very, very hard.

"I've been in love with Lacey for years," Brett gushed, his full cheeks pink with either new-love or early-onset rosacea. "Without your help, I never would have been confident enough to stand in a relationship with her."

Meredith bent her face into a smile, the struggle like trying to bend a metal spoon with her mind. "I'm so happy for you."

"And I can't believe I never noticed Brett before." The aforementioned Lacey, sweetly pretty in a colorful dress, stared at her new beau with gooey heart eyes.

If nothing else, it gave Meredith a second to roll her own eyes.

Bad form. Rude, Meredith. Pay attention to the client.

This was exactly the result people paid her for, after all. If nothing else, this soppy display of a happy ending would be good for business. She braced both hands on her desk and swiped an imaginary speck of dust off the immaculate wooden surface to give herself a moment to pull it together.

Darling, bland Lacey continued on. "But your coaching changed our lives! Thanks to that little bit of a push from you, I was able to see Brett in a whole new way. Thanks to you, I feel like I've found..." Lacey took a long, meaningful beat to gaze lovingly at her boyfriend.

Meredith clenched her jaw, bit a smile so sharp it could have crunched bone, and braced herself.

Please don't say soul mate. Please don't say soul mate.

"My soul mate!"

Lacey glowed with happiness. Brett swelled with such love and adoration as he stared at his girlfriend, he looked ready to float away. And Meredith swallowed down a gag.

"I'm so happy for the two of you."

Did that sound too obviously fake and mocking? Meredith thought it sounded wildly insincere.

The lovebirds didn't notice.

With a hearty chuckle, his arm wrapped possessively around Lacey's waist, Brett said, "Thanks for everything, Coach Hartman! We'll be sure to invite you to the wedding!"

Lacey laughed along. "Yes! Our guest of honor!"

Meredith grinned and nodded. A normal person would grin and nod at this moment, right? Although what did normal even mean, anyway? Clearly, these two were not normal. A normal person did not start planning their wedding to someone after going on four lukewarm, arguably-successful dates together. "I look forward to that!"

As Meredith stepped out from behind her desk and adjusted her pencil skirt, she gave herself credit for sounding like a sincere person instead of a cynical robot. *Job well done, Hartman. Now get them out of here.*

With a gentle but firm hand on Brett's shoulder, she steered them towards the door of her small, single-room office. Her heels clicked and creaked on the hardwood, and she brushed the ends of her long blonde hair back over her shoulder. "Thanks very much for letting me know how it went. You've been a great client, Brett. I'm glad the coaching I gave you helped you improve your confidence and your dating life."

This part of the interaction, she could say with some sincerity. This was her business, after all, and she believed in the necessity and efficacy of her product, if nothing else. True love? Soul mates? Nonsense. But improving the quality and success rate of a first date through sociologically- and psychologically-backed coaching? That, she believed in. That, she was good at.

"You've been amazing, Coach Hartman." As Brett reached out and shook Meredith's hand, he kept his other arm firmly planted on Lacey. As if he still couldn't believe she was real, was with him. As if he was terrified she would run away the second he let go of her.

Meredith's stomach turned and twisted with something sickening and sour at the sight.

She shut the door to her office behind the happy couple, and good riddance to them. Behind the safety of the thin, frosted glass door, Meredith sighed and sank as she released her pent-up tension. The beginnings of a migraine pricked at her temples, and she pressed her fingertips against her forehead to relieve the pressure.

They probably would get married, to be fair.

Meredith bet five years before they imploded in inevitable divorce.

Five years before Brett's possessive insecurities drove Lacey to a breaking point. Five years before Lacey realized that nice and treats me well were not lofty, high standards for an ideal man, but were instead bare minimum, dirt-floor basement requirements for a partner.

Five years. Max.

But for now, she was done with the two of them. Done with trying to coach Brett through the basics of consent, small talk, reading nonverbal cues, etiquette, grooming, manners, and other essential human patterns necessary for a successful dating life that any grown man should have learned by now. And yet, many of them had not. It was shocking, the level to which society would excuse men their bad behavior, would let them get away with a lack of socialization and empathy.

Thankfully for her, she supposed. Otherwise she wouldn't have a business.

And thankfully, many of them were not bad people. Her clients may lack some basic learned empathy and social skills, but those things could be taught to someone willing to learn. The men who came to her as clients were, by her own rules and investigations, not bad people. Their self-awareness that they needed to change, needed to learn how to treat people better, and how to think of women as people instead of some terrifying prize, was a good start.

She had to accept her own limitations, though. She wasn't a therapist—to achieve that, she would have actually had to have finished that master's degree instead of dropping out after one semester. There was only so much she could do to nudge people in the right direction.

She shook off the uncomfortable, lingering unease of the saccharine, sickening meeting, straightened her back and shoulders, and went back to her desk.

Of course, to be fair, not all of her clients were miserable lumps like Brett had been. As Meredith flipped through her appointment book, she considered her upcoming afternoon appointment and had to give credit to the occasional outliers to her business. Her two o'clock, Mr. Jack Benson, was definitely not a lump. A thirty-something man who had recently come out as gay, all he really needed was a bit of support and advice as he stepped into a dating world that was completely new to him. She also took on the occasional middle-aged or older client, a newly-divorced man or woman, nervous to get back onto the dating scene after so many years off the market. Once in a while, women who had been burned by past partners came to her for guidance on how to know if a date was looking for something serious, or just a fling.

Most of her clients were lumps, though. Decent guys, for the most part. Not hopeless cases. Not miserable or cruel or gross. Just a bit lost. Guys who wore baggy jeans and t-shirts printed with nerdy references. Guys who understood being nice wasn't enough, but also didn't know what else they had going for them or how to show it. Guys who had spoken to an actual human woman once or twice, and daydreamed of doing it again someday. Those guys were her bread and butter. They paid the bulk of her rent and student loans. She had two more of them on her schedule for the week.

But not this afternoon.

A thick knock rattled her door, exactly on time at two p.m., and the shadow of a large, looming figure, built like a linebacker, darkened nearly the entire window. "Come in!"

Mr. Benson stepped into her office and ducked his head to avoid brushing his scalp against the door frame. With a shy smile, he waved a big, dark brown hand at her in greeting. "Hi, Meredith."

"Hey, Jack!" At this greeting, Meredith's smile was authentic, warm, and easy. "Come on in. How has your week been?"

After a few minutes of small talk across the desk, Meredith slipped a folder out of one of her side drawers and got the appointment rolling. "Now, I know one of your biggest concerns when we spoke last week was where to meet potential dates, since you're not interested in going to bars or clubs, and you don't want to join a dating app right away."

Mr. Benson shrugged his wide shoulders. "Can you imagine me at a club? I would scare everyone off. They would think I was the bouncer."

Meredith laughed, but she sincerely doubted this client would have trouble finding someone to hook up with at a club. Tall, dark, and handsome, he was not an unattractive man. However, Meredith knew from years of coaching people on dates that comfort and confidence were half the battle. It would not be a smart move to send Mr. Benson into a scene where his discomfort would show. And besides, she knew from their initial consultation that Mr. Benson was more looking for someone to watch a football game or walk in the park with, less someone to party with. Thankfully, she had prepared for this. She slid the folder across to him, and he opened it gently. "I did some research, and I found a few options for you. These are clubs and social groups for gay men and LGBTQ people across the city."

6

As Mr. Benson flipped through the print-outs and flyers she had gathered for him, his eyes narrowed and he nodded along. He hummed a thoughtful noise in the back of his throat. "Gay Men's Choir. Gay Men's Soccer League. Association for Black LBGTQ Professionals." He paused at one and held it up, his mouth quirked in a smirk. "Gay Basket Weaving Club?"

"That one seemed like a bit of a longshot for you," Meredith conceded with a laugh.

"Probably." He winked at her and slid that one to the back of the pile. "But the rest of these look great! There's some really interesting groups here. I never knew most of these existed."

"I think it would be good for you to join something like this. For one thing, it could be a good place to find potential dates. But also, it would be nice for you to make some friends and build a support network, now that you're out."

Mr. Benson nodded, sincere and sure. "I do want to get more involved in the community." He gave a self-effacing, charming shrug and a smile. "And if one of the gentlemen in the Association for Black LBGTQ Professionals happens to be handsome and single and looking for a burly lawyer to cook him brunch…"

Meredith grinned. "Then all the better!"

As she worked through the rest of the meeting, Meredith's face stayed soft and relaxed, and her headache faded. Mr. Benson was the sort of client she loved working for. Open, honest, self-reflective, socially-aware, just in need of a little boost. If, someday, he came to her office to invite her to his wedding, she would probably even manage to be truly happy for him. She probably wouldn't even make bets on his chances of divorce.

Probably.

No promises, though, considering the absurdly high divorce rate in this country, not to mention the sickening fallacy of true love, commercialized and shoved down the throats of every man, woman, and child in the form of diamond ads and romanticized holidays.

But, probably she would be happy for Mr. Benson someday.

Chapter Two

"Mm-hmm. Yeah." Ryan nodded and stared at the pretty, petite brunette who sat at the table across from him while she talked about her latest project at work. "That's really interesting."

"Isn't it?" Kelly asked, her soft pink mouth quirked in a smile that didn't quite reach her round eyes. "It's right up my alley, too. I know a lot of people find them tedious, but contracts and negotiations are totally my jam! I really love…"

And Ryan paid attention. Really. He did! He did not share her enthusiasm for contracts and negotiations, but he appreciated her zeal and passion. Always, he liked hearing people talk about the things that interested them, and her animated story was endearing. And she was pretty. Overhead, the dim golden lights of the neighborhood bar illuminated the soft and shiny waves of her brown curls. She had nice eyes. A great smile. She was, objectively, attractive.

So why the hell wasn't he attracted to her?

While she talked, he lifted his cold beer glass and gulped down a swig of pale ale. He nearly missed the coaster when he thunked it back down, and the misstep had his heart picking up speed. Not in a good way.

He just had to try harder. He smiled—forced a smile. Nodded. Studied the way her hands moved, her fingers quick and animated as she spoke.

Nothing.

No chemistry. No attraction. No tingle or spark or fireworks or fluttering or anything. While an objectively beautiful woman sat across the table from him and lifted a martini glass to her plush, pink lips, Ryan felt nothing.

Again.

What the hell was wrong with him? Why could he never get this right?

He grit his jaw and had to look away for a moment. While she set her glass back down, he fidgeted and rubbed his fingertip through the drops of condensation on the woodgrain tabletop.

Cheap woodgrain. Cheaper lacquer, unevenly applied. Bad craftsmanship.

"So, what is it you do?" she asked.

"Oh." He took another sip of his beer. Set it down. Picked at the edge of the coaster. "I build furniture."

Eyes wide, unsure how to respond, she nodded. "Cool! That's…great. What sort of…?"

"Stuff for houses, mostly." His response was short and stilted and nothing else came to him. There was plenty more he could say! Like, that he custom designed each piece? Like, that he was really passionate about his work and loved doing it, that he put a lot of time and energy into everything he did, that he loved experimenting with different materials and sometimes went walking through the local forests for inspiration? Like, maybe, he could mention that he ran his own business? That he had a shop? That people from across the country contacted him for specially designed dining tables and cabinets? Maybe, literally just…anything? All of it caught in his throat. Probably, she wouldn't care. He shouldn't talk too much about himself. And besides, he could already feel this date was going nowhere, so it didn't make much sense to share anything personal. Anything about himself. "Yeah. That's what I do."

Kelly's pretty face fell and she forced a cheap, plastic smile. "Great."

A few more awkward minutes of small talk, and then Kelly made her excuses. It was nice meeting him, thanks for coming out, she'd had fun but it was a work night, so she'd better get going…The usual.

Out on the sidewalk outside the bar, the streetlights were just coming on and the early fall evening chilled as the sun went down below the line of office buildings and restaurants in Dupont Circle. "This was nice," she said as she forced a smile and shoved out her hand for him to shake. "But I don't think either of us was really feeling it. So I won't lie and say I'll be calling you again."

"Yep." Ryan shook her hand. "Totally understand."

With a little wave and a smile over her shoulder, she pulled her coat tighter around her frame while she walked away. "Have a nice life!"

"You too!" he called after her, and then felt awkward and stupid about it. Dammit. He stood on the pavement outside the bar and kicked the toe of his beat-up sneaker against the pavement with his hands shoved down in his pockets. He had to walk in the same direction to get to the metro station, and he didn't want to act creepy and tail her for three blocks. It was fine. He would just wait. By himself. Lonely and miserable.

He was being dramatic. She was just a nice girl he'd matched with on Tinder. They'd texted a bit and decided to meet up after work. Nothing grand and sweeping, nothing super romantic. Neither of them had high expectations. It was just a date. Nothing more.

But Ryan had never been able to get the hang of dating. While the people around him paired off, hooked up, went out, he constantly felt out of step. Not majorly so. Just like he was half a step off, never quite feeling what he was supposed to be feeling, never quite able to connect with the people he tried to date, never quite right. It was frustrating. Exhausting.

When enough time had passed to give Kelly some space, he set off at a walk around the park and rode the long escalator down into the Dupont Circle station for a metro ride back home. On the train, he stood and held onto one of the handrails, stared down at the blackened, rubbery spots of ancient gum permanently stuck to the dingy orange carpet, and felt lost. What was wrong with him?

It was fully dark and getting cold by the time he creaked open the little gate in front of his rented Eastern Market rowhome. A squat old two-story brick building with a small yard, the trees out front were just beginning to turn yellow. Golden light poured out from the front window as he walked up the path and fumbled through his pockets to find his keys.

The door swung open.

He looked up and found his roommate and best friend standing in the doorway in her pajamas. Loose joggers and a big, oversized sweater that hung off her shoulders drowned her tall, thin frame in soft and casual fabric. Her chestnut brown hair was pulled up in a sloppy bun on top of her head. Naomi blocked the whole doorway and studied him with a skeptical look while light shone behind her. One of her eyebrows lifted. She tilted her head to the side. "You fucked it up."

Ryan sighed. "I fucked it up."

Tender and mocking, she shook her head and stepped to the side to let him in. "There's Chinese takeout on the counter."

"Did you order for me?" Ryan asked as he stripped off his coat and sneakers and left them in a pile by the door. "Because you knew I was going to fuck it up?"

Naomi patted his shoulder and nodded as she walked past, the tread of her footsteps heavy and sure on their squeaky old wood floors. A few minutes later, armed with a giant bowl of lo mein noodles, he plopped down next to her on their couch. While he sighed long out his nose and stared at the book she'd left propped open on the coffee table, she asked him, "Want to talk about it?"

He shrugged. "Nothing to talk about, really."

"What went wrong this time?" She tugged her legs up underneath her and sat curled on the other end of the plush old sofa. It was lumpy and run-down. They'd had it since they'd bought it off of Craigslist in their junior year of college, for their first apartment off campus, and it desperately needed to be replaced. Ryan didn't work with textiles, though. Didn't know how to sew well enough to manage it. Over the years, he'd made most of their furniture. The coffee table in front of them, plus the matching side tables in a gorgeous light pine he'd shaped and sanded to perfection. Their long, asymmetrical dining table, with the rough edges of tree bark and swirling grains of wood pattern still visible, was one of his favorite pieces. He'd used scrap for that, unwanted and useless materials, and filled in the imperfections in the wood with slivers of turquoise. Couches, though, he couldn't do. So while Ryan filled the living space of their row home with personalized furniture, and Naomi covered the walls with original paintings and framed photos and decorative throws, their couch remained a sad and lumpy eyesore.

Really, he should just buy a new one. They both had the money now.

Maybe they kept it for nostalgia.

She gave him space. Let him take a few bites of his food. There wasn't much to say. "It went the same as it always goes. I don't know why I even try anymore."

"You didn't feel a connection at all? Didn't feel attracted to her?"

Ryan shook his head. "And then I panicked and shut down and grunted answers and acted like a complete bore. So, you know. The usual."

Naomi huffed a little laugh.

"I just wish it wasn't so awkward!" He thunked the bowl down on the table and leaned forward to rest his forearms on his knees. "Why does dating have to be this weird, formal interview process, where you sit across from someone and study them to determine whether or not you'd like to sleep with each other? It's so forced! I just want to be friends with someone first. You know?"

Naomi nodded. Peered at him. Raised an eyebrow.

Ryan sighed. "What?"

"Nothing!" She shrugged, the oversized teal sweater slipping down off her bronze shoulder. "I didn't say anything."

"No, but I can hear you thinking." He glared at her. "Just tell me. You know you're going to tell me."

It only took a second of hesitation for Naomi to pop out with it. "Have you considered that you might be demisexual?"

"No." Ryan blinked. "Because I don't know what that word means."

Naomi managed to look only a little bit smug, and her voice shifted into teacher tone. She spent her days as a coach and counselor at a Spanish language community center for girls, mentoring them and teaching them leadership skills. The switch from supportive friend to competent instructor was instantaneous. "It's a person who only feels sexual attraction after they already have a strong emotional connection with someone. So if you're demi…" She shrugged. "You wouldn't feel attracted to someone on a first date. Ever. There's nothing wrong with that, but if you feel like it's wrong, then it makes sense that you would get in your head, and panic, and shut down."

Ryan's eyes narrowed as he considered this. "What? No. Really? Is that really a thing?"

She nodded. Her brown eyes twinkled with kind amusement. "Yeah. It's really a thing."

With a groan, Ryan dragged his fingers through his hair and pushed his honey brown curls off his forehead. Did that make sense? Was that who he was?

Maybe.

It had always been like that for him. Always.

He'd had one serious girlfriend in college. And then another serious girlfriend a few years ago. Both of them had been people in his friend circle, and romance had grown slow and steady out of friendship. Never had he been the type to hook up, to date casually, to mess around. It just wasn't who he was. He didn't see anything wrong with casual hook-ups for other people; he had just never felt the urge himself. He liked relationships. Thrived in them. Wanted one now. And couldn't seem to meet the right person. Nothing ever clicked. He tried online dating because what the hell else was a twenty-something in DC supposed to do? He matched with people. He went on dates. And he felt no spark, no connection, nothing. Like something was wrong with him.

Maybe Naomi was right. Maybe it was because he just wasn't wired to feel that sort of spark right away. Maybe he was the sort of person who needed time to get to know someone.

Maybe he had been going about dating all wrong.

Maybe he was…whatever she had called it. Demisexual.

With a long hiss of breath, he sighed. "I'm assuming you have a pamphlet or something about this?"

Naomi snorted. "Of course I have a pamphlet. I always have a pamphlet. I'm going to the LGBTQ health center tomorrow for my support group. I'll grab you a whole bushel of pamphlets."

"You're the best." He groaned as he stretched out and shoved up the sleeves of his sweater to reveal strong, tan forearms. "If only you were attracted to men or I was a woman, I think we would be soulmates."

Naomi winced. "You think I'd be attracted to you if I was into men?"

"Ouch!" Ryan laughed. "Hurtful!"

"No, no, no, you're great! You're totally a catch!" She rushed with a laugh and sat up higher on her knees with her legs tucked beneath her. Her whole face lit up as she teased him. "But any possibility of me ever being attracted to you in any imaginable realm died in our first week of freshman year! Remember? You know why!"

"No!" While his face flushed red, Ryan hissed and snorted laughter into his hands. Ever since the all-knowing algorithms at George Mason's student housing office matched them and stuck them together in a run-down dorm room as freshman roommates, Ryan and Naomi had been inseparable best friends. They clicked. Got each other. And they had been there for each other through times good and bad, from Ryan's issues with his parents, to Naomi's health and emotional challenges while transitioning to live as her true gender, through break-ups, bad grades, stupid choices, and big accomplishments. All of it. And that meant that, unfortunately, Naomi had seen some shit. He waved a hand to try and stop her, but he knew exactly what was coming. "We don't speak of that, you traitor!"

She drove on, unhesitating to embarrass him. "First weekend of the semester. I barely knew you. And I came home to find you...? Remember? Remember what you were doing? Sitting on the floor in your underpants, crying into a bowl of microwaved mac and cheese, while looking at pictures of baby pandas in your biology textbook."

"They were so small!" Ryan shouted in his defense, through shaking laughter. "And also, that was the first time I ever got drunk! Don't be mean!"

"I'm not being mean!" She laughed, rather meanly. "I'm just saying. That killed any sliver of potential you ever could have had with me. That incident firmly cemented you into doofy, idiotic brother status in my mind."

"Yeah. That's fair."

"Hey." The laugher fell from her face as she scooted closer on the couch and took one of his hands. "You trust me. Right?"

"Of course." Ryan gave her hand a squeeze. "You're literally the only person I do trust."

"That's sad. But okay." Naomi took a breath and Ryan tensed as he couldn't help but notice it looked like she was bracing herself for something. It came a second later. "I made you an appointment."

Ryan winced and pulled back. "Therapy? I really don't want to go to therapy."

"Why don't you want to go to therapy? Everyone goes to therapy these days! It's the hip thing to do. Therapy is the new brunch!" She scoffed at him, shook her head, and changed the subject. "Anyway, no. Not therapy. I know you have been in a rut. I know you've been lonely. So I made an appointment for you with a dating coach."

"No. No, no, no." Disgusted, Ryan's face scrunched up in distaste as he shook his head and pulled away from her to squish against the arm of the sofa. "A dating coach? Naomi, no! I don't want help from some sleazy, chauvinistic men's rights pick-up artist who's going to teach me how to score. That's gross!"

"Excuse me!" She flicked his forehead with a long, manicured fingernail. Fast and tripping, she admonished him with a glare. "Did you get hit on the head? Did you forget who I am? Do you think I forgot who you are? What universe are you living in that you think I would ever send you to someone like that?"

"I don't know!" He grabbed her wrist and held it safely down on her lap so she couldn't flick him again. Those nails were sharp.

"It's not like that. First of all, this is a woman. She uses psychology and sociology to help people get over their hang-ups, work through their issues, and connect on dates. And if you talk to her about how you want to be friends with someone first, she'll be able to give you recommendations for new ways to get out and meet people. Is that acceptable to you?"

Skeptical, Ryan said, "Maybe. Still kind of sounds like therapy."

"Tough shit. You're going. And you're going to be grateful that I didn't make you an actual therapy appointment. Yes?"

It sounded kind of terrible.

But...

He was having trouble. Trouble meeting people, trouble connecting with people, trouble with wondering if something was wrong with him.

Maybe it wasn't such a terrible idea. Naomi had never steered him wrong before. As he said, he did trust her.

Ryan sighed and relented. "Yes. Fine."

"Good." Naomi smiled and went back to her own side of the couch, though she did stretch out her legs and prop one foot up on his lap. "I think it will be good for you."

"Good for me...or good for you, because if this is successful, you'll get the house to yourself more often?"

She shot him a beaming, beatific smile. "Both!"

He snorted a laugh and reached for the remote. "Want to Netflix and chill?"

"That doesn't mean what you think it means."

"Sure it does." Ryan shrugged and faked innocence, because he obviously knew what Netflix and chill meant, but also he liked to rile Naomi up. "It's self-explanatory. Netflix and chill, you know? Watch Netflix. And chill."

Long and dramatic, Naomi sighed. "It's like you're a baby bird. A sweet, stupid little baby bird."

Ryan laughed and flicked the arch of her foot with a calloused finger.

"Ow!" She kicked him, but they both laughed and settled in while he turned on the TV.

Before they went their separate ways for the night, Ryan thought to ask her, "So when is this appointment, anyway?"

"Tuesday," Naomi told him. "At noon."

"Okay." It was Thursday. Which meant he had the weekend to mentally prepare. To talk himself into it. Or to talk himself out of it.

Chapter Three

First meetings were always the worst. Meredith hated them more than just about anything, and the lead-up always made her nerves jangle. Tense, her stomach clenching in anticipation, she sipped on a coffee as she walked back to her office building. Thank goodness for the Starbucks across the street. With a new client meeting rapidly approaching, she couldn't handle proper food.

And he had scheduled it right for noon, of all times. Apparently she was skipping lunch today.

Meredith keyed in the code to get back into her building, and the pane glass door of the renovated townhouse beeped as it gave her entry. Through the narrow hallway and up two flights of creaking old stairs, she ran through everything she needed to keep straight in her head. First meetings were important. And potentially conflict-ridden. She had worked hard to build up her reputation, and her website made it pretty clear what sort of services she did—and did not—offer, but still, the occasional creep snuck through. In addition to explaining the packages and products she offered, she would have to analyze this new guy—his motives, his attitudes, his reasons for being here. Was he genuine and decent? Or was he a jerk with a backwards view of women? And if he ended up being the latter, could she kick him out of her office and refuse service without getting stab-murdered? It was a lot to figure out in a first meeting, and she—

Nearly ran into someone standing on the landing outside her office door.

Her coffee sloshed through the lid and splattered droplets onto her hand as she jerked backwards, surprised. "Whoa!"

"Sorry!" The guy reached out a hand to catch her and stop her from falling backwards down the stairs, but she regained her footing and his hand stopped short of actual contact. "I'm so sorry! Didn't mean to take you by surprise."

"It's okay," Meredith laughed as she tried not to be annoyed. Great. Now she had a coffee stain on the cuff of her white blouse. Her heart slowed its frantic pace, recovering quickly from being startled. It took a lot to startle her. Even more to ruffle her. This was no good. Like armor, she pulled her composure back on, drew in a breath, and pushed her blonde hair back behind her ear. With a pleasant smile and friendly tone, she said, "You must be my noon appointment."

"Yeah." The guy smiled, though the look might have been more of a bashful grimace. "Sorry. I'm a bit early."

"It's fine!" Quick and considering, she flicked her eyes up and down his body, took in his frame, his clothes, the features of his face. Cute. Strong. Tall. Nice body. That was unusual enough for her clientele to make him stand out right away. Most of the guys who came to her were a little pudgy, a little soft—not bad looking by any means, but not attractive enough to skate by on looks alone. This guy, though? Handsome. Chiseled, even. He had broad shoulders, a strong chest that tapered into a narrow waist. Nice arms. Nice face, too. Kind brown eyes with crinkly little smile lines at the corners. A strong, cutting jaw line, but soft, full lips. A mop of curly honey-brown hair that flopped down over his forehead. Damn. Meredith blinked and cleared her throat, caught by his attractive strength, his affable presence for a second too long. This guy was good looking. Very good looking.

So what the hell was the problem? Why was he meeting with her?

Well. Meredith quirked an eyebrow and kept her thoughts to herself as she unlocked the door and led him into her office. For one thing, he had absolutely no sense of style. In ripped up baggy jeans and an oversized red flannel shirt with the sleeves rolled up his forearms, he looked…unpolished. Careless. That was an easy fix. And an extra fifty dollars for her, when she scheduled him for a clothing consultation.

Already, she was tabulating out her prices.

"Please, come in. Have a seat." As she stepped behind her desk and motioned for him to take one of the chairs opposite, he stood and looked around the room with pensive approval. She pulled out his file and flipped it open to check the details: Ryan McKenna, age twenty-seven, referred here by a friend, Naomi Martinez. His roommate and best friend, so she said on the phone. Over the top of the file folder, though, she lifted her eyes to peer at him, watched him as he took in the bright unshaded windows, the simple wood floors, the small blue couch and cream-colored arm chairs that created a little nook in one corner of the room.

He nodded to himself as he sat down. "Nice office."

"Thanks."

He was still staring. Looking around. Taking it all in. Avoiding looking at her.

She gave him another minute to simmer.

Interesting.

After a few seconds of awkward, full silence, he leaned forward and brushed his hand against the mahogany surface of her desktop. "Where did you get this desk?"

Odd. Not good at small talk. Uncomfortable in new social situations. Meredith made a few more notes in her head while she peered at him.

"Sorry." He grinned, his face bashful and charming. It lit up his eyes. With a wave of his hand, he explained, "I just noticed that all of the other furniture is different. Ikea flat-pack kind of stuff. But the desk isn't like that. It's nice. I like it."

Meredith nodded. "It came with the office. Whoever rented this place before me left it behind."

"Oh! So you didn't pick this?"

"No. And I wouldn't have picked it." She laid her hands flat on the dark, polished wood of the wide desktop. It looked too big, too heavy, too imposing beneath her long, ivory-pale fingers. Too masculine. Too aggressive. "It's fine. It's just not really my style."

"You would have picked something..." He leaned back a little in his chair and studied her, his head tilted to one size. She felt his eyes skim over the lines of her face, her hair, her collarbones, over the sharp cut of her high cheekbones and her gray blazer. She held herself poised, waiting, until he said, "Something sleek. Modern. Something lighter."

"Yeah," Meredith said, as she added perceptive to her growing list of client observations. That was good. A good quality, something she could work with and build on. "Exactly."

The conversation died there. Her client shifted in his seat and fidgeted, pressed the tips of his fingers together. Looked away.

Interesting.

Meredith brushed her hair back and threw the client a lifeline, since he was clearly too hesitant to keep the conversation going. "So. Ryan McKenna. Tell me about yourself. What do you do?"

He laughed a little bit and gave the desk a pointed look. "I design furniture."

"Oh! Okay. That makes sense." Meredith grabbed a pen and clicked it just to have something to do with her hands. "Tell me more about that."

"I…" He shrugged. "Have a shop? I make things. Furniture…things."

She clicked the pen a few more times and peered down the long line of her nose while the poor guy fidgeted and fumbled and tried to answer the question. She cut to the point, which had quickly become apparent. "You don't like talking about yourself."

He slumped a little, his shoulders sagging in relief, and laughed. "I really do not like talking about myself."

Interesting. "Why not?"

"Why not? Who likes talking about themselves?"

"Hmm. In my experience?" Meredith lifted one eyebrow and smirked. "Most people. Although, they pretend like they don't. You really don't, though. Why?"

Her client smiled to himself, bewildered and good-natured, and shook his head. "Because no one wants to hear it? No one cares. Who wants to listen to someone drone on and on about themselves? No one. That's awful. I don't want to be that rude and oblivious."

Meredith's eyes narrowed as she zeroed in on his word choice. "So you think no one cares about you, and that's why you don't like to talk about yourself?"

His brown eyes went wide and glittering, his mouth dropped open in an *oh*, and he barked a laugh. Meredith kept her face cool and impassive as he leaned forward and rested his elbows on the edge of the desk, folded his hands together. "See, I was told that this would not be therapy! But this is feeling a little like therapy."

"I assure you, it's not therapy. I'm not a therapist."

He scoffed and nodded at the wall over her shoulder. "I don't know. That thing on the wall there looks very much like a Psychology degree. From Georgetown, too. Good school. They could probably teach you a lot about therapy."

"It's a B.A. I never got my master's or doctorate." She stopped herself from explaining any further—from explaining that she had started her M.A. but dropped out. Her clients didn't need to know that. It made her seem weak. Incapable. Incompetent. She was not those things. "And I am not here to help you work through your issues. I here to help you improve your dating life. Sometimes that means helping you get to the root of how you're holding yourself back. Not therapy. Dating advice."

His eyes narrowed. "With some psychology."

"Is there anything in this world that doesn't involve some psychology? You just analyzed my personality to determine what sort of furniture I would prefer. You think that didn't involve psychology?"

He leaned back and crossed his arms over his chest. "Touché."

"Alright." Meredith straightened her file folder and held her pen poised over the client sheet, ready to make notes. "Let's get back to this, then. Tell me about yourself, and please remember that you are literally paying me to listen. What do you do for a living?"

With a breath and a pause, he explained that he designed and made custom furniture pieces, that he owned a small shop and workspace. He gave a few details about what sort of designs he created. And then cut himself off with a wave of his hand. "Anyway, that's all there is to it. It's not that exciting."

"Really?" Meredith clicked the pen a few more times. "Because I'm hearing that you are a craftsman, an artisan, someone who owns his own business, someone who works with his hands. There's a lot of interesting stuff there."

Interesting...and attractive. Women he went on dates with would eat this up, if only he felt comfortable sharing it.

She picked his brain and background for a few more minutes, got him to share tidbits about himself. He didn't offer much freely, but he answered without fuss when faced with direct questions.

That was a good sign. Trainable. Already, she had ideas for how to develop coaching for him.

She made a few notes on the sheet and then got down to serious business. "So why are you here, Ryan? Tell me about your dating life."

"I..." He cleared his throat and looked down at his hands. But answered simply. Without any complaining. Already, within fifteen minutes, she was chipping away at the walls he had up and getting him to talk a little more freely. All it took was some direct questions, some deliberate signs of interest. Yes, definitely trainable. She could work with this guy. He explained, "I have been trying to date. I've met people online, gone on a bunch of dates. And they never go well."

"Okay." Meredith pushed, prodded. It was what she was good at. "How do they go badly?"

"Well…I never feel a connection. And then I get in my head about that, and that makes me nervous, so I don't open up or share anything."

Meredith paused. Her eyes narrowed. "Don't you think that might be a bit self-fulfilling? Connection has to go both ways. How can you expect to feel anything if you don't open up at all?"

Ryan sighed and winced, his nose scrunching up while he bit back a sardonic smile. "Maybe. You might have a point."

"I always have a point."

"Okay, but it doesn't quite feel exactly like that, though." He leaned forward, energized. "I feel like there's a little more to it than just that."

"You never feel a connection." Meredith considered this, considered the reasons for it. "Have you dated or had relationships in the past?"

"Yeah. I've had a couple serious girlfriends. But both of them started off as friends. You know? I think I might be the sort of person who needs a little more time?"

"Ah." Meredith nodded. "And so dating apps in DC are really not doing you any favors."

"Yeah. Exactly. I hate the whole way that it happens."

"Okay." Workable. Definitely workable. For sure, she could help this guy out, if the problems really were what he said they were.

She grabbed some paperwork and flyers from a desk drawer and slid them across to him. "Well, I definitely think I can help you out. For you, I would recommend a basic package, which is six weeks of personalized coaching. Based on what you're telling me today, I would focus on some of your communication and self-esteem issues—"

"Self-esteem issues?"

Meredith forged onward. "Workshops and practice sessions to help you open up, feel more comfortable sharing things about yourself. I'd do a few chemistry and attraction sessions, to help you identify what attraction means to you and how to help yourself feel it. I'll coach you on alternatives to online dating, options that will let you get to know people first. That basic package also includes four practice dates with me or with one of my associates, so we can get a feel for how the coaching is going and what we need to adjust. The prices for that are listed here…" She tapped at the paper while he glared down at it. "And I would also recommend a few add-ons. Not much for you, honestly. Based on my experience, you seem very coachable. But I would suggest you add on the make-over package, so I can shop with you and help you look your best."

His eyes widened a fraction and he glanced down at himself. "I don't look my best?"

"No," she whispered unequivocally and shook her head as she sized up the awful, disheartening sight of that ratty old flannel shirt hiding his muscled frame. "No you do not."

"Oh." Ryan nodded to himself. "Okay. I mean. These are work clothes."

"Mm-hmm." Sharp and pointed, she questioned him. "So you don't wear things like that when you're going on a date?"

"Maybe?" He winced while she smirked. "Alright, alright, fine! You know what? Fine. Do the whole thing. The basic package. Plus the add-on where you take me to the mall and turn me into a hot princess."

"Yeah." Meredith nodded, amused but trying not to show it. "That's exactly what will happen."

He nodded and laughed and held eye contact while he said, "Great. I look forward to it." And it sounded genuine. Sincere. "You really think this will help? First impression: I'm not doomed to die alone?"

She laughed. "First impression? You're fine. You just need a change and a little push. I do think this will help you. First thing's first, though." She grabbed her phone and sent off a quick text to her friend, roommate, and sometimes-business-associate Richelle to confirm her schedule. Richelle got back immediately. "I'm sending you on a practice date with a friend of mine. She's going to test you out, see if she notices anything else we should be working on. I'll design the coaching based on what you've told me, and also on whatever she picks up on. Sound okay?"

"Perfect."

"Great." Meredith looked down at her phone and texted Richelle back while she spoke to Ryan in a dull, uncompromising tone. "This is not a real date. She is not interested in dating you for real. She is not interested in dating men at all. Treat it as close to an actual first date as you can. Try your best to act natural. Flirt, if you feel the urge—she will probably flirt with you. It's fake. It's a test. If you are rude or inappropriate with her…" She finished up the text, hit send, and looked up at Ryan. "I'll cut your balls off. Okay?"

He blinked and nodded. "Got it."

"Great!"

It only took a few more minutes to finalize everything. She set Ryan up for his test date with Richelle on Thursday evening, and then for a follow-up back at the office on Friday. By Friday, she would know for sure whether or not she would actually work with him—Richelle helped her pinpoint areas for improvement and blind spots, yes. But mostly she tested to make sure the men who came to her as clients really were people Meredith wanted to work with. Ryan seemed like a decent sort, and Meredith had pretty good instincts after running this business for three years, but you could never really know at first.

"You can close that on your way out," she said from her desk when Ryan left, armed with his paperwork and Richelle's contact information.

"Have a good day," he told her. Again, sincere. Friendly. Warm. He had a nice smile. "Thanks for meeting with me and for not thinking I'm completely hopeless!"

Self-deprecating, self-effacing—maybe a little too much. Sense of humor. Several good things. Lots to work with.

She watched him leave, thoughtful. It was early, but she had a good feeling about this one.

Once the door was shut and she was left alone in her quiet, sunny office, she scribbled down a few more notes—observations and thoughts about how she should tailor his coaching, what she would focus on.

By the time she remembered to drink it, her coffee had gone cold.

Chapter Four

On a street corner outside the Eastern Market metro station, Ryan stood with his hands in the pockets of his jacket and tried not to feel like a total doofus while he waited for his fake date. All around him, the sidewalk bustled. People in suits on their way home from jobs on Capitol Hill. Hip young artists with streaks of blue in their hair, pushing strollers and carrying canvas bags of groceries. And then him. Uncomfortable and awkward, in a shirt that was too tight around the arms, and his least ripped up pair of jeans. After Meredith's rather pointed comments about his wardrobe, he'd gone home and considered his options…and realized that he didn't have any. But what was wrong with that? He wore what he was comfortable in.

Except this time, with Meredith's sharp, condescending look fresh in his mind, he had pulled on an old shirt—a green button-up flannel that was a little nicer than the others. It didn't quite fit. So he wasn't comfortable, now was he?

Thanks to Meredith.

She was…something. Spiky. Pointy. Not afraid to jab and prod and pick someone apart. It was refreshing, to be honest. He didn't hate it. Kind of appreciated it. Too many people he'd met tried to skate around issues, to soften a blow before hitting him. It could be frustrating. He liked that Meredith Hartman seemed to know her own mind and wasn't afraid to speak it. It made it easier to trust her in this weird coaching process, and to know where things stood.

A gust of wind picked up and crept through the outer layer of his jacket, and he hunched in tighter to ward against it. A few more weeks, and the weather would be freezing.

"Hi! Are you Ryan?"

He looked up from the pavement and found a woman approaching him. With a big, soft halo of natural black curls, a bright smile, and pretty brown eyes, she looked beautiful and friendly. "Hi. Richelle?"

"That's me!" She held out her hand as she closed the distance between them, and he shook it while greeting her. Grinning, she looked him up and down and nodded to herself. "Okay. Okay. You're cute! Nice and tall. Like the hair. Not my type, mind you, but definitely someone's type!"

"Thank you!" Ryan said cheerfully, though the compliments made him feel even more awkward and small than he had felt when Meredith told him his clothes were horrible. "And thanks for meeting me!"

"Sure thing!" She gestured over her shoulder. "There's a good bar up the block. Want to head there and grab a drink?"

"Perfect. Lead the way."

As they walked side-by-side up the sidewalk, dodging around evening neighborhood commuters on their way home or out to restaurants, Ryan had no problem with small talk. Richelle was bubbly, effusive, and easy to chat with. He asked about her day—a little hectic, but fine—and about how she met Meredith—college, in a sorority. "I know she seems all cool and collected now, but Meredith was quite the peppy little blonde princess back at Georgetown!" Richelle laughed at the bit of teasing gossip.

"Wow." Ryan shook his head, amused. "I have only met her the once, but that is hard to picture."

"Right?" Richelle nudged him with her elbow, though the padding of her stylish navy blue pea coat softened the jab. "Let me guess; she was wearing a blazer when you went in? Pencil skirt? Heels? Looked real sharp?"

"Yeah." Ryan nodded after he thought about it. That had been exactly her look—very sleek and professional. A little sharp. A little intimidating. It had matched her personality. "Is she always like that?"

"Always! Even at home. She's a great roommate, though. The two of us have a place up by U Street. Great place, but old, you know? I send Meredith out to be our bull dog whenever the landlord tries to pull one over on us. How about you?" she asked. "Where are you living? You have roommates?"

"I'm, like…" He looked around and tried to orient himself. There was the park. So that meant… He pointed to the right. "Four blocks that way. Right around here. And I do have one roommate. Naomi. She's my best friend."

Richelle glanced at him. "You live with a woman?"

"Yeah. For a while now. Since college, actually. We've had other roommates over the years, but right now it's just the two of us."

One of Richelle's eyebrows lifted. "You ever think that maybe that's part of why you're having trouble dating? Your dates feel threatened by you living with a woman?"

Ryan prickled a bit at that, defensive. It was a little on-the-nose, too. He'd broken up with Rebecca, his college girlfriend, partly because she couldn't handle how close he was to Naomi. Naomi was more than a friend—she was family to him. He tried to keep the edge of annoyance out of his voice when he said, "She's really important to me, so I wouldn't want to date someone who couldn't understand that. And anyway, she's gay, so it would be pretty ridiculous for a woman I was dating to feel threatened by her."

This stopped Richelle short. "Your best friend and roommate is a lesbian?"

He nodded and rubbed at the back of his neck.

"Something you and Meredith have in common!" Approval of this rolled through Richelle's body. Eyes closed, she lifted her hands in a little sign of praise. "Ryan. You are speaking my language. We're going to have fun tonight. I can tell."

"Thank you."

As they approached a drug store, she pointed and mentioned, "I need to run in here real quick, if you don't mind."

"No, of course not."

"Oh, dammit!" Right outside the entrance to the store, the bright fluorescent lights spilling out onto the pavement through the automatic glass doors, she stopped and stomped her foot. "I totally forgot! I have a really important email I need to send to my boss. Could you do me a huge, huge favor?"

"Sure." Ryan watched while she dug through her purse and pulled out her wallet. "What do you need?"

Brusque, while pulling out her phone with her other hand, she shoved a ten-dollar bill into his fist. "While I send this off, could you run in and buy me a box of tampons?"

Ryan blinked at the abrupt exchange, but quickly said, "Yeah, no problem. Preference on size, brand?"

"Regular. Store brand is fine." She winked over her shoulder while her thumbs flew and clacked over the screen of her phone. "Thanks, you're a doll!"

Money in-hand, mission in-mind, Ryan made it halfway down the personal hygiene aisle before the complete absurdity of this scenario struck him. He paused. Stared at a clip of pink and purple poufs that dangled precariously from a rack of shampoo. This was weird, right? It was weird for a woman he'd just met ten minutes ago to send him off to buy tampons.

Oh.

He laughed to himself.

This was a test. It had to be. What had Meredith said? That her friend would test him out? Confident in his realization, Ryan walked onward and found the right box. He would feel proud of himself, satisfied that he had passed, but honestly, what sort of loser wouldn't buy a woman a box of tampons? Did they really have people who failed that simple test?

Weird.

He paid and went back outside, where Richelle was waiting, no longer on the phone. "Thank you so much!"

"This was a test, wasn't it?" Ryan handed over the box, receipt, and change, which she dumped unceremoniously into her large, slouchy purse.

"Yep." Richelle grinned and popped the p at the end of the word.

"And you passed. So, well done!"

"Seriously?" Ryan asked as they kept walking. "Who fails that?"

With wide eyes that suggested she had seen horrors he could only begin to imagine, she shook her head. "You'd be shocked by how many men refuse to believe women have actual, living bodies. Although, since you live with a woman, I'm sure you're used to that sort of thing."

"Yeah." It took a second for Ryan to shake off the sad, heavy disappointment in his own gender. "Well, she's trans. So never this scenario in particular."

Richelle looked surprised by that detail, too, but didn't comment on it as she swung the worn wooden door to the bar open and ushered him inside. He grabbed them a high-top table and ordered—a beer for him, a wine for her. And they chatted.

To Ryan's shock and pleasant surprise, the "date" did not fall apart in the first five minutes.

It didn't even fall apart in the first thirty minutes.

When Richelle mentioned she was hungry, they ordered mozzarella sticks to share and talked and laughed over a couple of drinks. It was great. Fun. Easy, even though Richelle had a quick mind and a quick tongue, and it could be hard to keep up with her.

Richelle groaned as she bit into a snack, the cheese oozing in a string as she pulled it away from her mouth. "These are great. You know what this sauce needs, though? Fresh basil. I've just started teaching myself how to make pasta."

"You make your own pasta? That's really cool! Isn't that hard?"

"No, not really! It just takes some patience. Lots of practice to get the kneading and the cutting right."

"Why did you decide to start doing that?"

"Oh, well…" While Richelle explained the origins of her pasta obsession, Ryan sipped his beer and nodded along. She was engaging and interesting. Fun to listen to. "What about you?" she asked. "Do you cook?"

"I do cook! I don't make my own pasta or anything that impressive, but I know my way around a kitchen."

Richelle set her wine glass down. "So what's your specialty? If you were going to cook your best dish for me, what would it be?"

"Crepes," he answered without hesitating. "I make a good crepe. I recommend the Nutella and banana. It's the perfect food, too. Good for breakfast, good for hangovers, good for dessert. I also make a decent shawarma. Pretty good at tacos." He cocked his head to one side, thoughtful. "Apparently, my specialty is thin bread-like materials that you fold in half and fill with things?"

Richelle laughed and announced she was coming over to his place for dinner.

"So what do you do?" she asked.

And he didn't panic or shut down. They were laughing, they were talking, it was fine! He didn't need to go spilling his whole life story or monopolizing the conversation, but it felt okay to tell her, "I build and design furniture. I have a shop and a workspace a few blocks from here."

"What?" She slammed her hands down flat on the table and rattled their glasses. "That's amazing! What kind of furniture?"

He shrugged. "All woodworking. Table sets and armoires. I do a lot of custom doors. Like, front doors, for people who want something unique for their house. It's…yeah." And there it was. Too much. It all caught up to him. Before he could choke, he cut himself off and smoothly adjusted. "It's neat. What do you do?"

She noticed the discomfort, the rapid deflection and change of subject, but allowed it. "I'm a teacher. I teach art at a private elementary school."

"That's incredible! That must be pretty challenging?"

"Oh yeah. You have no idea. The kids are great! Amazing and creative. It's the parents who give me trouble, but not too often."

"That's awesome. My roommate works with kids too."

"Oh yeah?"

He nodded. "She works at a Spanish language community center, in an after-school program for girls. She teaches them leadership skills and coaches their soccer team. She's great at it!"

"She's good with kids? And she speaks Spanish?" When Ryan nodded, Richelle pressed a fluttering hand to her collarbone and batted her long eyelashes. "I do love a bilingual woman."

"You would really like her, actually." Ryan was biased and thought that everyone on the planet should like Naomi. But also, as he leaned back and considered it, he thought they would get along well. Both were vibrant, vivacious, interesting, and beautiful women. Both worked with kids. Both liked art and culture. Both were loyal friends. The more he thought about it, the more he realized they probably would really hit it off. "You two should meet."

Richelle smiled and shrugged one shoulder. "Maybe I will, when you invite me over for Nutella crepes!"

The whole thing went so well.

Ryan enjoyed it.

Until all of a sudden, with a heavy, twisting dread that tangled up in his throat and sank down to sit writhing in his lower stomach, he realized that he had fucked it up.

He was supposed to think of this as a date.

But it didn't feel like a date at all. It felt like getting to know a new friend, with no strings and no expectations, no rules and no egos. Definitely no expectation of sexual chemistry for him to miss, to bungle, and to feel wrong-footed about.

Dammit.

He gulped down a mouthful of cold beer.

"Okay, I have to ask." Richelle drained the last of her second glass of wine. "What is the deal here? I don't get it. You're sweet. You're funny. You know how to cook and clean and take care of yourself. You have a good, interesting job. You respect women you're not interested in sleeping with, and more than that, you seem to genuinely enjoy and value friendships with women. You're a bit shy and not willing to talk about yourself much, but that's literally the only note I have to give to Meredith so far. So what gives? What's the catch?"

"I...ugh." Ryan groaned and hung his head in his hands. Laughing, but annoyed with himself, he explained, "This isn't real! I messed this all up. This has been awesome, but I knew it wasn't real from the start, so I didn't feel any pressure to...feel attracted to you? I guess? I don't know! You're really fun and nice, and I just get along well with lesbians. I'm sorry. This was a failed scenario."

Full and warm, Richelle threw her head back and laughed at him.

Her smooth dark brown cheeks bunched up into perfect apples above her grin, and her eyes squeezed shut while she shook her head. "You're cute, Ryan."

"I'm hopeless. But thank you."

"Not hopeless." She reached across the table and patted the back of his hand, gentle and kind. "This was still useful. I'll tell Meredith you passed all my tests with flying colors."

"Thank you. I feel like I should be angry that every topic of conversation you brought up tonight was a secret test, but I'm not. I'm just amazed that you managed to flow all of that into conversation so smoothly. Impressive."

"Thank you, thank you." She gave a little tip of her head. "Hold on, though. You said you feel pressure to feel attracted to people? Is that what makes dating hard for you?"

Ryan chewed on the inside of his lip and nodded. "I never feel that spark right away, and then that makes me nervous. Like something's wrong with me."

"And then you shut down?"

"Yeah."

Richelle studied him for a long second. "Huh."

Ryan tried not to squirm under the attention. And then he didn't quite know why he said it. Maybe because Richelle's gaze was too piercing, too all-seeing? Maybe because he wanted an excuse to talk up Naomi some more? He added, quietly, "Naomi recently brought to my attention that I might be demisexual."

"Okay. Okay." Richelle nodded, her round brown eyes sincere and kind. "You know there's nothing wrong with that. Nothing wrong with you. Lots of people are somewhere in that spectrum. Way more than you'd think."

"Yeah. Thank you." He fidgeted and drew in a breath but didn't look away or pull back. She was too kind. He didn't want to bristle too much. And honestly, it didn't feel like that big or life-changing of a deal. Just...maybe something he was. Maybe something that made dating a little harder. "I've been reading a lot about it, and it makes sense. Naomi gave me a bunch of pamphlets."

Richelle leaned back and smirked. "Naomi sounds wise and insightful. And like she's a good friend."

"She is, she's the best." Ryan jumped on the opportunity to change the subject, to get attention off of him...and also maybe to play matchmaker a bit. "Plus, she's gorgeous."

"Subtle." Richelle fake glared at him for a moment while he tried to look innocent and unassuming. Finally, she laughed and rolled her eyes. "Okay, I'll bite. Is she single?"

"She is single! Want me to call her? She could meet us here." He reached into his pocket and pulled out his phone while he spoke, and flipped through his gallery until he found a nice picture of Naomi. One of his favorite shots of her, it showed his friend in shorts and a tank top, her long brown waves of hair up in a loose pony tail, grinning like the sun while she coached her soccer team to victory. "Here, that's what she looks like."

"Damn." Richelle's eyes went wide. And then closed. And then wide again. "Wow. Okay. Yes. Fine. Call her."

So Ryan did, and he laughed to himself while the phone rang and Richelle went to get herself another glass of wine.

"Hey, how did your fake date go?" Naomi asked on the other end of the line.

"Great! Still going, actually. Are you in your pajamas already?"

"Obviously, yes."

"Okay, throw some clothes on and get over here as fast as you can. I'll text you the address." He glanced at Richelle, who was just out of hearing distance up at the dimly-lit bar, her figure soft and curvy under her tunic and leggings. He lowered his voice anyway, a little thrill of excitement zipping up his spine as he conspired. "I have your next girlfriend here."

"Ryan! I can't just—"

"She's a gorgeous, brilliant, funny, artistic lesbian woman who works with kids and has a good job and wants to meet you. Her jaw about fell off when she saw your picture. So put some pants on and get your ass down here."

Naomi only hesitated for a second before she announced, "I'm on my way."

A loud thunk on the other end of the line, followed by a muttered, *ouch, fuck,* told him Naomi had just tried to leap over the coffee table to get to the stairs. Good. Good hustle. He laughed to himself as he hung up and texted her the name of the bar.

When Richelle approached with her hands full—she had thoughtfully grabbed him another beer while she was up there—he told her, "She's on her way."

Richelle squealed and did a silly little wiggle dance as she sat back down. "Oh lord. I can't believe you talked me into this. This is not how these test dates are supposed to go, my friend! You're going to get me in trouble with Meredith."

Laughing, Ryan raised his hands in surrender. "If you two hit it off, I will gladly take the blame and deal with Meredith's wrath."

"Good luck." She snorted into her wine glass. "Although, my report will soften the blow. I'm going to tell her you passed all my tests. You seem like a good one. She's going to be happy to work with you. We'll help you find true love, don't you worry."

And Ryan tried not to smile too much, because for the first time in a while he didn't feel completely hopeless about his love life.

Chapter Five

When Ryan McKenna knocked on her door and popped his curly head into her office, Meredith greeted him with a bright smile. No one was catching her off-guard this time. She was ready for the meeting. "So? How did it go last night?"

"It went great! Really, really great." As he pulled out a chair and sat down across the desk from her, he spoke with animated enthusiasm. "We went to a bar and had a really nice time. She's lovely. Seriously, she's such a great person—so funny, and charming, and kind. So we had a good time talking and laughing over drinks. And then the night ended with a rousing bout of very loud, hot sex!"

Shocked, Meredith held herself very still, her mouth pursed. She blinked. "Excuse me?"

"With my roommate. I was not involved." The sardonic, amused smile grew across his face as he nodded and said quietly, "She hooked up with my roommate. The two of them really seemed to hit it off. But I had a nice time, too!"

A surprised huff of laugher snuck out through Meredith's cool exterior before she could help herself. "Wait, seriously? Is that why Richelle didn't come home last night? She told me she was staying out, but she stayed over with your roommate?"

Warm and a little mocking, Ryan nodded. "It was fun. She and Naomi woke me up at four in the morning and asked me to make them crepes. I think she had a nice time. They were talking about seeing each other again soon."

"Okay." She sized him up, took in the same style of beat-up clothes he had worn to their first meeting, the bit of stubble on his tan face, the cheeky smile. "I'm not sure if you did that very wrong or very right."

"Fair," he conceded. "Sorry if I wasted your time, though. Like I told her last night, I don't think that was representative of how it would normally go for me."

"It's alright." Meredith shrugged a little. "The first test date is to get insights and see if Richelle's perception of things unveils anything you might have missed, yes. But a lot of it is just checking your general attitude towards women. If you don't respect women in a basic way, then I can't help you date them. I can't help because…I really can't help in that regard. I'm not qualified to undo deep misogyny. As we've established, I am not a therapist. But also, I simply don't want to work with people who have values so dramatically antithetical to my own."

He nodded. "So if I had refused to buy that box of tampons for Richelle?"

"That's not an automatic disqualifier. I will work with people who seem generally decent but who have some internalized bias. I don't mind helping good guys challenge that part of themselves, so long as they're willing to do the work." Conspiratorially, she leaned over the desk a little and hissed in a condescending stage whisper, "But you would be surprised how many guys throw a tantrum right then and there on the street when suddenly confronted with the notion that women have bodies—when all their lives, they thought that women are bodies."

Ryan's face scrunched up in distaste. "Is that safe? For Richelle to put herself into situations like that?"

"It's never safe to be a woman. Even less safe to be a black woman," Meredith said with dull, blunt simplicity. "I have a few friends who do the test dates for me. I never send them out unless I know they're going to be in a public space and they're comfortable with a taser. Richelle, especially, I only send out with guys who don't ring any alarm bells. I knew your best friend was a Latina woman, since she was the one who called me in the first place, so Richelle and I agreed you didn't have any obvious warning signs. We labeled you low risk."

While Ryan considered this, he nodded thoughtfully but said nothing more. He looked pensive.

As he should be.

All men, even the good ones, should be more thoughtful about the sorts of things women had to think about, had to burden themselves with, just to exist safely in the world. Things that would never cross a man's mind—or a straight, cis, white man's mind, anyway. Things like whether it was safe to meet someone online, whether their drink had been tainted, whether they should leave early so they weren't the last person in the parking garage. It was exhausting. A big part of Meredith's job was dealing with men who were good people—who were decent, and respectful, and fine—but who had never considered that lived reality looked very different for people of other genders, races, and sexualities.

All of those things applied to this guy, and the more insight he could have on his own, the better.

Although…he wasn't precisely straight, was he? He was something a little-to-the-side of straight.

When Ryan McKenna had first walked into her office, she had taken one look at his clothes and his muscles and had assumed he would be another typical, oblivious guy client. He wasn't. Her meetings with him, plus all of Richelle's notes and reports, confirmed it. He was one of the ones outside that normal box. One of the ones that was a relief and a pleasure to work for. He was a thoughtful person who had recently discovered something new about his sexuality and who needed a little help figuring out how to live that new discovery in the best, healthiest, most validating way.

It was unexpected and pleasant. Already a little fond, Meredith cut him a break and teased him. "Well. We both agreed that the risk to Richelle's safety was low. What I didn't expect was that you would be a risk to my business. So you're a competitor, huh? Trying your hand at helping people get a date? That's supposed to be my job."

Ryan laughed. "It wasn't date coaching. It was matchmaking. A separate but complementary service to your business. And anyway, I'm out of the game. It was a success, so I don't want to ruin it. One and done."

"Yeah, you'd better be, McKenna. I won't have you poaching all my clients from me." She glared at him and then gestured to the couch and arm chairs in the corner of the room. "Come on. Let's go get started."

Once they were situated, her perched on the petite blue sofa with her ankles crossed, and him in one of the arm chairs, leaning back and trying to look comfortable, Meredith launched. She took a few minutes to explain that based on his comments, Richelle's notes, and her own observations, she was going to tailor his coaching with a three-pronged approach. One: broaden his social circle and embrace that there was nothing wrong with looking for a slower, more natural connection. Two: work on his confidence and willingness to open up and talk about himself. And three: tease out the differences and commonalities between connection and attraction in his mind, so even if he didn't feel attraction immediately, he could work on building connections based on things that were important to him.

"Richelle tells me you're demisexual. Why didn't you mention that the other day?"

Ryan shrugged and looked down at the floor, rubbed one big hand through the hair at the back of his neck. "Because it's really new? I'm not a hundred percent sure it fits me. I only just started considering it as a possibility a week or so ago. I've done a bunch of reading on it, but it's still new for me."

"Okay. And that's completely fair. Do you think that even if that label is not one hundred percent perfect, it still has some truth for you?"

It took him a moment. He bit his lip. And then nodded. "Yeah."

"That's great." Meredith deliberately softened her voice. Normally, she was all business, straight-forward. She wasn't here to hold hands; she was here to get results. But she had compassion for this guy. It was obvious to her that he had gone through the world feeling like something was wrong with him, just a little out of synch, for a while now. A big part of success in this case was going to be helping him accept that he was wasn't wrong—just a little bit different. "All of the coaching I'm suggesting is keeping that part of you centered. Respecting it, celebrating it, and seeing it as a strength you offer, and not as some hurdle you and your partners have to overcome. Does that sound okay to you?"

"Yeah." He bit his cheeks in and nodded along, said nothing more even though his brown eyes were distant and it looked like he wanted to speak. Meredith didn't rush to fill the moment. She let him sit with it, let it linger. Her patience paid off when he cleared his throat, looked away and smiled a little. "Yeah. Thank you. For a while, it has felt like…I don't know. Like everyone was dancing to a different song than I was, maybe? It's never felt like some big disaster or anything. Just kind of…off. It's frustrating. I don't know how you saw that so fast, but thanks."

"It's what I'm here for." One corner of Meredith's mouth lifted in a gentle smirk. "And now look at you, sharing things! What a world of difference a little bit of insight and understanding makes."

He laughed and avoided looking her in the eye, shy and on the spot. Which was fair. Baby steps. They barely knew each other. That was, after all, one of the big goals of this session.

"Now. With that in mind. What dating apps do you use?"

"I'm just on Tinder."

"Great. That makes this easy. Take out your phone. Right now." When he lifted his hips to get at the back pocket of his jeans, the edge of his gray t-shirt rode up and revealed a sliver of taught, tanned stomach. Meredith flicked her eyes away from the sight and admonished herself. Clients were not for ogling. Although, she had to admit that on a purely aesthetic basis, he was a bit ogle-able. Once he had his phone in hand, she ordered, "Delete the app. Now. I don't want you using Tinder or anything like it again. That whole set-up is just going to be toxic and frustrating for you. That style of dating is never going to give you the opportunity to be your best self."

"Done." A dimple crinkled in his cheek as he smiled down at his phone and then up at her, and damn if that wasn't adorable. "That felt pretty good."

"Right? You had a terrible time with it. No need to keep yourself trapped." She crossed her legs in the other direction, flipped open her notepad, and clicked her pen a few times. Once she was settled, and once she had ripped her eyes away from that stupid dimple on his cheek, she got them back on track. "Now. In this session, I'm going to get started delving into the beginnings of those prongs we talked about—places to meet people, how to feel comfortable in your own skin and open up, how to forge meaningful connections. This won't be very structured. We're going to have a conversation and let it go where it goes. But a big part of this is also you learning to open up and get comfortable with me. Right? Because if you don't trust me and share with me, I can't help you."

"Fair. Sounds like therapy. But okay."

"Not therapy. And trust me, once we get going, this won't feel like therapy." She sent him a sugary sweet smile. "I'm too mean and blunt to give you therapy."

He snorted a laugh and looked some combination of amused and threatened.

"So let's dive in. Tell me about your social circle. Who are your friends?"

As he spoke, Ryan leaned forward in his seat and rested his elbows on his knees. He mentioned a few people he had been friends with since high school and college, who he cared about but didn't see often. Plus Naomi. "I'm not great at maintaining a big social circle. I'm pretty introverted. But Naomi has a lot of friends and she has parties at our house once in a while. I get along well with all of her friends. We hosted a wine and paint night last month, with a bunch of her girlfriends."

Interesting. She clicked her pen a few times and peered at him through narrowed eyes. "Are they your friends, or are they Naomi's friends that she lets you borrow sometimes?"

He winced. "Maybe more that one?"

Meredith hummed in the back of her throat. "And where does Naomi meet people? How does she have such a big circle? What is she involved with?"

He considered this. "Most of her friends, she has met either through work or through the LGBTQ+ center where she volunteers."

For a long, unblinking moment, Meredith froze and stared at him. "Ryan. Are all of them lesbians? Was that wine and paint night you, plus a houseful of lesbians? Is your entire social circle lesbian women?"

Laughter burst out of him, sudden and loud, and he blushed and hid his face in his hands while he cackled.

It might have been endearing.

He only laughed harder when Meredith harassed him, and that made her smile. With claps of her hands to accentuate each beat, she shouted, "Do you see the problem inherent in this?"

"Yes! Alright, yes. Maybe." Still giggling to himself, he uncovered his face and shook his head. The laughter had cracked squinty little lines in the tawny, tanned skin around his eyes, and his teeth were white and sharp with a clever bite when he grinned. "You might have a point. I might need to widen my social circle a bit."

"A bit. Yeah." Meredith smirked, but then said more sincerely, "I think it's great that you're the sort of man who is genuine friends with lots of women you're not interested in sleeping with. But if you want a romance to grow naturally out of friendship, you need to start spending social time and becoming friends with women who might actually be interested in you at some point."

"Yep. Fair. Got it."

"Alright, so--"

"Sorry." He cut her off with an apologetic look. "Do you mind if I stand up? This whole set up, with the sitting and the talking, feels really inauthentic and weird."

It took her a second to recover her footing after the interruption. "Of course. Do whatever you need to feel comfortable talking about yourself."

As he stood, he flashed a grin. "Oh, so you have lots of vodka you're planning to share?"

"No." She glared. Quirked an eyebrow. "And I'm more of a whiskey kind of woman, anyway."

"Of course you are."

"What is that supposed to mean?"

"It's just your aura." Laughing, he raised his hands in a pose of surrender. "Whiskey is for bosses. You seem like a boss."

She thought about arguing, but it was true. She was a boss. She was the boss. So she rolled her eyes but gave a little shrug of acknowledgement. "Now. Let's talk about attraction and what that looks like for you."

He groaned and flopped his head forward while he paced slow and steady lines across the wooden floor of her office. As the afternoon sun cast a long comet trail of light through her western-facing windows, he stuck to that lit-up path like a cat and bounced from one end of the room to the other, constantly in motion. Not antsy. Steady. But always moving.

And he did answer her questions. With a lot of laughter, deflecting, and incomplete responses, yes. But he answered. And the more she prodded, the more he opened up.

She stayed seated on the couch and watched his constant movement back and forth, back and forth. "You're not going to feel instant chemistry, and that's fine. But a connection is different than just sexual attraction, and I think it would help you to intentionally try and foster connection right off the bat. You can connect with someone on a lot of things—your values, sense of humor, shared experiences. So what are some of the qualities you want in a partner? What do you need to see in a person to start a connection with them?"

"Like…ideal woman kind of thing?"

"Sure." Meredith's eyes narrowed as she studied him. "What are those ideal woman traits?"

His whole face scrunched up as he thought about it. Ryan McKenna had a very expressive face. Every emotion writ plain across his features, in the lines around his eyes, in the twists of his mouth.

He drew in a deep breath. Puffed out his cheeks. Let the air out in a long sigh. Raised his eyebrows and widened his eyes. Glared at the floor. And his whole body got into it. As he walked and thought, he absently swung and stretched his arms out in an arc, behind and in front of him.

Meredith tried not to laugh. She had never seen someone who looked so physically invested in their own thinking process.

Endearing, she thought, not for the first time about him.

"Competence." After all that thinking, that was what he finally came up with. "Yeah. That's number one. Most attractive. Most…ideal. In a partner. For me, anyway. Competence."

"Competence?" One of Meredith's brows lifted in skeptical mockery. "Seriously?"

He nodded, plain and earnest. "What? Do you know what I mean?"

"No, I know what you mean!" She shrugged and shook her head. "I get that. I just don't think I've ever met a man who wanted the woman in his life to be competent above all else. Most guys want someone who needs them."

Ryan stopped short and peered at her. "Are all of your clients terrible?"

That took Meredith by surprise, and she snorted a laugh before she could stop herself. "A little, yeah."

"Yeah. The business you are in kind of self-selects guys who are not the best." Cheeky and amused, a smile snuck its way across Ryan's face. "Maybe you need to expand your social circle a bit."

Meredith glared at him and rolled her eyes, but bit back a smile as she turned away. "Don't turn my advice back on me. We're here to focus on you. So, competence. What else."

He shrugged and rocked back and forth on the soles of his beat-up sneakers. Awful, atrocious low-top black Chucks, which were nearly drowned by the too-long hem of his frayed jeans. Only emo teenagers going to a Fall Out Boy concert in 2006 could get away with shoes like that, and Meredith looked forward to replacing them very soon.

"Sense of humor. I want someone who makes me laugh. Doesn't everyone?"

No. Women want someone who makes them laugh. Men want someone who laughs at every half-hearted, stale old joke they make, like a VIP audience at the exclusive comedy show of their life.

But Meredith bit the insides of her cheeks and kept her mouth shut. Maybe he had a point. Maybe she was just a tad cynical. "What else?"

"I don't know. All the stuff you mentioned? Similar values, stuff like that." With another big, dramatic sigh, he paused and glared out the window. The light caught tiny hints of red and gold hidden in his honey brown hair. Precise, his voice modulated and rhythmic, he explained, "I want to be with someone who doesn't need me. But they want me around anyway. You know what I mean?"

Meredith stayed very still and fought to control her reaction. Her face was cool and passive, unaffected, her expression unmoving. But if Ryan had known her better, he might have noticed the tightening of her eyes, the slight flare of her nostrils she couldn't quite control. Something sour wriggled in her stomach, an old and near-forgotten tumor, a disease, a poison she'd once swallowed gleefully at someone else's urging. The poison of being needed, the cancerous growth of needing in return. She'd cut it out, cut that needy-needing-needed man and all of his tendrils and hold out, a long time ago. Still, the reminder taunted. That bitter, twisting thing in her stomach lurched and mocked her at the reminder of what she had once let herself become, of what that man all those years ago expected her to give, the quivering, bloody chunks he'd expected her to carve out of her soul and self in the name of his need. Regardless of what either of them had wanted.

People like this client, who understood the poison of need, the health of want, were few and far between.

Maybe it was just lip service. Maybe Ryan McKenna was just the sort of person who knew how to say all the right things. Who knew if he'd actually live up to them?

In her experience? Based on all the people she had known? All the men she had dated? All the relationships she had seen, both through her work and through her friends' experiences?

Probably, he was full of shit.

But…

A small voice, timid in her sharp mind, insisted, maybe not. Probably. But maybe not.

Impassive, giving nothing, she said, "Yeah. I know what you mean."

"Alright, Coach." Ryan sighed, good natured, and waved his hands in a come at me, bro, gesture. "What else you got?"

Meredith paused for a moment and collected her thoughts. With the information he had given her, she could start to develop specialized coaching sessions. Maybe they should—

"You know," he said, interrupting her train of thought. "It doesn't seem entirely fair that you get to ask all the questions."

She lifted a brow. "We're not here for me. We're here for you."

"Yeah, but I'm supposed to trust you, right? It feels pretty unbalanced."

"Fine." Her own answer surprised her, and she rolled her eyes as she gave it. But she told him, "Fine. One for one. You can ask whatever you want."

"Deal. My turn?"

When she nodded, he tilted his head to one side and pointed across the room, to the far wall behind her desk. To her diploma from Georgetown, proudly framed and displayed above the leafy green spray of a potted plant. "Why no master's degree? Or doctorate?"

"Why would you assume I would even want a master's degree?"

"Now look at who's being evasive!" He laughed, the sound round and full, with no malice. When she said nothing, only peered at him, he shook his head and said, "Like I said earlier: you seem like a boss. You strike me as ambitious. High achieving. Like you hold yourself to a high standard. It just kind of makes sense, based on my first impression of you."

Fair point. She looked away and bit back a smile at his astute observation. It was true. She was all of those things, aspired to be all of those things, and liked that he had noticed. But her tiny smile faded as she stared at the shiny silver edges of the clean diploma frame and considered her answer. "I was in a master's program. Clinical Mental Health Psychology, at George Washington." She paused. Composed her face. When she was sure no hint of memory, of disappointment would leak through the cracks in her features, she finished. "But my circumstances changed unexpectedly, and I had to drop out after my first semester. I would like to go back someday, but for now it's not financially feasible."

True. All of it, true. He didn't need to know exactly what the circumstances were.

But without missing a beat, he asked, "What were the circumstances?"

Meredith scoffed and glared at him. "One for one, remember?"

"You've asked me, like, thirty questions already!"

"Those don't count in this arrangement." She shrugged one

shoulder. "The terms are not retroactive."

His eyes narrowed and he crossed his arms over his chest, but his mouth pressed into a thin, lopsided smirk. "You drive a hard bargain, Hartman."

She asked him another question about his preferences, about what he wanted in a relationship, and he responded without much fuss. And then he immediately smirked, a cheeky, shit-eating look, and Meredith knew to brace herself.

He asked again, "What were the circumstances?"

She rolled her eyes at his tenacity, his attempt to be sneaky and catch her off-guard. Her mouth fell open, the answer poised on her tongue, but she held the story firm and tight in her throat. He didn't need to know about the man she'd built her life around, about how she had chipped herself down for him until she felt so small she could hardly reach her own ambitions. He certainly didn't need to know about how that man had treated her, how he'd cheated on her, how he'd expected her to allow it and be grateful. No one needed to know any of that, especially not one of her clients. Her friends barely knew all of it. It was not something she talked about. It was something she had worked hard to move past. That man, Michael—and she hated saying his name, even thinking it, even now years later—had run a slow and inexorable bulldozer over her entire self. She left. She worked hard to build towers and turrets and glorious spires out of herself, to make herself tall and strong and unconquerable. She liked the person people saw in her now. She liked, very much, that this client took one look at her and pegged her as a whiskey-drinking boss woman, someone who would want a master's degree, someone with nerve and ambition and high standards. She liked that she presented herself to the world in that way.

No one needed to see the cracks and filled-in spots in her foundation.

Especially not a client.

"I had money. And then suddenly, I did not." Careful, her words precise and measured, she added, "I was engaged. And then suddenly, I was not."

"Hm." He looked thoughtful but said nothing more than, "I'm sorry to hear that."

"It was a long time ago." She brushed her hair back off her shoulder and sat up straighter. "How do you know when you have a good connection with someone? What's the level of connection you have to have before you might start feeling romantic attraction to them? I mean, what does that feel like for you?"

He considered this for a second. "When I would fight a bear for them, then I know we're solid friends. Once I get to that point with someone, then maybe more could develop."

"A bear?" Meredith bit back a smile and asked, very seriously, "What kind of bear?"

"Any kind of bear. But not a panda. They're too sweet and pure. I would never fight one. And not a polar bear, either. They're endangered. That's bad form."

"Only a bear?" Meredith asked, teasing, though she kept her face and voice deeply serious. "Not an alligator or a baboon or a harbor seal?"

His eyes went wide and sad, horrified. "Why would I fight a harbor seal? I would never! They're like a dog mermaid!"

"Good answer. Seals are the best animals. Plus, you wouldn't stand a chance in a fight with one. They're too wily and strong. It would drag you to the bottom of the ocean and you'd drown before you could get a single punch in."

"Yeah! Exactly!" He laughed and nodded in furious agreement, although his eyes were wide with a hint of confusion. He hadn't expected her morbid response.

"Your turn," Meredith said more quietly. He was funny. Fun to talk to. To tease. It usually took a lot longer to build up a good rapport with a client. "Ask me something."

He paused and took in a deep breath, let it out in a sigh. "I'm allowed to ask you anything? You don't have boundaries here?"

A warning bell clanked in the back of Meredith's head. Cool and aloof, she said, "You can ask me anything. If I don't want to, then I won't answer."

He nodded. And burst out with, "Why did your engagement end?"

"Oh my God." The abrupt question took her by surprise. "You are a menace."

Ryan winced and looked bashful, but something about his tone was teasing, challenging, when he said, "Sorry! You don't have to answer if you don't want to!"

Of course she didn't. She didn't have to do anything if she didn't want to. This was her office, her job, her session. She was in control. Thoughtful and pinched, she bit the inside of her cheek and considered giving him nothing, no answer at all.

But that would be tantamount to admitting something terrible had happened; something bad enough that it was still clawing at her, years later.

So she said, bluntly, "He cheated on me."

"Ouch." Ryan's nose scrunched up with a look of distaste. "Sorry. That's rough."

"Yeah." And then she kept talking. For some reason. Why was she talking? Why was she telling him this, telling anyone this? Maybe just to prove to herself that she could. Her voice was calm, no tremors and no sliver of emotion, completely matter-of-fact, as she explained, "He was older. My mentor. A rather well-respected therapist with a private practice here in DC. I met him when I interned with his office, my senior year of college. I was twenty-one. Too young to know all the warning signs. We were together four years before I discovered I was not the first, last, or only college-aged girl who caught his eye. He was gross."

A thoughtful look came over Ryan's face while he hurried across the room and sat himself back down in the chair across from her. Leaned forward, his elbows on his knees, he peered at her and asked, "So is that why you started this date coaching business?"

"A lot of things happened all at once and led to this." She nodded and kept eye contact while he urged her to continue. "Once we split, I was suddenly homeless. He had paid most of my bills while I was working on my master's, so suddenly I had to get a job. And in the meantime, I went on a bunch of dates. Frivolous. Just trying to throw myself back out there. And they all went horribly, because online dating is the absolute worst. All I could think about, every time I had a bad date, was that just a little bit of coaching or intervention could have prevented it. These guys were doing stupid, little things that were so obviously wrong—talking way too much about themselves, not dressing appropriately, being too chivalrous and not letting me pick or plan or pay for anything. All of it was so fixable! They'd be able to do better, if only someone would tell them. So I started telling them. Several were not happy about that. But a few appreciated it. And that's how I realized I had a business." She waved her hands out to gesture at the office. "Here we are."

"Here we are," he agreed. Kindly, he smiled and said, "That's cool. You have an interesting origin story. Like a super hero, with a call to action."

At being compared to a super hero, Meredith huffed a little laugh. Super hero, she was not. Super heroes were not typically so cynical.

"You just asked way more that your one question. That was several in a row. And they were big ones." She lifted a brow. Considered him. Collected herself.

The confessions and discussion of her past left her on uneven footing, like she no longer knew the ground. Like she was vulnerable.

She hated that, hated the little twinge of stripped-down insecurity.

But she could easily parry and recover her footing. All she had to do was go on the attack with something precise, targeted, and sharp. That was a game she knew how to win.

"Alright, alright." He lifted his hands in surrender, good natured and completely unaware that she would be out for blood. He had gotten her to spill too much of herself, had made her feel vulnerable in her own office. That simply could not stand. "Ask me anything. I owe you, after prodding like that. Sorry."

A wicked, cold smirk ran like cracks in ice across her face. "Tell me about your sex life."

"Rude!" Bewildered, his mouth fell open in a dramatic oh. "Wow! You are defensive, aren't you? Way to deflect and get back at me for asking you something uncomfortable. Which I didn't mean to do, by the way! You didn't have to answer!"

With wide blue eyes dripping fake innocence, Meredith batted her lashes and said nothing. She let him simmer.

Though, she might have been a little impressed that he saw her moves and strategy so clearly. A little put off. But a little impressed.

Ryan sighed and slumped in his chair. "I should have seen this coming."

"Probably." Meredith grinned. "Now spill."

He smiled a little. Said nothing for a long moment. Stared out the window. But then laughed, and said, "Fine."

And he did, as she had expected him to.

What she hadn't expected was the warm fluttering sensation she'd get deep in her stomach as she watched this big, strong guy blush and laugh and open up.

That was not something she had controlled for.

Chapter Six

A loud, screeching hum filled Ryan's entire world as he carefully rocked the work bench forward towards the spinning buzz saw. Slow. Deliberate. Sweat beaded on his upper lip and in his hairline, more from the tension of concentration than from any physical exertion. Each piece of red oak plank precisely measured, he cut them down to size. The humming saw screamed louder each time he rocked the wood to the blade, the sound a near-animalistic, mournful wail. In a burst of chips and sawdust that speckled against the screen of his protective goggles, he and the blade quickly cut the wood down to size, and soon he had six planks that would become shelves for his newest contracted project.

He studied each one, checked the sizes, ran his gloved thumb along the edges to make sure there were no inconsistencies. A few bumps and imperfections that he would sand down later, but for now, the pieces were perfect. Nice quality, too. The darker grain patterns ran in soft, pointed whorls through the lighter wood. He smelled wood smoke while he studied it, a sense memory so strong he might have sworn it was real. Campfires. Autumn nights out in the hills of Virginia, bonfires and hayrides near the farm where he'd grown up. He smiled with the nostalgic flash of memory—the memory of welcome warmth in the midst of shivering cold—and knew he had something to work with. The couple who contracted him to build them a custom cabinet for their dining room gave him specifications on size, on materials, and on timeline. But they gave him freedom with the design. He was an artist, and they wanted a custom piece. It had taken him a few days of thinking, but the idea came to him eventually, as it always did. Fire. That was the theme. Not raging or destructive. Warm and homey and welcoming. He'd sketch out the design tonight, and already he could envision the gentle curve he'd give the legs, the softly pointed crown at the top.

He set the planks into place, stood them on end against the wall of his workspace, and then turned off the loud saw.

"Hello?" A voice, thin and harassed, called from up front. "Mr. McKenna, are you back there?"

"Shit," Ryan muttered to himself as he tore off his goggles and smacked sawdust out of his hair and off his shirt. "With you in a moment!"

Who was in his shop this early? Ryan started each day with several hours of design and construction work. Most of the time, he was in his workshop buzz-sawing planks or sanding wood or sketching pieces. The actual shop front, he only opened for a few hours each day. It was for show, mainly, and for advertisement. The small shop floor only showcased a few pieces at a time, all of them experimental: things he had made just for fun, or to test out a new material, or to teach himself a new technique. Most of his money and sales came from custom orders.

He toweled off his face and then tossed the towel over his shoulder. It landed with a flop on the bare concrete floor behind him as he swung open the door and strode out into the store front. "Hi. Sorry. I had a saw running and couldn't hear anything. I hope I didn't keep you waiting long?"

"Oh, not too long at all. And the wait gave me time to admire all of the pieces you have for sale here in your shop!" An older gentleman in a black suit, with a portly figure and thinning gray hair, stuck out a thick hand for Ryan to shake. "Thank you for meeting with me, Mr. McKenna. I am George Anderson, Director and Curator of the Washington, DC Artisans Guild."

"Oh. Great." Ryan had not heard of the Artisans Guild, and he certainly had not agreed to meet with this man, but he stayed pleasant and shook his hand. "It's nice to meet you. Welcome to my shop."

"And what an impressive shop it is!" The man beamed, a cheesy and polite smile that Ryan was sure was at least half forced. With a wave of his arm, he gestured out at the collection on display. "Are all of these originals, created by you?"

"Yeah. Every one of them." Ryan rubbed at the back of his neck and nodded along, wondering what this was about. Not a client—clients always got to the point much more quickly. Ryan scanned the small room, the bright clear wall of windows at the front that illuminated his store. Cabinets and armoires lined the walls—some dark and heavy and traditional, some light and airy and whimsical. A small, round dinette table with four beech wood chairs, vines carved into the breezy legs and base, caught the morning sunlight, and the smooth lacquer gleamed. The small space filled with several furniture pieces was a tight fit, but not cluttered or cramped. It had a cozy feel to it, with each of the carefully crafted pieces displayed on an assortment of patterned rugs. While the man studied his displays, Ryan said, "I mostly do custom orders, but everything on display here is for sale. Are you looking for anything in particular? Is there anything I can help you with?"

That broad grin still in place, the man blustered and ignored the question. "You're younger than I expected! How old are you, exactly? It's impressive that you have such skill, and such a fine business at this age."

"I'm twenty-seven," Ryan answered. Smoothly, without faltering and without going into too much details, he explained his credentials in a way he hoped came off as charming and trustworthy. "I've been building most of my life, though. I taught myself how to design and build furniture in the old barn out on my parents' property when I was fourteen. Then, I went to college and got a business and marketing degree so I'd be able to sell what I made."

"All self-taught?"

Ryan nodded.

"Impressive. Quite impressive. And exactly the sort of young, creative energy we need in the Guild." Mr. Anderson patted his breast pocket, searched around for a second, and then pulled out an embossed business card. Ryan took it. "I believe you showcase your work at local craft fairs, yes? One of my associates met you a few weeks ago. She said you had a display here at the Eastern Market."

"That's right." Ryan nodded while he studied the card, his hesitance and uncertainty fading by the second. This could be an opportunity. He ran a small business in DC, where cost of living and working was very high, so he was always looking for those. He wasn't struggling, but he did have to hustle and constantly search out new contacts and clients to make it month to month. "I set up a stall there and sell sometimes, on the weekends. It's a good way to meet new clients."

"I'm sure it is. And I'd like to invite you to join us for an opportunity that will undoubtedly put you in contact with many more clients, and many more wealthy clients, than you could possibly meet at a little neighborhood flea market!" Mr. Anderson pressed a hand to his generous belly and laughed. A rich, white man's laugh, it could only be described, unpleasantly, as a chortle.

Ryan winced, bristled, at the guy's attitude. The Eastern Market was a historic and cultural treasure, a community center that showcased some of the best artists and crafts people in DC. Sure, it was a little touristy sometimes. Sure, it was a bit of an unorganized free-for-all. And sure, the quality of some of the goods sold ranged from handcrafted heirlooms to cheap knock-offs with the Made in China sticker barely scraped off. But that was part of its charm! Standing out in the sun, meeting people, shaking hands, getting to know neighbors, sharing kebabs and fresh produce with the other vendors, watching young white hipsters attempt to haggle; he was quite fond of the whole experience. And he never left without a sale—either a ready-made piece he had lugged over for the day, or a contract for a new custom design. Ryan's pieces were not cheap. He didn't like what this man was implying.

But he said nothing. Let the guy laugh to himself. Waited.

Once he had chortled himself out, Mr. Anderson announced, a bit grandiosely, "We at the Washington, DC Artisans Guild would like invite you to display your work at our Autumn Showcase, as a featured creator." Another trip into his pocket, and he pulled out a glossy, tri-fold pamphlet. "This is a black-tie event with an exclusive guest list, all collectors who appreciate fine craftsmanship and pay well for original pieces. The event is something of a blend between a craft fair and a showing at an art gallery. You'd present your work to groups of guests, show your samples, and talk a bit about your process and inspiration. No hard sales. Our guests love a good story, and I suspect they'll want to hear all about your journey!"

Another chortle, plus a friendly clap on the shoulder, and Ryan was reeling. A formal event where he was supposed to put himself on display instead of his work? Talk about himself? Talk about his inspiration? For an instant, he panicked, his throat tight. How the hell was he supposed to talk about that? What was he supposed to tell all of those fancy, wealthy potential clients? That he grew up an only child with parents who wanted nothing to do with him, so he taught himself how to build to stave off crushing loneliness as a teen? Great story! Super relatable! That didn't make him want to throw himself into the Potomac River and submit to the mercy of its toxic pollution at all!

It did not sound like his kind of scene.

"Uhh…" Ryan looked away and laughed a little bit to himself, shook his head. Maybe he was being dramatic. He had bills to pay, and he needed a steady stream of contracts to keep him doing the work he loved doing. He was scheduled through the next month and a half, but he really should have more Christmas orders on the books than he currently had. He loved his work. He loved his business. He was in the habit of taking opportunities as they came and saying thank you for them. Maybe he shouldn't shut this down so quickly. "Thanks so much. That's a great opportunity. Can I give you an answer in a day or two?"

Mr. Anderson's face fell, and he took a half step out of Ryan's personal space. "Of course! Of course. But don't think too long about it! This is a very prestigious event, and we do have a back-up list of artisans."

So he was replaceable to them. Great. That gave another note of sour nuance to the nasty taste in his mouth.

"I just need to check with my…" He cleared his throat. He needed to check with his best friend, who always knew how to help him sort out his feelings from his thoughts. He needed her opinion on this. And maybe a few other opinions. In a half-ignored flash of thought, he realized that Coach Meredith would probably give good advice on this—especially since she had a lot of thoughts on how he should open up and talk about himself more. He shook off the urge to call Meredith right now and demand some of her blunt, clipped, sharp-eyed advice, and focused instead on Naomi. Thankfully, when he had first opened his shop, Naomi had given him ten bucks to buy a pack of pens and paper, and from then on she insisted on calling herself an investor. "My business partner. I just need to talk it over with my business partner."

"Wonderful!" That seemed more palatable to good old Mr. Anderson. "I look forward to your call tomorrow!"

Once the guy was gone, having been politely shooed out the front door and bid farewell by the pleasant little tinkling of the shop bell, Ryan stood alone in his quiet storefront, surrounded by the steady furniture. What the hell was he supposed to make of this? A good opportunity, yes. Lots of potential new clients, on the one hand. But also, on the other hand, it seemed unnecessarily pretentious. And it required him to wear a black-tie tuxedo and talk about himself with a bunch of strangers. Not his cup of tea. He studied the pamphlet and read details about the Guild and about showcases in years past. It highlighted the numerous artisans who had presented their work. Big names. Ryan recognized a few of them as DC powerhouses. Glossy photographs showed elegant people in tuxedos and gowns, soft and glittering in gentle golden light, as they laughed and drank champagne and listened to an artisan clock maker give a presentation.

Awful.

He tugged his phone out of his back pocket and texted Naomi, "Do you know anything about the DC Artisans Guild? They just invited me to present at their Autumn Showcase. Formal thing. I think it looks too stuffy for me, yeah??"

With that sent, and with his mind unsettled and spinning from the encounter, Ryan went through the swinging door back to his workshop. Functional and unassuming, the wide-open room was nothing special. All of his tools, his workbench, and his stacks of raw materials rested and waited to be useful. He grabbed his sketchbook and plopped down onto the ratty old sofa he kept in one corner of the room, next to the mini fridge and side table.

His mind calmed as he sketched.

Two hours later, he had a mock-up for the custom cabinet. The fire theme was subtle and evocative. Not too literal. Soft and light and hearty. He would stain the wood to bring out and highlight the natural red oak color, and maybe he could use a new technique he'd been wanting to try to char and harden some of the panels. That would create some nice color contrast, some interesting patterns.

And then it was still only three o'clock.

He could go home, but that seemed like a waste of a day. He could keep cutting and measuring and sanding pieces for the cabinet, but that seemed too rushed. He had done all the basic sizing work, and he wanted to sit with the design for a little longer, just to make sure it was perfect.

So instead, he flipped to a fresh page in his sketchbook and started something new. He was always collecting new ideas, seeing them and filing them away in the nooks and corners of memory until he had a chance to sit and sketch and let his mind wander.

His pencil marked out clean, precise lines. Bold and cutting, strong, and clean, and elegant. He let the lines guide him for a while until he got a feel for the style, the pattern.

It reminded him of Meredith.

Meredith, who hated her office desk. Meredith, who said on the first day she met him that she would prefer something more modern, streamlined, and elegant.

Meredith, who embodied and personified modern, streamlined, and elegant.

He sketched and tweaked, tried a few different designs, a few adjustments, and within an hour, he had a mock-up for a new desk to replace the one Meredith hated. In ash, he thought. Strong and pale, the color striking, simple gray. Almost blonde.

He looked across the workroom at his stock. He actually had some ash wood, ready and available, stacked in a neat pile.

"Hm." He hummed as he peered at it, and then back at the sketchbook. He had other things to work on. Other things clients had paid him to work on. Plus, it was probably a little weird, a little extra, to build a desk for a woman he had just met a few days ago.

But he liked Meredith. She was cool. Funny. Interesting.

And anyway, he wasn't even going to make the desk. Not now.

Not right now, anyway. He was just thinking about a new design.

He dragged a few sheets of the ash out of storage, over to his workbench. Just to measure them and get a sense for what he had available. Just to get started.

It didn't mean anything. Or, at least he told himself it didn't.

When he locked up and walked home that evening, he thought more about the showcase. It really did not suit him. Naomi had never texted back, probably too busy with work, but he didn't think he needed her advice after all. Something like that, with so many rich, pretentious people saying things they didn't mean, laughing over glasses of bubbly champagne…it sounded terrible to him. He was not that kind of person. And nothing he could say would connect with them. They would have nothing in common. His pieces spoke for themselves, and it would do the work a disservice if he had to speak for it instead. What would people like that even talk about? *Oh, Richard, this sideboard would look simply marvelous as a display for all of our diamonds and caviar! Splendid, Muffy, let's order three of them from this silly little peasant wood worker!* And then they would laugh—no, chortle— into their champagne glasses. And he'd have to act grateful; he'd have to think of something witty and interesting to say about himself, while looking ridiculous in a tuxedo. No. No way. He didn't need that.

He was going to tell them no.

By the time he opened the gate and walked up the leaf-strewn path to his front door, he had decided. He wasn't going to do it.

Their glossy, navy blue front door swung open as he jogged up the steps, his breath ghosting in misty clouds in front of him, warm effort in the cold. He looked up. Naomi stood in the doorway, wearing workout pants, a big hoodie, and a scowl. With both arms stretched across the doorway, the light behind her spilling golden into the darkening evening, she blocked his entrance. "Ryan."

He blinked and dug his hands a little deeper into the pockets of his jacket. "Naomi?"

"You'd better not be thinking about skipping that showcase."

"I thought about it. I really don't think it's a good—"

She cut him off with the wave of her hand and a roll of her eyes.

"Ryan McKenna! Do not be ridiculous. This is a really big deal! Do you know how big of a deal this is? Did you look into it at all?"

"No," he said as he nudged past her into their house. She allowed it, but followed close behind him. "But I already know it's not my kind of thing!"

"Oh, so money is not your kind of thing? Getting new clients is not your kind of thing? Tons of exposure is not your kind of thing?" She chased him all through the ground floor of the house, while he shucked off his coat and shoes in the foyer, while he rifled through cabinets in the kitchen to get a glass of water. "So help me God, Ryan, you are doing this showcase and you are going to be spectacular. This is a big deal! This group is a big deal, and it's a big deal that they want you to join!"

"I…" He sighed. Her face was so sure, her eyes so bright and beseeching. She had every confidence in him. He gulped down water, the glass strange and slippery in his too-cold hands. Quietly, he asked, "You really think I can do it?"

She softened and nodded, just a little smug as she smirked and crossed her arms over her chest. "Yeah. I really think you can do it. And I really think you should do it."

"He said…" The words caught in Ryan's throat, the true source of his nerves a spiky, anxious burr. "He said they don't do hard sales, and that everyone would want to hear my story. He said I'll have to talk about how I got started."

"Oh. Okay." Understanding washed through Naomi, and all of the smugness melted out of her. Her arms swung towards him as she crossed the kitchen, her bare feet padding across the dingy linoleum. "I'll help you," she said as she reached up and braced both hands on his shoulders. "I'll help you prep for it. We'll come up with some talking points, some basic, superficial stuff that you're okay sharing, and I'll help you rehearse. Okay? I won't send you into the fancy, rich people viper pit without some practice." She squeezed his shoulders and then let go. "But I really do think you should do it."

He closed his eyes and let her words, her promises and reassurances, sink in. "Okay. Yeah. Okay. I'll do it."

One corner of her mouth lifted in a smile. It scrunched up her nose. "Good."

"And anyway." He sighed and leaned back against the edge of the counter. "Part of what I'm working on with the date coaching is getting more comfortable opening up and talking about myself. Maybe that will help a little bit with this, too."

He could mention it to Meredith. See if her suggestions could be broadened a bit. Obviously, this showcase wasn't a date. But it did sort of feel like he was going to have to romance a crowd of people into finding him charming enough to buy from him, so maybe she would count it as under her purview.

"Oh. That's a good point." Naomi winced as she stepped back and gave him space. She leaned against the opposite counter, the meat of her hip digging into its sharp edge with her legs out long. She had long, slender legs, accompanied by the knobbiest knees he had ever seen.

That always made him smile to himself a little. She was so dear. So dear to him. Their closeness was a rock, and the glimpse of her, so tender and real and unassuming, made him feel at home. So much so that he nearly missed the thoughtful, pinched look on her face. "What? What's a good point?"

"You can't go to something like this alone." She shrugged. "You have to bring a date."

"How can I bring a date? This is definitely not a first date kind of setting."

She winced, her whole face scrunching up. "Exactly."

"No." Ryan's heart fell heavy into his stomach. "No! Really? You think? I can't just go alone?"

"To a big high society debut?" Naomi shook her head. "Not unless you want to look sad and pathetic. People like that will gossip, and they will pry. If you're alone at this huge career-changing event, they'll wonder why."

Deadpan, Ryan announced, "I don't want to look sad and pathetic."

"Then you need to bring a date." Naomi paused and then added, "A date could help deflect some of the attention off of you, too. Help make it go smoother for you, if you're nervous."

Ryan nodded and felt rather dismal. "But it's not a first date kind of thing. It's a third date kind of thing, at least. It's a serious kind of thing. And the event is a month away."

Dull, Naomi said, "Yep."

"I have a month to find someone to be in a potentially-serious relationship with." Ryan looked up at her and pinned her with a stare that felt wide-eyed and slightly panicked, though his voice was dull and heavy. "Or else everyone at my big, career-changing society debut is going to think I'm sad and pathetic, and I'm going to freak out."

"Yep."

Ryan considered this, considered the chance of it all coming together for him, and proclaimed, "I'm fucked."

"Not necessarily." Naomi pushed forward off the counter and patted him on the shoulder, before she set to work gathering supplies for dinner out of the cabinets. It was supposed to be his night to cook. She was kind, a goddess, his hero, to take over for him while he was very busy considering his imminent doom. "You've always been good with a deadline! Never missed one, right? You'll be okay. Talk to your date coach about it. Let her know there's a time crunch now. I'm sure she'll understand."

Ryan snorted a laugh, because Meredith was helpful, insightful, and clever. But flexible? That was not a trait he'd pin on her.

But what choice did he have? If he was going to do this showcase—and he could always not do the showcase, he supposed, but then Naomi would kill him, so he was going to do the showcase—he didn't want to walk into it alone. He did want someone there with him, by his side. It would be nice. Nice, to have someone there with him, someone he cared about. Someone to snark and tease and laugh with, to make fun of all of the pretentious Richards and Muffys with when no one was looking. Someone to catch him with a smile offered, with a hand held, with a word interjected, if he stumbled or got tangled up and nervous while putting himself on display. Someone he felt comfortable enough with to want to get dressed up for. It would be nice, to have someone to share it all with.

It was a longshot, but it was worth it. He'd have to tell Meredith. He might have to pay for an upgraded coaching package. She would not be pleased. But she had been fun and easy to talk to so far, surprisingly so, and her sharp sense of humor seemed to respond well to his lighter teasing. He'd have to make her laugh when he told her. That would soften the blow.

Still, she might eviscerate him for it. As long as she helped, he didn't think he would mind.

Chapter Seven

Meredith stared at the man on the other side of her desk with calculated consideration. He kept eye contact. But he also fidgeted and picked at a loose string on the cuff of his plaid flannel shirt.

This was not ideal. Not a catastrophe. But not ideal.

"So, you didn't think to tell me about this big, fancy event you need a date for in less than six weeks, because…?" She lifted one perfectly shaped blonde eyebrow, her face cold and impassive.

Ryan chewed on the inside of his cheek, but then shrugged and flashed her a cheeky grin. "Element of surprise? To keep your life interesting?"

Meredith rolled her eyes, but she also bit down on a smile. Ryan McKenna had just taken her carefully structured work schedule, set it on fire, and thrown it into traffic, true. But those damn dimples helped soften the blow. She pulled up the calendar on her phone and added the new deadline: four weeks from tomorrow. While she typed, she muttered, "For future reference? I hate surprises."

"You would hate surprises." He folded his hands and leaned forward onto the desk. "Why do you think that is? Something in your childhood?"

"I'm not going to answer that question." She looked up from her phone screen long enough to glare at him. "I know what you're doing. Stop trying to divert. We're here to talk about you, not me." She set her phone back on the desk and kept talking before he could get another word in. "Well, this new deadline is not ideal, but I can work with it. Normally, the package you paid for with the coaching sessions, practice dates, and matchmaking options would require six weeks. We'll cram it into four. And you will do your best to listen to everything I say, take all of my advice to heart, and do all the work I ask of you. Are you willing to do that?"

Ryan tilted his head to one side and peered at her. "You know, I was planning to ignore you and do the opposite of whatever you advised when we had six weeks. But now that we have four? I'm really going to buckle down."

Meredith glared at him. Unblinking. Dull and dead eyed, like a shark.

Ryan stared back, a rotten little twinkle of amusement in his brown eyes.

Locked together, the silence stretched between them for a long moment until Ryan gave in. Of course he did. No one had ever been able to beat her in a staring contest. Meredith smirked at the victory while he raised his hands in surrender and said, "Yes. Of course. And I am sorry for the rush. I only just got the invitation to this event a couple of days ago."

"Good. I make no guarantees, but you show some promise. With some luck, we'll be able to get you a serious date for this showcase." She rolled her chair back across the polished boards of her office floor and stood up. "Today, we need to start by updating your look. I'm taking you shopping, and you will try on whatever I tell you to try on. Got it?"

Ryan stood and waved his hands up and down to gesture at his body. "What's wrong with my clothes?"

"Nothing!" Meredith offered him a polite, plastic smile as she gathered her purse, wallet, and keys. "If you have a time machine and you're planning to find your next girlfriend at a Nirvana concert in 1993."

"But flannel is a thing! Plaid! Plaid is a thing! Hipsters wear it. And jeans?" He followed her across the office floor and stood to the side, still gesticulating and arguing with a good-humored grin. "Jeans are fine! What is wrong with jeans? Everyone wears jeans!"

True, everyone wore jeans. But not everyone had a body like Ryan McKenna. With those broad shoulders, muscular thighs, and perfect ass? This man in a pair of loose, baggy jeans was a crime against humanity. The U.N. would pass a resolution banning him from wearing oversized, ill-fitting clothing any day now. God, what Meredith wouldn't give to wrangle him into a suit.

Not that she was thinking about wrangling him. Nothing wrangle-related. Wrangling, tangling, or falling into bed with? No. Hard no. Not with a client. Preferably, not with anyone she knew by name. She gulped and pushed her long hair back behind her ears to cool the sudden flush of heat up her neck.

Ryan did not notice and kept whining that jeans were perfectly acceptable date attire while he followed her down the creaking old staircase to the ground floor of the building. Meredith ignored his claims and instead thought about what sort of women might be drawn in by his current style failings. "Maybe that look would be fine if you're hoping to date a fish woman, new to life on land who can't perform basic tasks on her own. She'll be so grateful to you, she won't care how sloppy you look!"

"Hurtful." Ryan paused on the stairs a few steps behind her, but then thundered down to catch up, the rubber soles of his beaten-up sneakers squeaking with every stomp. "And inaccurate! I wouldn't take a fish woman home! I would return her to the sea, where she can be happy."

Meredith smiled and shook with a silent laugh, glad he couldn't see her face. "Or! Maybe the perfect match for you is a robot woman who only just gained sentience yesterday but is somehow still sexy, and also she has a programming flaw that makes her unbearably attracted to people who wear jeans three inches too long for them!"

"Wow! You are on a roll." At the foot of the stairs, Ryan hopped the last two steps and dodged to swivel around in front of Meredith. Face to face.

With practiced perfection, she schooled her expression and hid any hint of laughter. She didn't want him to know just how stupidly charming she found him. She didn't really want him—or anyone else—to know anything about her.

He crossed his arms over his broad chest and smirked down at her. The front fringe of his curly, honey-brown hair flopped down onto his forehead. "You got any more?"

Meredith's heart sped up as that insufferable smirk of his widened, as it tilted up one corner of his full mouth. And there was the dimple. Damn those stupid dimples! Cool and serene, she shook her head. "I think I got it all out of my system."

"Really?" He blinked, taken aback. "Because I'm wearing flannel. The whole world of lumberjack humor is open to you, and you're not going to go for it?"

The words slipped out before Meredith could stop herself, all sweet and tender. "Look, Ryan, if that's your type, then maybe you should find another dating coach. I'm not going to help you screw a lady Sasquatch." Her earnest, concerned façade did not crack as she reached out and patted his cheek, his stubble prickly against the palm of her hand. "Bestiality's not a dating preference. It's a sin."

Ryan snorted a loud, abrupt laugh. When she turned and walked across the lobby, he stayed rooted to the spot. Another victory in this strange, back-and-forth teasing game he had somehow drawn her into. She didn't quite know how this had become a competition, each trying to one-up and make the other laugh, but they were in it now and Meredith was determined to win.

He jogged to catch up and made it in time to hold open the door for her. "Even if they're anthropomorphic? I think a Sasquatch is more of a monster than an animal."

Out on the sidewalk, Meredith squinted against the bright afternoon sun, adjusted her blazer, and shook her head. "Why would you make a distinction for a monster? I'm not going to help you fuck a werewolf, either!"

Ryan fell into step beside her as they walked to Meredith's car, her heels clicking on the pavement.

Thankfully, he had the good sense to wait for a little old lady in big sunglasses to pass in the other direction, and then he stepped to the side to let a young mom pushing a stroller go ahead, before he leaned in towards Meredith and quietly announced, "I wouldn't just fuck her! We'd go on a nice moonlit date."

"Are you saying you would actually fuck a werewolf?"

"Not during the full moon!" Eyes wide with offense, Ryan shook his head. "But while she was just a normal, nice woman who had some extra facial and body hair and didn't mind me wearing baggy jeans—"

Meredith cut him off. "I just figured out your dating problems!" She dug around in her purse for her keys, and her car beeped when she hit the button to unlock it. As she approached the driver's side door, she said, "You'll never be satisfied with a natural human woman. Only the supernatural will suit you."

Ryan stared at her unmoving, with his hand on the handle of the passenger's side door. His forehead scrunched and his mouth pursed in a thoughtful pout. He sized her up, peered at her, sunlight catching the gold flecks in his brown eyes. Meredith stared back and kept her face unreadable.

Until he asked, "Do you charge extra for that?"

She broke and laughed. At the sight of his own victory, Ryan beamed.

Meredith rolled her eyes at him. "Get in the damn car, McKenna."

She drove him out to the Pentagon City Mall and then dragged him inside. He grumbled and complained the whole way, though it was mostly good-natured and teasing. Once inside the huge fashion complex, she did not even bother to try some of the younger brands she'd used for other clients. She wasn't going to force him into anything too out of his comfort zone or make him change everything about himself. She wasn't a monster.

Although, based on their conversation earlier, that might make her more appealing to Ryan's tastes…

Laughing to herself, she shook off the little tremor of blush that thought evoked and dragged him into the first in a series of stores.

In the wide-open doorway of the mall shop, Meredith and Ryan stood side by side and took stock. High overhead fluorescents beamed down on the gleaming white tile floor, cool and bright and detached. Headless mannequins contorted into slightly inhuman positions and modeled outfits, while sales associates—heads attached—folded and sorted misplaced wares back into their homes on hanging racks or on the wall displays. Everything was simple, clean, and adult. No glaring colors, no wild prints. A few flannel and plaid shirts caught her eye, and she knew that Ryan had noticed them too, because his grumpy grimace softened into hesitant approval.

"See?" Meredith said. "Not so bad. Right?"

"Maybe. I'll withhold judgement until I see what weird princess-makeover clothes you're going to make me try on."

"Nothing too crazy," she promised. "I'm mostly trying to give you polished, nicer versions of what's already in your comfort zone. But you need a few rules. Number one: work clothes are work clothes. You keep your ripped up, ill-fitting jeans and your ratty old flannel shirts for as long as your heart desires. At work. You should have a separate wardrobe for work."

Ryan sighed, but nodded. "Fair. I do get kind of a lot of splinters because I never can quite get all the wood shavings out of my sleeves."

Meredith glared at him. "And you just…live with that? All the time?"

"Builds character?"

"You're a nuisance. First? Jeans." At a clipped, sure walk, her heels clicking pleasantly sharp and sure on the tile, she led him through racks and along pathways until they reached a wall of denim. As she scanned the piles and sought out the right size, she explained, "For your physique, you need to be in a slim fit. Nothing baggy. But also not a skinny jean. Skinny is different than slim. Slim will look nice and tailored on you. Skinny…" She turned to glance at him, to run her eyes up and down his muscled figure, his broad frame. Just for sizing purposes! That was all. She turned back to the jeans and tugged a pair out. "Your thighs are too strong for a skinny fit."

Without warning, Ryan thunked a shoulder against the shelf right in front of her and positioned his smirking, dimpled grin right in front of her face. "You think my thighs are strong?"

Startled, Meredith barked a laugh, which she quickly covered with one hand. She smacked him with the folded-up pair of dark wash denims in her fist. "Menace! Move! You're in the way!"

He fell back, laughing to himself, and didn't argue when she shoved a pile of five pairs, all different washes and styles, into his waiting arms.

"Go. Go try those on." As he walked towards the dressing booths on the far wall, Meredith called after him, "And don't you dare think you can get out of modeling them for me! I need to see how they fit."

"Right!" Ryan glanced over his shoulder while he smirked. "So you can get a better look at how strong my thighs are!"

Dammit.

Meredith bit back a grin and shook her head, too amused for her own good. Even more amused when he, too proud of himself and too busy teasing her to watch where he was going, ran right into a circular rack of women's sweaters.

When he popped back out of the dressing room a minute later, with his hands raised to the sides in question, Meredith took one quick look and announced, "No. Those are still too long. Go a size smaller."

And then a minute later, "Ugh. No. I hate the buttons on those."

"Then why did you give them to me to try on?"

Meredith ignored him and shooed him back into the dressing room with the flick of one finger.

Another pair, and, "Ew. No. You are not meant to wear light wash jeans. Stick to darks and mediums."

"Now who's the menace?" Ryan grumbled under his breath as he dutifully trudged back in.

Meanwhile, Meredith busied herself grabbing shirts and over-wear options. When he stepped back out again, Meredith paused.

In slim, dark jeans that hugged his hips and clung just tight enough to his ass and thighs, Ryan looked...

Meredith bit her lip, but her eyebrows climbed a little higher on her forehead against her will.

She had no complaints. Far from it.

She gulped. Her throat had gone hot.

"Well?" A tentative tremor in his voice, he waved up and down at his body. "What's wrong with this pair? What do you hate about these?"

She held herself very still. "How do they feel? Do you like them?"

He took a moment to step back and survey them in the mirror. He tilted his head side to side, considering, and spun in a slow circle to study the fit from a few angles. "Yeah, actually. They feel good. I think they fit right. And they make my butt look pretty good."

With a long, hissing exhale, Meredith closed her eyes and shook her head.

"What?" he asked. "Do you disagree?"

Composed and very proper, Meredith looked him up and down and nodded. "These are the ones I professionally recommend."

He smirked. "Because of the butt?"

Yes. Obviously. His ass was a world wonder. She rolled her eyes. "I'm going to add an extra nuisance surcharge to your bill. Fifteen percent seems fair."

Ryan laughed and disappeared back into the changing room, and he settled on two pairs of the jeans.

With little fighting, but rather more teasing than she had expected, she helped him pick out a few more basics: two more pairs of pants—khakis and gray trousers, both of which could be dressed up or dressed down; a few simple, solid color t-shirts—which actually fit him, and which looked obscenely good stretched taught over his pecs, dear Lord, she was in trouble; a couple dressy-casual patterned dress shirts—a little nicer than his typical flannel, but still casual enough to roll up the sleeves; and a few light sweaters for layering. She spent a few minutes showing him how to mix and match, and how to put together an outfit for a date. This was enough to get him started and to set him on the right track.

"Alright. I think that's all you need for now. Anything else you think you need? Anything else you want to try on?"

Deadpan and unhesitating, he lifted a t-shirt off a rack and held it aloft. It was white. With a giant, very realistic picture of a soft pink cockatoo stretched across the entire front. Its beady little black eye stared at her.

She glared. "Ryan!"

He laughed and shoved the shirt back onto the sales rack. "I'm sorry! I'm sorry! I swear, I've been paying attention. It was just so ridiculous, I had to see how you'd react." His wild, sharp grin softened in a smile more real, more tender, more fond. "Sorry. I know I've been harassing you all day while you're trying to help me. It's just that you're so composed and put together. It's fun to rile you up."

"Ugh." She pressed her hands to her hips and shook her head. Mock disgusted, she scoffed and said, "I might be mildly entertained by you."

"Thank you!" He pressed his hand to his heart. "I might be mildly entertained by you, too!"

"Now seriously. Anything else you need?" The urge to dress him up again tempted her. Something way down in her id longed, in a deep and visceral way, to get this big, muscle-y, works-with-his-hands guy into formal wear. Nonchalant, she asked, "You don't have anything you need to wear a suit for, right?"

"Oh." Ryan bit his thick lower lip and chewed on it, thoughtful. "Actually…"

"Wait, really?"

"Yeah. That event I told you about? The one I kinda need the date for in a month?" Uncomfortable, no longer the laughing, teasing, goofy little sunbeam he'd been all afternoon, he rubbed at the back of his neck. "It's kind of a formal thing."

"Really?" Now that was an exciting little coincidence. Maybe she would have her excuse after all. "How formal? What's the dress code?"

"Black tie. I'm not sure that it's the same for me, though?"

"Why wouldn't it be the same for you?"

"Because I'm not really a guest. I'm…more of a vendor? But not quite that either."

"Okay, what is this event exactly?" Meredith cut through his fumbling half answers. "I need to know more about it before I can help you pick something to wear."

As Ryan explained the showcase, downplaying his role in it with every word he chose, the picture started to become clear in Meredith's mind.

"Wait. This guild picked you to be one of their featured crafts people? How many are being featured?"

He brushed his hair back and hunched his shoulders forward. "There are twelve of us."

"Twelve?" Meredith blinked several times, her eyes wide and hazy with the burn of the stark fluorescents in the shop. She had known Ryan was a craftsman, and that he designed and built custom furniture. She hadn't realized that he was so good at it. That he was, like, being-recognized-at-a-huge-fancy-showcase level of good. "That's amazing. Seriously. That's really incredible. Congratulations."

"Thanks," he said down to the floor. Then, he corrected himself and looked up at her. With more conviction, he tried again. "Yeah! No! Thank you. I am pretty honored that they asked me. It's a big deal and a really good opportunity. But I'm really stressed about it. Because it's such a big deal, and everyone there is going to be kind of judgmental, and I don't know if I'll be able to find a date by then, so everyone will think I'm a miserable loser. And I'm supposed to talk about myself, and I'm not good at that. And it's just really not my scene. Not my kind of clothes, not my kind of people, not my kind of thing."

It was a lot. The whole confession came out of him in an unsure rush, and suddenly Meredith understood the whole picture. Why he was nervous, why he suddenly needed to move up the timeline on his date coaching. "Hey." While he fidgeted and forced a smile, Meredith reached out and grabbed his wrist. Gently. But firmly. Always, Meredith was at her best when she had a goal, and she didn't stop to question why helping him prep for a career event felt like a mission she needed to take on. But it did. She wanted to help him shine, and she knew that she could. "I'll help you. Okay? It's going to be great. We'll focus more in our coaching sessions on opening up and talking about yourself in a way that feels authentic. I'll find you something killer to wear. And I'll help you find a good date." Lower, teasing, she added, "So none of the rich men think you're a loser, and none of the rich women try to grab your ass while their husbands aren't looking."

He laughed. "Thank you. You're the best. Seriously."

"I know," Meredith said simply as she let go of his arm and took a step back. "And you say that even before I tell you the good news about what you're wearing to the showcase!"

"Oh? What am I wearing to the showcase?"

Meredith grinned. "Not a tuxedo."

Ryan looked shocked and near-giddy at this. "Really?"

"Really." She led him back to the men's formalwear section of the store. "They want you to present yourself, right? Since you are there as one of the crafts people, presenting your work, and since your work is so hands-on and rooted, and physical, and artistic, I give you permission to dress down a little bit. Just a little bit! We're going to put you in a suit. Which is way better than a tuxedo with a cummerbund and all that nonsense."

Ryan stood back and let Meredith live out her wildest dreams, though he didn't know that's what he was doing. Methodical and careful, she scanned the racks and took in each color and style option. Designer would be better, obviously, and tailored. But they would work with the time and budget Ryan had. These were off the rack, but fitted, modern, and not bad options. She could do some good work with these, and Ryan's body was a glorious canvas.

No black—too stuffy and formal for him, too traditional. No wild colors—nothing he would feel too showy or well-seen in.

Now that…

That could work.

A blue—not quite navy, little bit of gray to it—wool blend. The shade would look lovely with his warm brown eyes. It looked very modern, but still classically attractive. That was the one. She grabbed a plain white button up and shoved him back into the dressing room.

Outside, alone while she waited for him, Meredith chewed on her thumbnail. Why was she nervous? Was she nervous or excited?

Maybe a little of both.

This client was going to kill her.

He was too…

Everything.

In a good way. He was genuinely caring, and funny, and charming. He was skilled, and impressive, and creative. Insightful. Thoughtful. Clever.

He had his insecurities and hang-ups, but so did everyone. Too often, people tried to hide their insecurities, and that desperate need to hide their own weakness, to never face it, never acknowledge it, made them unkind. Or it made them blind, deliberately ignorant to the ways they needed to grow. Ryan's hesitancies were sweet, and soft, and tender. They made him unsure sometimes, but never mean. He wore them with self-awareness.

He would make a great partner. A great friend. A great lover.

To someone.

Someone else.

Someone who could be sweet, and soft, and tender in return. Someone whose insecurities hadn't made them mean. Someone very much not like her.

She cleared her throat. Sniffed. Blinked a few times.

A plan. That was what she needed. A plan! This client needed her help. He was a good one. Circumstances were tougher than normal. She would need a plan. A proactive approach. While Ryan took his sweet time getting changed, Meredith ran through a mental list of any friends and associates who might fit the bill, any clients or former clients who might be a good match. She scrolled through her contact list on her phone for inspiration.

Stephanie Marks. Now there was a thought. Huh. Stephanie was lovely. Kind and warm. She'd just gotten back into the dating world after a divorce, and she wanted to take things slow. Meredith still had a few more coaching sessions with her.

It would be tough with the timing, but the two of them might just—

"So?" The flimsy dressing room door creaked as it swung open. Ryan stepped out. "How do I look, coach? Completely ridiculous? Reasonably respectable? Somewhere in between?"

Meredith's mouth went dry. Completely against her will, her lips parted and she quietly panted for the breath he had just stolen from her. Up and down, and then back again, her eyes scanned his body.

Damn.

Hot damn.

The suit fit him perfectly—showed off every muscle, every strong line of him. His jaw was a classic, daring cut above the crisp and polished collar, and his broad shoulders and powerful legs were thick and strong within the confines of the fabric, barely and perfectly contained. The close fit showed off his strength, but the clean and sharp lines also served to accent the softer parts of him. His round, pert ass, his lush, soft lips, his tumble of gentle brown curls, his bashfully hesitant smile and pose, were all highlighted and made more charming, more gorgeous by the clothes. This, this dichotomy of the soft and hard of him, was precisely why she had wanted to get him into formalwear. The sight of him did wonders, made her breath hitch, made her neck flush, made her want to…

To mess him up.

And actually…he did need to be messed up a little bit. Fully buttoned, his shirt looked overly prim. Uncomfortable.

Too brave, though her breath quivered in her lungs, she pinned him with an uncompromising stare and walked towards him on confident, sharp heels. He froze. Waited until she was close, very close to him, close enough to feel the warmth of his body radiating

94

through the wool of the suit. He watched her all the while, looked down to meet her eyes, and lifted his brow to ask a silent question. But he didn't stop her. He quirked a smile.

She smiled back, predatory, hunting, and smug.

With sure, unhesitating fingers, she reached for the buttons of his white dress shirt. With a flick of her fingers, a firm pop and a flash, she undid the top one. Slid down lower. And undid the second one.

"Wear it like this," she commanded in a low murmur. "With the top two undone."

He held his breath that whole time. Meredith could feel his tension. His submission to whatever she wanted. It made her feel powerful, buzzing with electric energy.

It made her too bold.

Once those few inches of his bare, tanned chest were exposed, she dragged one fingernail gently down his skin, let it hiss, let him flinch. And then she smirked, bit her lip, and stepped back.

His lips parted on a breath, the first he'd remembered to take in a long moment, and one corner of his mouth lifted in a helpless smile. "So?"

"You look hot as hell."

"Really?" He grinned, shy and pleased. "Do I really? You're not just saying that?"

"Really."

She watched him, the lines of his back and legs, too closely as he returned to the dressing room. Once she was alone again, in the wide-open store, she shook herself. What the hell had just come over her? That was not appropriate. That was…

Maybe a little exciting.

He was a menace! Ryan McKenna was an absolute menace to her composure, to her professionalism, and to her libido.

She needed to get this guy a girlfriend and get him out of her hair before she lost her damn mind.

On the walk back to the car, Meredith ran her idea past him. "What are you doing tomorrow?"

"Working. But I make my own schedule, so I'm flexible." He glanced at her, his eyes shining with a smile. "Why?"

"How do you like hiking?"

"I love hiking, actually. It's one of my favorite things to do for inspiration. Especially this time of year. Why?" His smile grew a little softer, a little hesitant. "Are you...?"

"I have a client I want to set you up with."

"Oh! That's great!" he said. But Meredith didn't think she imagined the little flicker of surprised disappointment in his eyes, the tiny falter of his smile. She ignored it and looked away from him, focused on the sidewalk ahead of her, while he asked, "You think I'm ready for that? You said early on you don't do any matchmaking until a little further into the coaching."

"Normally that's true. But with your timeline being short, we need to speed things up a bit." She flicked a look at him and crossed her arms over her chest like a shield. Against the chill in the air. Against whatever feelings might sneak out of her. "And I trust you."

He smiled at that. "So how does hiking come into it?"

As she walked and dug through her purse to find her keys,

Meredith told him a little about Stephanie—and especially made note of how she was kind, she was a little shy, and she wanted to take things slow and find someone serious. They were compatible in those ways. "And you both like hiking, apparently. She recently joined a social group that gets together on weekends to do outdoorsy, adventure stuff around DC. They're going on a hike in Rock Creek Park tomorrow morning. You should join." She beeped the key to unlock her car as they approached, and she kept talking as Ryan split off to walk around to the passenger's side. Over the blue roof of her little sedan, he leaned against the car and watched her as she said, "It would be a great place to start. Lots of people around, everyone's there to make friends, low pressure, and an activity you enjoy. You could meet her in that environment and see if you feel any potential for bear-fighting friendship-possibly-romance vibes."

He hesitated for a moment, and Meredith stood poised and waiting for a reaction.

She knew what reaction she wanted: her client opening up, taking her advice, and pursuing a new dating path. Obviously. That was her business.

But a tiny, foolish little goblin in her brain suggested that maybe, just maybe, the best thing would be if Ryan told her, *Nah, I'd rather go to this big, fancy showcase thing with you!* And wouldn't that just be a disaster. He was a sweet little cinnamon roll. She was a bitch queen. She would destroy the poor guy.

Probably.

Maybe.

Probably.

Definitely, it would not be professional or fair to give herself a chance to find out.

"Yeah," Ryan said after a moment of thought, and Meredith nodded. Good. Fine. That was good. It was good that he agreed with her plan. The car door creaked on its hinges as he opened it and plopped himself down into the seat. "I'll go and meet her tomorrow. Thanks, coach."

"You're welcome."

Driving him home, the car was filled with far less banter than it had been on the way out. Polite conversation. Friendly. But none of the easy, prickling teasing that had followed them all day. When she dropped him off, he left with a wave and a sincere thank you, his arms laden with shopping bags, and she shook off her unease.

This was fine.

Stupid to even think about, really.

She didn't need Ryan McKenna taking her to showcases or fighting any bears for her. She could fight her own bears, thanks very much.

Back at her townhouse, she battled for a parking space on the street and then headed up the steps of her front stoop. The large trees up and down this street had just started to change colors, and she pulled her blazer tighter around her middle to keep out the chill that crept up when she stepped out of direct sunlight.

Barely two steps inside, Richelle ran down the stairs in her socks and pajamas, her hair wrapped in a soft scarf, and stopped her with a look. A fearful look. Worried. "Don't freak out."

"Okay." Meredith hung up her keys on the welcoming little clip they kept by the door. "What's wrong?"

While Richelle trudged down the last few steps, her face was pinched and worried as she stared at Meredith, her arms crossed over her chest.

Meredith's blood ran cold. She forced herself to take a breath, to stay steady, though her heart raced and her eyes darted every which way in search of answers. "What is going on?"

Richelle took a deep breath. "You had a visitor earlier. Your ex. Michael. He came by, looking for you."

The whole world froze in place, silent and immobile, as Meredith stared at her friend and tried to make sense of the words. Her heart beat on. Her breathing sustained her. But everything else had stopped, her brain included. In a small, confused voice, she asked, "He came here?"

That couldn't be right. Richelle must have misunderstood. Misremembered. That wasn't possible.

But Richelle nodded and chewed on her lower lip. She reached out for Meredith, brushed her shoulder. "He said he needed to talk to you. Obviously, I told him to go away."

Panic seized her, cold, and vicious, and sudden. She sucked in short, hitching breaths through her nose as she tried to hold in the reaction, the fear, the unsettling sense of wrongness that screeched up and down her bones.

Michael knew where she lived.

The man who had nearly ruined her, who had belittled her, who had manipulated, and gaslighted, and controlled her for years, knew where she lived. How did he know where she lived? He wasn't supposed to know. He wasn't supposed to come looking. It had been four years since she had even spoken to him.

He wasn't supposed to be able to just walk back in whenever he pleased. He wasn't supposed to be able to swoop in and make her feel like this on a whim.

A tingle in her spine, a brush of discomfort, nudged her, and she had the sudden urge to turn around, to look over her shoulder, to check the locks on all the doors and windows. She did not. Every muscle in her core locked tense and rigid as she held herself together. "Okay. Did he say what he wanted?"

Richelle shook her head. "I told him if you wanted to talk to him, you would call. And I told him to never come back here."

"Okay." Meredith nodded and squared her shoulders. Richelle's lower lip quivered and the worry in her eyes was bright and wet. More than anyone else, Richelle knew about her history with Michael, knew what he had put her through. She reached out, the beginnings of a hug, and there was a flash of concern, of hurt on her face as Meredith brushed past her and went up the stairs. It made her feel guilty, but she didn't turn around. "Thanks for letting me know. I'll call him and deal with it."

And she would.

She could.

She could deal with her ex. She could talk to him without breaking down, without crying, without screaming. She could face this with her head on straight, cool and collected, in control.

Even if the mere thought of speaking to him triggered a repulsive, unsettled reaction so strong that she felt like millions of insect larvae were wriggling around under her skin, ready to consume the bloody mess of her alive.

She could hide that, control it so no one saw her weakness. That was what she was good at.

Chapter Eight

"It went well." Ryan nodded and watched Meredith across the desk in her office. She did not react. This whole meeting, she had been strange and distant. He studied her face closely for any hint of a reaction and saw only the firm set of her jaw, the tightness around her blue eyes. It didn't feel like her normal professional veneer. It felt cold. Withholding. Upset. Ryan gulped down a rising quake of nerves. "I think it went well, anyway."

Meredith rolled her eyes. It was not playful. "It went well, or you think it went well?"

"It went well," he rushed to say, and the back of his throat burned hot. Something had changed. They had been getting along so well, laughing and getting to know one another. A few days ago, when she had taken him shopping, he had really enjoyed the outing, enjoyed spending time with her, watching her in her element. While she had clipped around the store, ordered him into clothes, her blue eyes had sparkled bright and clear, and she had smiled that brilliant, sharp smile as she teased back as good as she got. She had been in charge and engaged. Now, three days later, she just seemed...

Wrong.

Like something was wrong.

"Is everything okay?" Ryan asked. "Did I do something wrong? Do we need to talk about something?"

She looked away and sighed, a low huff of annoyed breath. "We need to talk about what you came here to talk about." Abruptly, with cold, laser focus, she zeroed back on him and glared. Dead-eyed. No sparkle. Her long, silvery blonde hair was knotted in a tight bun, so tight it made her face look unusual and stiff. "So talk. Stop fucking around, stop avoiding the subject, stop making this about me. Just answer the damn question. How did the group date with Stephanie go? Is this something worth pursuing?"

Silence hung heavy in the still, quiet office after her questions, clipped and severe. Ryan's mouth slipped open, his lips parted in bewildered upset at her tone, and he stared off into the distance to give himself a moment. Dust motes danced in the thin, gold light from the tall windows, and Meredith stayed statuesque and unmoving. It was so sudden. So unexpected. He'd been getting to know Meredith for a few weeks now, and he had seen enough to know that she was not a particularly effusive, or warm, or bubbly person. But she wasn't unkind. She wasn't vicious or mean.

The rapid turn made him feel off-kilter and small. Like he was twelve years old again and had no idea what he had done wrong.

But Ryan wasn't twelve anymore. Wasn't a kid. He knew how to set boundaries.

"It was fine," he said, slow and calm. And it was true. He had enjoyed the group hike over the weekend. It was nice, to get out in the cool autumn weather and explore nature with a group of like-minded people. He'd had fun. And Stephanie had been nice and friendly, and easy to talk to. They had some interests in common. It had felt like a good start. But it was way too early for him to know for sure, and Meredith should have known that by now.

Surely, she did know that by now. He knew she had been paying attention, that she was thoughtful and wanted to help her clients. This cutting shut-down was out of the ordinary. He explained, "We had a nice time and we agreed to meet up for dinner one night this week. But it's a little early for me to know anything for sure. You know that. We've talked about that."

She scoffed.

So Ryan pushed his chair back and stood up. This was unusual for everything he had seen of her so far, out of character, unlike the person he was getting to know. Something must be going on, and he could have compassion for that, could give her the benefit of the doubt. But he didn't have to sit here and let her claw him. That wasn't necessary, healthy, or productive. "I'm going to go."

"What?" A shocked, angry look came over her face, a flash of raw and twisted emotion. "You just got here five minutes ago. I thought you were serious about this. You're really going to waste—"

"You're clearly going through something today." Ryan pulled on his coat. A tremor of anxiety at the near-confrontation shook his voice, the scared inner kid who didn't know what he'd done wrong. But he'd had a healthy friendship with Naomi long enough to have learned how to set boundaries, how to address a conflict without feeling like it was going to destroy his whole world. He waved back and forth between himself and Meredith. "This? This is not helping anyone. I'll make another appointment for later in the week, when you're ready to talk."

Something cold and distant came over Meredith. All the anger and frustration melted off her face as she schooled her features and hid all of her feelings behind a mask. Unreadable. "Fine."

At the door, Ryan hesitated. He wasn't angry. Maybe a little hurt.

But not angry. He didn't want to lash out or snap at her, so he should probably just leave. Clearly, she didn't want him around right now. Instead, he gripped the knob and looked back over his shoulder. "I hope you have a better day."

He shut the door carefully behind him when he left and took the stairs at a quick, jogging pace. His chest felt tight. Too warm. A sudden shut-down, emotional stone-walling, and cold disdain were strange for him, weird and awful new territory. Not as awful as fighting, yelling, and big emotions would have been. Things like that were too loaded with memory, but they were at least familiar. This strange encounter left him shaky and unsettled, like his bones had swelled and his skin didn't fit quite right. It was fine. They didn't know each other well.

But he had kind of thought they were becoming friends.

It took him by surprise, was all. Shook him. He'd go back to his shop and spend the day working. Drowning himself in the careful flow of building, shaping creations into the world, owning the whole process, had always soothed him after the big, angry, loud explosions growing up. The same would help now, even though this strange run-in with Meredith had been more of an implosion. He reached the landing at the bottom of the stairs.

"Ryan!"

Startled, he stopped still. From three stories up, Meredith chased after him. Strong and steady in her gray high heels, with loud sharp clicks on each step, she quickly made her way down and didn't stop until she reached the landing. Panting breaths, from exertion or nerves, heaved her chest as she marched up to stand face-to-face with him. "I'm sorry."

"It's okay." Tentative and hopeful, Ryan smiled. The sight of Meredith, a few blonde fly-aways zipping out of her perfect bun, a flush of pink on her high, pale cheekbones as she ran after him, did something to him. The uncomfortable tight feeling in his chest soothed, and the crystalline clear apology in her eyes warmed him like a balm. "You didn't have to run."

"No, I kind of did, though." She sighed and shook her head, annoyed, but this time at herself. Her movements were quick and jerky, and she raised one hand to push her stray hair back into place. It didn't hold, the fly-aways too fine and frizzled with static in the cool, dry air. So she grabbed onto her hair tie and yanked it away, a forceful tug that sent her sleek blonde hair tumbling down around her shoulders and half-way down her back, a ripple of shining quicksilver. As she shoved her hair back and scraped her fingernails against her scalp to try to get it to lay flat, she glanced at him and said, "I was a real asshole to you, for no reason. I'm sorry."

"It's okay." Ryan shifted his weight from foot to foot and stared, distracted, at her hair. It looked corn-silk fine, all kinked and bent like a sheet of dented aluminum from the pressure of the hair tie. There was something endearing, something captivating, about watching her drag her fingers through the tangles and nervously fluff her hair back and forth, trying to tame it but only succeeding in making it a mess of soft waves. Every other time he'd seen Meredith, her hair had been sleek and shiny, perfectly straight or pulled back. This cascade of silvery blonde hair didn't match the polished rest of her—the stylish, feminine black blazer, white blouse, and gray pencil skirt, the perfect smooth make-up. For half a wild second, he was tempted to grip her wrist and gently pull her hand away, to tell her to leave her hair be, because somehow this softer look suited her just as much as any more polished one. He didn't. He tore his eyes away from the loose, tangling wave of her hair. "I could tell you're having a bad day. It's fine. I do appreciate the apology, though."

Meredith nodded and chewed on her lower lip, forced a smile that looked pained and fake, and kept fussing with her hair. "Thanks."

As her fingers worked through each tangle, she pulled a little harder, yanked at her own scalp, and frustration mounted on her features—her nose scrunched up with every pull, and her jaw tensed. Like she was getting upset that she couldn't control this, couldn't make it do what she wanted it to do. It was so unlike the calm, cool-fronted woman he had seen so far. Meredith was not an emotions-on-sleeve kind of person, and the little unguarded, unintentional glimpse into her emotional state had him asking, before thinking about it, "Do you want to talk about? Whatever it is that has you upset?"

She froze, her fingers still wrapped around a stray lock. Her lips parted as she stared at him and considered the question, her eyes darting up and down from his face to the floor.

"Sorry." He raised his own hands in a gesture of surrender. "I know it's not really my business. But we're kind of friends, right? You seem like you're having a bad day. Do you want to talk about it?"

"Maybe." Both of her hands fell to her sides and she sighed, defeated. She rolled her eyes and then looked out over his shoulder, to stare at the line of brass mailboxes mounted on the wall inside the building's entrance. "I can't believe I'm telling you this. But my ex showed up at my house the other day. I haven't spoken to him in four years. It put me in a weird head space."

"He showed up? Without warning? Where you live?" Ryan's voice lifted higher, more disbelieving with each question. "I'm so sorry. That's really disturbing. Why was he there?"

Meredith sighed again. Something like peaceful acceptance had settled over her after she decided to talk, and her nerves no longer jangled. But it was obvious she felt strange talking about this. Was it because Ryan was a near-stranger? A client? He wasn't sure. But he didn't push, and even though she sounded low and dejected, even though she crossed her arms protectively over her chest and didn't look at him, she kept talking. Like maybe she needed to. "He is planning to propose to the girl he cheated on me with, and he wanted to ask for my engagement ring back."

Ryan stared at her. "What?"

"Yeah." She grit her jaw and nodded. Some sort of rotten, awful amusement twisted through her and the nod turned into a disbelieving shake of her head, and bitter smile. "Yeah."

"He's giving her the same engagement ring he gave you?"

"Presumably."

"What a cheap piece of shit!" Ryan shook his head and glared up at the dusty, crumbling line of crown molding at the top of the wall, at the pale brown water stain in one corner of the ceiling. Anger that wasn't his own quickened his heart. This was what had gotten Meredith—calm, cool, competent, boss lady Meredith—so upset? This cheating, no-good guy from her past, swinging back into her life like she owed him something? Four years without speaking, and he showed up at her house without warning? That was invasive. Scary. What kind of guy must he have been while they were dating to think something like that was okay? With the little bit Ryan knew about this guy—that he was clearly someone who did not respect boundaries—and with seeing how shaken-up Meredith was at his reappearance in her life, a dark little tendril of fury snaked through his stomach. He must have been bad. For Meredith, who seemed so unflappable every other time he'd spoken to her, to be so affected, this guy must have been bad to her.

Now that Ryan knew the context, he could see Meredith's earlier cold shut-down for what it was: she was spiraling a little inside, set off by this guy's sudden reappearance, and she was trying hard to put up walls so no one could see how upset she was. It had backfired. But Ryan understood. He was glad she had opened up to him a bit, glad she had told him.

Righteously angry for her, too warm and worked-up, he asked, "You don't actually still have the ring, do you? Please tell me you threw it in the river."

Across her chest, her arms tightened in a little closer, her elbows a little pointier. "I do still have the ring."

"Why would you keep that?"

"Because I very much wanted to throw it in the river!" she snapped. "I hated feeling like that, like it still had so much power over me. So I decided to keep it until I no longer felt the urge to throw it into the river."

Ryan pressed a hand to his face and rubbed at the stubble on his chin, thoughtful. It made sense. It made sense for her. She liked to be in control. "Are you going to give it back to him?"

With a tiny, almost invisible nod, she said down to the scuffed-up tile floor, "I'm meeting him for coffee tomorrow."

A much bigger, more frustrated reaction threatened to burst out of him, but Ryan contained it. This was not his fight. He hurt for her. But she was new to his life, barely even a friend, and he didn't need to start swinging on her exes or her ability to take care of herself. But still. He was worried. If the lead-up to the meeting had her so upset, what would sitting down for coffee with the guy accomplish? Nothing good, he thought. Nothing good had ever come to him from giving his tormentors and the people who hurt him another doorway into his life, from giving them another swing at his heart. Boundaries: he very much believed in them. He did ask, "Why, though? Why would you do that in person? Can you send a friend? Could Richelle get it to him? I could take it, for God's sake! I wouldn't mind! Why does it have to be you?"

Alight and burning, she zapped out of her distant hesitation and glared at him full on. Her blue eyes were blazing. "Because I am a grown ass woman! I have moved on! I make a living giving people advice about dating, for God's sake. What does it say about me if I can't handle an unpleasant conversation with my ex?"

"It says you don't want to torture yourself?" When she scowled, Ryan leaned back a little to give her space, and said, "Meredith, I get it. You don't want him to have control over you and your emotions anymore. But you don't have to put yourself through some painful test to prove that you're better than that! You don't have to do this."

For a long, heavy moment, she narrowed her eyes and considered him. He gulped and tensed under her gaze but stayed still. Finally, she said, quietly and with conviction, "Yes I do. I do have to do this. You don't know me. You don't know my history. You don't know what's going to make me feel empowered, or safe, or free of it all."

Shame heated Ryan's cheeks, an unflinching and immediate recognition that she was right, and he lowered his head and nodded. He liked Meredith. His heart thrummed with sympathetic hurt when he found out why she was hurting. But they were only at the beginnings of a friendship, and a strange one at that. She was right. He didn't know her well enough to have an opinion here. She certainly didn't need him telling her what she needed. That was why he liked most about Meredith: that she was thoughtful. Competent.

"Of course. You're right," he said. "I'm sorry."

"It's okay. If you can forgive me for being such an ice bitch, I can forgive you for being weirdly overprotective." With a little laugh, she added as an afterthought, "You sound like Richelle. That's basically exactly what she told me after I talked to him and set up the meeting."

"I know you can handle yourself." Sincerely, he told her, "I hope it goes okay. I hope you get what you need to get out of it, or that you prove what you need to prove."

"Yeah." She bit her lip and looked away. "Me too."

She was nervous. It was wrecking her. Ryan didn't know her well, but that much was obvious. A painful flash of memory came to him: the time just after college that his grandmother had begged him to reach out and reconcile with his parents—the parents with major anger management problems, the parents who spent most of his life whining about how his very birth had ruined everything, the parents he had not spoken to once since he moved into the dorms freshman year. But he loved his grandma, and it had seemed important to her. And he had been hopeful, that maybe he would get some sort of resolution or absolution from the meeting. So he had done it. He went to their house, met with them, and had one of the worst days of his life. Never again. Boundaries. He'd only gotten through that day without screaming and crying and throwing things because Naomi had gone with him, had squeezed his hand during all the awful, cutting comments, had stuck up for him when he forgot how to do it himself. He hadn't wanted her to come with him at first, told her he needed to do it alone. By ten minutes in, though, he was more than grateful to have her by his side.

The memory dripped into thought. Into an idea.

"What time are you meeting him for coffee tomorrow?"

"Ten. So I should be free by eleven, if you'd like to reschedule after today's disaster. I have some time." Her tone shifted and she smiled, a small and pleasant offering, when she said, "I'm excited to talk properly about how things went with Stephanie. You set up a dinner date? That's awesome. I'll be ready to help you with some ideas for how to make that go smoothly."

"Thank you. That sounds good." He shoved his hands in his pockets and rocked from foot to foot, uneasy and full of strange energy. "I'll see you tomorrow."

When he left, he did not go to his shop.

He went to Nuestros Niños community center to find Naomi.

When he pushed open the glass door, a little bell tinkled and announced his arrival. A gaggle of four middle school-aged girls looked up from a table where they had laid out stacks of books and homework. They all flashed him shy, sweet smiles and waved hello with pencils in hand. They were girls in Naomi's troupe; she was the mentor and coach for the middle school aged tweens, and they looked up to her like the fantastic, fashionable, badass big sister she was to them. Some of them, he recognized. He had gone to most of Naomi's soccer games, to cheer her and the kids on. And last Christmas, he had carved a bunch of little gifts—picture frames, star-shaped ornaments, plant boxes, whatever he could think of. The girls had painted and decorated the raw wood into sparkly, colorful gifts they gave their parents and siblings. He had made quite a few little friends with his carvings and his smiles and his broken attempts at Spanish.

He greeted them and asked, with his stiff, stilted white-boy pronunciation, "¿Dónde está Naomi?"

They pointed him in the right direction, and he found her down the hall in the arts and crafts room, standing high up on a step ladder to put away boxes of paints and markers. A riotous rainbow of colorful supplies all sat piled on the floor below her. She saw him and asked, "What are you doing here?"

"Need your help with something."

"Great." She nodded down at the puddle of crayons and acrylics and said, "Trade you. Help me re-organize this shelf while you talk."

He dropped to his knees on the cold, paint-splattered concrete floor and sorted the mess into piles, handing her whatever she asked for as she was ready for it. "You're still seeing Richelle, right?"

"Yes. The rest of the paints, please." Quick and snappy, he passed her little bottles of paints one by one. She grabbed them and slid them onto the shelf with alternating hands, turning at the waist with each pivot. She smiled. "I am still seeing Richelle."

"It's going well?"

The smile grew into a grin, but she didn't slow down her motions. "It's going well. It's going really well. I really like her."

Teasing, in sing-song, he asked, "Is she your girlfriend?"

"Maybe!" He handed her the last bottle of acrylic. As she shelved it, she pointed and said, "Brushes."

So he passed her those too, and they plunked out a staccato rhythm as she sorted them by type into plastic cups.

"Good. I'm glad. She seems good for you." As she finished up with the brushes, Ryan looked around the room. Desks and easels everywhere. A big mural on one wall of a bunch of little girls holding hands and smiling, the words Sí, se puede! painted in big, looping letters below. A little bit of mess, a few paint splatters, a few stray bits of glitter sparkling on the floor. The smell in here was so distinct too, and that chalky, dusty tang in the air brought back sense memories of elementary school art class. Naomi did everything with the group she mentored—arts and crafts, leadership, school tutoring, soccer. She liked all of it, but she was a physically active person, and Ryan knew the soccer coaching was her jam, the art a little less so. He wondered if she had been hanging out in this room a little more, reorganizing it, because of Richelle. "Has she come by here yet? To see where you work?"

"No. Not yet."

"She should. I bet she would like it."

"Yeah, I bet she would. Glitter glue, please!" She grabbed a fistful of the shiny tubes from Ryan's hand. "I don't know, though. I don't want to move too fast emotionally, you know? I'm definitely not pulling up with a U-Haul. But I am kind of parked outside her place with a nice, midsize Subaru full of feelings. You know?"

Ryan's forehead scrunched up as he tried to envision how many trips it would take to move all of Naomi's stuff in a Subaru. "That would take at least ten trips back and forth. Two just for your shoes! So, metaphorically, what, like ten dates before you're ready to have a hand-fasting ceremony and adopt a dog together? That seems reasonable! That's not super fast!"

"Thank you! That's what I think, too! Hopefully she's on the same page." She held out her hand so Ryan could help her climb down the step ladder. "Now, what are you here about? I know you didn't come by just to talk about my love life."

He ran a hand back through his hair. "I kind of need to talk to Richelle about something." He explained what was going on with

Meredith and what he planned to do.

Naomi smirked at him. "That's a lot of effort. You're going all out for this girl? I thought she was just your date coach."

"She is! But I like her. We're…not quite friends. I think we could be friends, though. We're almost friends."

"You could be friends…" Naomi shimmied her shoulders and winked. "And then you could be a little something-something else?"

Ryan laughed, embarrassed, and he looked down at the smear of dried pink paint on the gray floor by his shoe. "No. I don't know. I don't think so? I don't know! Maybe. Maybe? I could maybe see it being a possibility. But I don't know if that's an option, you know?"

"Okay," Naomi said skeptically, one eyebrow lifting. "So you're just doing this to be a friend to her?"

He sighed and studied her face, the strong line of her jaw, her kind eyes, the way her dark hair cascaded in waves from her high pony tail. Carefully, he said, "The way she talks about her ex reminds me of how I talk about my parents."

Naomi shivered, repulsed at the mention of his parents. "Ew."

"Yeah. And when she told me she had to meet with him, all I could think about was that time you came with me to see my parents, when I felt like I needed to meet with them and talk things out."

Naomi nodded, her eyes pinched and distant. With a sardonic smile, she nodded and said, "Ah yes, that day. The day your mother declared she could have still been winning beauty pageants, if only you hadn't ruined her life and her physique." She took out her phone, dialed, and said, "Yeah, alright."

After she greeted Richelle and told her what was going on, she passed the phone to Ryan. He explained the situation, how Meredith had told him she was planning to meet with her ex the next day.

"Oh, God, Ryan, please tell me you have an idea for how to stop her from doing that!" Richelle shouted on the other end of the line. "Because I have been trying to talk sense into her for the past two days, and she is not budging!"

"I'm not going to talk her out of it. If she says she needs to do it, then she needs to do it."

Richelle groaned. "Not you too. So what are you calling me for?"

"I was hoping you might have a way of knowing when and where she's meeting with him?"

"Of course I do. She always lets me know where she's going to be if a man is involved, just in case of murder. She texted it to me." She paused. "And also, even if she hadn't, I know all of her passwords."

There was a pause on the other end of the line, with clicking and tapping sounds as Richelle scrolled through her messages to find the information. Ryan stood still and waited, watching as Naomi dragged desks and easels across the floor to rearrange them in a circle.

"Got it!" Richelle told Ryan the name and neighborhood of the coffee shop. He held the phone in place between his ear and shoulder and scribbled down the information with the first thing he could grab, a broken orange crayon. "Wait, so what are you planning to do? I'm not going to let you go busting in and chasing this guy off, or any other he-man nonsense, no matter how much I want to ram an open umbrella down his throat."

"I know, I know. I'm not going to do anything like that." Ryan folded up the scrap of construction paper with the address on it and tucked it into his jacket pocket. "I'm just trying to be a friend to her. I'm not trying to be her knight in shining armor or any of that crap. I know she doesn't need or want one of those."

"So what are you going to do?"

"Well. I paid for date coaching that included a bunch of practice fake dates." He huffed a dry laugh and shook his head, ran his free hand back through his hair to push it off his forehead. "So I'm going to use one of them. I'm going to be her fake date."

Chapter Nine

Across the café table, the man Meredith had once planned to marry ran his eyes up and down over her figure with a soft and leering smile. "You look good, Meredith. Really good."

She said nothing.

Dr. Michael Wilson looked every bit the forty-something, successful professional he had looked when she first met him and when she left him. Tall and slender, with a chiseled jaw, his stylish dark hair had the perfect amount of silvery gray at the temples, and his neat suit and tie announced to the world that he had money. Handsome, if she disconnected.

But she saw memories of their time together reflected in every line of his face, every smarmy, knowing curve of his smirking mouth. And those memories made him repulsive.

Tense and wary, Meredith sat with her back straight and firm against the chair, her hands resting deliberately on the plastic surface of the table, right beside her untouched latte. She cleared her throat. "How have you been?"

"I've been great." He leaned back and affected a casual shrug. But that close and focused look never left his eye, and he kept an unbroken stare on her figure. He had that habit. His gray eyes pale and glittering, he used to make Meredith feel breathless and wanted, like she was the whole center of his universe with that enraptured attention. Now, she saw it for what it was. A predator's look. Calculating. A trap. That attention was less about admiring her and more about keeping her pinned in place. It always had been, even in the days she had thought were good.

While he gently bragged about how his practice was booming and his life was great, Meredith held herself poised and forced herself not to scream. Not to throw hot coffee all over his face. Not to react at all. Low and deep, her stomach burned hot and heavy with twisting dread, with a tendril of sickening panic. Her breath felt short and shallow, but she forced slow, calm inhales through her nose. Her face betrayed nothing.

"Enough about me. Tell me about you!" He smiled and leaned forward a little to rest his elbows on the table. Every muscle in Meredith's core wanted to flinch away from him and pull back, but she did not. "You look like you're doing well. And I have to tell you: you sounded great on the phone, Mer. That pretty voice of yours just brought so many memories flooding back."

"I'm fine." Fine? No. Fine would not cut it. She was better than fine, and she wanted to make damn sure he knew it. She took a breath and forced a smile, though she did notice the quirk of his mouth as his smirk deepened and it made bile creep up her esophagus. "I'm great. I'm doing really well."

"Yeah?" He lifted an eyebrow. It was supposed to be a charming sort of look. Probably, all of the young women he brought on as interns found looks like that charming. Certainly she had, once upon a time.

A barista nudged by their table with a broom and dustpan. While pleasantly warm, quiet coffee shop music played through the speakers overhead, Meredith froze and held Michael's searching, piercing, penetrating gaze. The barista behind them dragged the plastic bristles of the broom across the bare wood planks of the floor with a quiet, *swish swish.*

"I was so disappointed to hear you had dropped out of George Washington."

It was a cut, the slice of a rapier, expertly wielded and intended to wound. Furious, angry heat flared up and down Meredith's spine. She crossed her legs and affected deliberate movement to hide the involuntary wince that had staggered her. "I'm not sorry," she said simply.

And it was true. She wasn't. If her master's degree was the price she had to pay, the thing she had to sacrifice to get out from under his unyielding thumb, then so be it. Shame did prickle the back of her throat, though, at the reminder of how foolish she had been. She had trusted him too fully, put too much faith in him, and let herself become completely reliant on him for her financial security. It had been terribly naïve, to let Michael pay for her housing, her clothes, her every need while in school, and to think that those were gifts of support and belief in her, given in love, to think that they didn't have strings attached. Foolish. Her eyes narrowed and burned, emotion building up within them. She cleared her throat. "It wasn't the right time. But it opened a new path for me, and I've done well for myself without the degree."

"Good. Good." He tilted his head to the side and smiled. "So much wasted potential, though. You would have made a good therapist."

"I still will someday." Her hands were balled into fists. When had that happened? Forcibly, she unclenched her fingers and rolled them out away from her palms. "I have plenty of time. I'm young."

Michael's smile hardened just slightly, and he caught the insult inherent in her words. She was young. He was not. Not anymore.

"Well. You're not that young, Mer."

Twenty-nine. She was twenty-nine, and already an old maid as far as he was concerned. Girls barely out of their teens were more to Michael's tastes; they were easier to manipulate and mold into the perfect partner of his liking. Girls who were intelligent, but not yet smart. Girls who were feisty, but not yet strong. Girls he could gently sink his claws into and shape to his own mold. That had been her. That had been his type. Still was, if the fact that he was marrying yet another twenty-something-year-old former intern was any indication.

Bile crept up the back of her throat.

Thank God she had gotten out.

He sipped his coffee and set the paper cup back down. "If you have any hope of running your own practice someday, you need to have certain things in line by the time you're thirty. Otherwise—"

She cut him off. "I own my own business. I already have a strong client base, should I ever decide to transition to therapy."

Once upon a time, his professional opinions and efforts to mentor her had felt genuine and helpful, and she had welcomed them. Now, she saw the comments for what they were. Control. Always, it had been about softly exerting power over her, carefully, and with a steady, gentle hand that increased pressure measure by measure, so she never noticed how constricting the squeeze had become until she was free of it.

"Good. That's great."

Her throat tightened and her cheeks heated as she realized her mistake. She shouldn't have mentioned the business. He would ask about it. And she didn't want him to know.

Her work paid the bills. It brought her some satisfaction. She enjoyed helping her clients, the good ones, and she believed in her product.

And also, she was ashamed of it.

Long ago, she had aspired to much more than just helping loser guys learn basic social skills. Still, she had those aspirations. She would go back to grad school. Someday. Ambition defined her. Back then, it had all seemed so clear. But now…

Why should she care what this bastard thought of her?

She didn't know. But she did.

The final chords of a strumming acoustic guitar faded as the café song changed. Foam hissed from a latte machine as a barista chatted with a customer and filled an order. Smartly-dressed Washingtonians clipped past the window on the sidewalk outside. A tinkling little bell over the glass entrance door chimed to announce a new arrival. And Meredith grit her teeth so hard her ears nearly popped while she panicked.

Michael smiled at her over their cups of coffee, the elbows of his gray suit resting on the edge of the café table, a question poised on his mouth.

She wanted to reach across the table and snatch the words from his lips before he could speak them. Wanted to rip them away, and his tongue with them.

Of course he was going to ask.

And she was going to have to tell her one-time mentor, one-time finance, the man who had known her every ambition and given her her first job, the man who had introduced her to her graduate school faculty advisors, the man who had once told her that she would get nowhere without his help—that she was average at best, but it was alright, because he could open the right doors for her—that man. She would now have to tell that man that she worked as a cheap matchmaker.

"What sort of business do you own, Meredith?"

As she stared at him, his smarmy, smirking figure, her eyes went fuzzy. Her heart sped up and her head spun, too hot and drowning with the rush of unsteady blood. She couldn't breathe. She couldn't tell him. Because to tell him meant admitting he was right. She had gotten nowhere without his help, and maybe that would always be true. "I—"

"Hey babe! I'm so sorry I'm late!"

Suddenly, the tension shattered and several things happened at once while Meredith's brain raced to catch up. Chairs were moving, scraping in loud screeching drawls as they were dragged across the floor. The table wiggled and sent a few droplets of her hot coffee, barely touched, splattering out through the hole in the top of the lid. Michael glared and looked bewildered, taken-aback. At her. At someone over her shoulder. At the whole coffee shop.

And Ryan McKenna, of all people, leaned down to pop a quick kiss on her cheek.

What the hell had just happened?

While Meredith blinked and used the opportunity of the bizarre distraction to suck in a long, calming breath, Ryan dropped into a chair beside her. He rubbed his hand in circles on her back and asked her, casual and warm, "How's it going, love? How has your morning been?"

Through narrowed eyes, confused and calculating, Meredith glared at him but gave nothing away. For a beat, she held his gaze.

One corner of his mouth lifted in a kind smile. Every feature on his face was held in thoughtful pause, asking her a question, radiating concern. Was she alright? That was what he really wanted to know. He'd swooped in here—pretending to be her boyfriend, no less!—because he thought she wouldn't be alright when faced with her ex.

That scheming, little son of a…

Something.

Maybe.

Maybe not.

Because for every second that she held his eyes, for every hot brush of his fingers across the knobs of her spine, she drew in a steadier breath.

Somehow, with him here on her side, she found the footing she had so nearly lost.

His presence filled her with calm reassurance, gave her some back-up, and threw off the whole uncomfortable back-and-forth pissing contest Michael had somehow trapped her in. She could do this. With Ryan here beside her, she remembered she could do this.

"I'm great." The smile she gave him was small and genuine, but sneaky, reluctant amusement threatened to crack her right open. He saw it and bit back his own grin. "Thanks for joining us."

"Yeah." Michael cleared his throat. "And you are…"

"Ryan. Meredith's boyfriend." Ryan's hand shot out like a barracuda and took Michael by surprise. With a big, squinty-eyed grin, Ryan shook Michael's hand and said, "You must be Trevor! So good to meet you!"

"It's Michael, actually."

"Oh! Sorry about that, Mitchel." While Michael sputtered and glared, and while Meredith worked very hard to contain her nasty amusement behind a smooth façade, Ryan waved one big hand over the table. The other, he kept gently on her back. Through the thin fabric of her blouse, she could feel the rough pads of callous on his fingers and palm. "Anyone need anything? More coffee?"

"No, I'm okay. Thanks." Meredith took the moment to sip her latte, which she had been too nervous and shaky, too focused on presenting a cool and unflappable exterior, to touch. It took a lot of effort, to hold up walls and contain all of the reactions that threatened to scream out of her. With Ryan taking some of the heat, drawing some of Michael's attention, she had room to breathe.

Room to remind herself that she was competent, steady, and proud. Room to remember that she liked her life, she liked her job, and she liked herself, whatever Michael might think.

While Meredith drank deeply and let the warm, creamy coffee soothe her throat, Ryan kept talking. "Been a long time since the two of you have seen each other, right? Lots to catch up on!"

"Mm-hmm." Meredith nodded and refused to look at Michael. He had trapped her too easily once before. Instead, she shifted in her chair so she could turn toward Ryan. Her knee bumped into his, and the smile he gave her at that brush of contact, of closeness, was warm and private. Her heart sped up again, just a little, and for entirely different reasons than before. In clothes she had picked out—those perfectly-fitted jeans, a nice green button-up with the sleeves rolled up over his strong forearms—and with that charming mop of brown curls, he looked gorgeous, and approachable, and strong. While he rubbed circles on her back and toyed with the ends of her hair, she straightened her spine and said, "Michael was just asking about my work."

"Oh yeah?" Ryan's eyes brightened, and he turned back to Michael. "Did she tell you she runs her own business?"

"She did." Michael's tone was clipped and sharp. "Though, she didn't have a chance to explain what, exactly, she does."

Poised and confident, Meredith forced a plastic smile and said, "I run a consulting service where I help clients improve their dating lives. I help people work on confidence and connection issues, and I coach them through lessons on how to be a more respectful, less selfish partner." One corner of her mouth ticked up in a smirk, and her eyebrow lifted to join it, pleasantly satisfied by the little twitch of muscle in Michael's jaw as she sliced back with a razored insult of her own. "I find it's quite a necessary service, these days."

A condescending smirk began to lift Michael's mouth. "Wow. That's…"

Ryan gave him no room. Grandiose and charming, he interrupted Michael and jumped in with, "She runs a great business. Has a gorgeous office, tons of happy clients." While Ryan bragged on her behalf, he grinned across the table at Michael. He gave her shoulder a supportive little squeeze. "She really knows what she's doing, too. Great success rate. How many of your clients' weddings do you get invited to every year? A dozen?"

Meredith laughed. "That's a bit much. It's more like two or three."

"Is that all? It feels like every other weekend we're going out of town for someone's wedding!" He leaned over the table and with a lop-sided grin said to Michael, "I'm telling you Richard, if she had a boat for every time a bride and groom toasted her in thanks at their wedding, Meredith would be admiral of her own navy!"

It was over the top. Ryan was definitely painting it on thick. But also, his boasting was not entirely inaccurate. Many happy clients had thanked her in their wedding toasts. Meredith rolled her eyes but laughed as she nudged Ryan. The gesture came naturally, a casually intimate press of her side against his, and the warmth of his body against her caught her breath when he wrapped his arm a little tighter around her. He was laughing. He was mocking Michael. He was drawing attention to himself. But also, he was completely in tune to her.

"That's Meredith for you, though." Ryan shrugged. "She's a powerhouse. From the minute I first met her, I've been constantly impressed by her."

She held eye contact with him for half a heartbeat too long, and the fondness and sincerity in his warm brown eyes was enough to send her spinning. In a surprised smile, her lips parted and her cheeks flushed. She had to look away.

Michael nodded along with everything Ryan was saying, though the longer Ryan talked and the more Meredith laughed and looked happy, the more his face fell. He looked a bit like he had just chewed up a raw egg and swallowed the whole thing, shell included. "And what is it that you do?"

"I also run my own business!" Ryan said without hesitation. "I design and build furniture. Have a shop over in Eastern Market."

"Oh." Michael nodded, his look sour. "So you build furniture. Who do you design for? Any big contracts? Do you sell to Ikea? Or Walmart, maybe?"

Big and boisterous, Ryan laughed at Michael's attempt at an insult and clapped Meredith on the back. "Good one, Stuart! Funny. No, no, I only do custom work. I'm a member of the DC Artisan's Guild. Maybe you've heard of us?" Ryan paused for half a second. "No? Well, that's alright. They're very selective. It's a pretty niche audience."

Meredith was tempted to laugh. Apparently, her coaching and lessons really had done Ryan some good. That, or he was much more comfortable talking about himself when it meant shutting down some condescending jerk who was trying to insult him.

Or trying to insult her.

With a warm little trill, Meredith recognized that he was putting himself on display, talking about himself—something he hated doing—for her. To help deflect criticism and attack away from her. To make her look good. To help her get through the awful reunion.

Ryan's voice was big and confident while he spoke, but his fingers tapped out a rhythm on the tabletop and his shoulders had gone tense. Nervous. Uncomfortable.

Meredith slid her hand under the table and squeezed his thigh, just above his knee, while she pushed her own coffee cup towards him. He hadn't stopped to get anything for himself. "Do you want some of this?"

He looked at her. Paused. And smiled. "Thanks, babe."

While he took a sip of her latte, drank something warm to calm some of his discomfort, Meredith kept her hand in place on his leg. "Ryan's a guest of honor at the Artisan's Guild Fall Showcase. They're hosting him a few weeks from now, so he can display his work."

"Is that so?" Michael said, tight and snippy. His smile remained unyielding on his face, but Meredith knew that false look well. He hated losing control of a conversation, especially one he'd expected to dominate. Snide, to Meredith, he said, "And you'll be one his arm for the big event, will you?"

Without thinking about it, without hesitating, Meredith smiled. "Of course."

Like a shark scenting blood in the water, the hint of an opening to hunt, Michael's smile lifted. "You always did make great arm candy at events, Mer."

Meredith tensed. Her cheeks heated and flushed and her throat constricted like it was closing with a sudden rush of memories.

Arm candy. That's all he ever wanted her to be at public events. Quiet and beautiful. A lovely, submissive, charming reflection of his power and dominance.

She had tried. That was the worst part of it all. Time and again, for years, Meredith had tried. Tried to be the perfect partner to him, tried to be more poised, tried to be less abrasive and opinionated, tried to fit in with his friends, tried to keep up with his demands, tried whatever he asked for in bed, tried to be what he wanted. Tried very, very hard.

It took some years of growing and distance to realize that no amount of her trying would ever be good enough. There was no final, perfect end product she could have shaped herself into that would have made him happy just to be with her. The trying was his tool and his payoff. He kept her in place with subtleties and nudges that promised there was a reward at the end of it all, if only she would try. And he got off on watching just how far she would bend and push herself and try.

She grit her jaw and bit back the long stream of insults that threatened to come hissing out of her. She controlled her face. Kept herself unreadable. Kept up the appearance that she was untouchable.

But Ryan flinched and held back no measure of disgust on his face. "Gross."

"Excuse me?" Michael glared.

"Meredith is one of the most badass, intelligent, competent people I've ever met. You'd reduce her down to arm candy?" He pressed his hand firm and steady against Meredith's back while he stared Michael down, uncompromising. "That's gross."

It was a breath. It gave her pause.

It was gross. Michael was gross. Why should she reign herself in? Why should she try to act like he hadn't hurt her? He had. And she was not that naïve girl anymore, desperately trying so hard to please him. She was not so easily manipulated or controlled.

And more than that: she wasn't alone in it. The hand at her back didn't feel controlling or possessive. It didn't feel like it in any way diminished her agency or power.

It felt like support. It felt, quite literally, like Ryan had her back. His palm pressed against the knobs of her vertebrae and reminded her that she had a perfectly good spine.

So she might as well use it.

Michael started to slash back at Ryan. "I don't think I like your tone. If you're trying to insinuate—"

But Meredith leaned further over the table and waved a hand through the air in front of his face to cut him off. "What public events are you remembering, Michael? The Psychology

Professionals banquet, where you shamed and humiliated me in front of one of my grad school professors because I dared mention I had read a research paper you hadn't heard of?"

Across the table, Michael leaned back in his chair to get some distance from her. His mouth fell open and he shook his head, disbelieving. With narrowed eyes, he glared at her. It was a familiar look. That look was the one he always used to wear when he thought she was being too emotional, too irrational. "Mer, come on!"

Meredith did not come on. Meredith did not settle down, or stop making a scene, or whatever it was he wanted. With Ryan's warm, heavy hand a solid presence on her back, she huffed a disdainful laugh and kept right on going, her voice steady and sure. "Or were you maybe thinking of that Christmas party you threw for your office, my senior year of college? Remember how you thought I was ignoring you, so you dragged me out in front of the bar and screamed in my face about how I was such an unconscionable bitch? And your admin had to chase you off, and she called me a cab while I cried on the sidewalk and tried to tell her you weren't normally like that? Remember that? Was I good arm candy then?"

Michael gawked, too taken aback to cut her off.

Meredith gave him no quarter, no room to lunge or fight back. "I don't think so. I was never arm candy for you. I was never the pretty, pleasant partner you wanted me to be. But that wasn't the point, was it? Because you sure as hell did enjoy the years-long process you spent trying to turn me into that girl. What's the point of dating a college girl half your age if you don't get to make her into whatever perfect imaginary woman you want her to be, right? And for the record? In case you hadn't figured this out yet? It didn't work."

"Jesus, Meredith!" Shocked and furious, Michael snarled. "What the hell is wrong with you?"

Oh, and wasn't that ironic? Now who was the one causing a scene?

All through her attack, Meredith had kept herself tight and contained, her words a precise rapier in the hands of a skilled and practiced fencer.

At hearing them, Michael sputtered and turned red, spittle clinging to the corner of his mouth as he raised his voice. Behind him, the young barista at the counter, a girl with tattoos and gauges in her ears, watched with concern. Meredith ignored her, ignored Michael, ignored everything but the heat of Ryan's hand on her back as she dug through her purse.

"Here." With a dull and final thunk, she banged the fuzzy little navy blue box down onto the table and ripped her hand back away from it. After several years collecting dust in the back of her underwear drawer, the case looked a little more beat-up than it had the day Michael had lowered himself far enough to get down on one knee for her, but the ring inside was the same. Platinum, with a glittering two-and-a-half carat princess cut diamond, that ring could have paid for a whole semester of school if she'd sold it. She hadn't. She didn't want one more thing from him, didn't want him to be able to claim even the tiniest sliver of credit for her future accomplishments. Maybe she should have thrown it in the river. It might have been satisfying. But this untethering, this return, felt like a freedom she had been waiting for, the release of a breath she didn't know she had been holding. "I wish you every happiness."

Cheesy guitar music drifted down over them, and for a moment that was the only sound in existence. Michael sat tensed and paused as he stared at her, bewildered anger radiating off of him. Of course he was bewildered, as well as angry. She'd never stood up to him so competently before. And besides, men like that never liked having their persona questioned. He'd created a vision of himself in his mind that was so out of touch with the reality of how he treated people, of course it was shocking and jarring to hear someone lay his faults bare. Nothing she had said would change him. Nothing she could say would make him see the subtlety and insidious depth of the wrong he had done to her; men like that were not capable of such introspection. But still. It had felt good to say it, for her own sake.

Michael shook his head and sneered, emotional, one corner of his upper lip lifting. "What am I supposed to say to that? Mer, what the hell are you trying to say? That I—"

"You should go now," Ryan said. All throughout the exchange, he had not shifted, had not moved an inch away from her side. Still, even now, his hand stayed on her back. "Clearly, she is done talking to you. You've got the ring you came for. So go."

Beseeching and strange, like his whole world had been knocked off-kilter, Michael stared across the table at Meredith. Cold and unblinking, face plain and smooth, she stared back and said nothing.

"Fine." He huffed as he grabbed the ring box. A loud screech filled the small, nearly-empty coffee shop as he pushed back dramatically and stood up. "Fine. If that's what you think, Meredith, maybe you should—"

While Meredith stayed stoic and focused on her breathing, Ryan cut Michael off again. "No one wants to hear your last words, Walter."

In a snarling, huffy attempt at dignity, Michael straightened his blazer and strode away. Meredith and Ryan both sat frozen and watched, tense and waiting, until they saw him leave the shop, get into a dark car, and drive away.

Chapter Ten

"Wow." Beside her, Ryan's whole body loosed and slumped a little, his shoulders giving way after the strain of the meeting. His hand stayed in place on her back, even though Michael was gone. "He was a real charmer, huh?"

Meredith couldn't shake off the tension, though. Couldn't let it go. Couldn't move much at all. As soon as Michael left, the full impact of what she had just done surged through her like a tidal wave and she was close to drowning in it. After everything he had said to her, everything he had done to her, every poisoned word, every hateful touch... To finally say it all to him, to finally be rid of that stupid, ugly ring...

Her breath hitched in her chest, a tiny squeaking sob that she quickly snatched back into her lungs. With trembling force, she pressed her eyes shut. The music and the rich scent of coffee all assaulted her senses, suddenly too much to bear, sending too many nerves firing.

"Hey. Meredith." Ryan's quiet voice was steady beside her, but the sound was muffled, her swirling thoughts so thick and raging in her head they were blocking sound. "Are you okay?"

And his hand was still heavy on her back. Too heavy. Too warm. She couldn't stand it, all of a sudden. Couldn't stand the touch of anything. Hands twitching and flailing, she shoved his arm away, and then waved her hand to issue a silent apology.

He slid back. Gave her some space. Let her breathe her way through it.

Awful, wretched memories crashed through her. Fear and humiliation and hopelessness.

Mediocre at best…

Never get anywhere without me…

Take it. Be a good girl for me…

Tainted goods. No one will ever respect you…

You should be grateful…

Stop crying. I can't enjoy it if you cry…

Try harder to…

Flashes of awful memory crashed through her and hit like lightning. She breathed through it. Fought her way through. Until the world inside her calmed, and the world outside her didn't seem too loud and tactile and vibrant to bear. Until the nerves of her sense memories stopped firing in a rapid onslaught.

Fluttering away built-up tears she refused to let fall, she opened her eyes.

Ryan was still there, beside her. With brown eyes as sweet, and rich, and dark as the coffee, he watched her with concern.

Why? He'd only known her for a few weeks. Why had he done

this?

And more importantly, how had he known exactly what kind of support she would need? Because she had needed this meeting. She had needed to face Michael, and she had needed to give the ring back, and she had needed to show off just how strong she was now. She had needed that. But if Ryan hadn't been there to back her up, to take the edge off, she might have drowned under the pressure. Some broken, bandaged little part of her brain remembered everything too well and reverted back in panic. Ryan had pulled her back up and stayed by her side while she fought her own fight. Got in few jabs of his own, sure, but only in support.

It was insightful. Balanced. Thoughtful.

All things she knew he was.

She just hadn't realized he cared enough about her to be the one by her side in this sort of moment. She didn't quite know what to make of that. But she was grateful.

While she sniffed, while she collected herself and blinked to keep tears from running past her eyelashes, she flung out her hand and smacked him.

"Ow!"

"What the hell are you even doing here, Ryan?"

"I thought you could use some back-up." He shrugged. "And anyway, I paid for the premium coaching package, which includes fake dates, right? I figured a fake date is a fake date, even if there's a few extra layers of fake on top of it."

Reluctantly amused, Meredith snorted a laugh and shook her head. Her eyes were still glassy and wet, and she kept herself faced forward, not looking at him. "You are such a menace."

"Wow, thanks, Ryan!" he said, teasing. "You really defused the tension for me, there. I'm so grateful to you for helping me out, I'm going to give you a discount on your coaching!"

"You're the worst." She glanced at him. "Thank you. I hated it. Thank you."

Sincere and sweet, he said, "Any time. I'm sorry I didn't believe you right away when you said you needed to do this. I get it now. You needed this. I just..." He cleared his throat. "I kind of know what it's like, facing someone who hurt you a long time ago. I didn't want you to have to go through it alone."

Emotion threatened to squeeze her again, and she tensed against it as she nodded.

"And hey. What you did just now?" The chair squeaked as he scooted a little closer, but he didn't touch her again. She half wished he would. "You kicked ass today. You were brilliant."

Again, she nodded. Her throat was too tight to speak, and her core clenched uncomfortably. She hadn't felt brilliant. She had just felt bitter and angry and broken. Her bottom lip quivered.

With sudden movement, Ryan lifted up higher in his seat and looked over her head out the window. After a second of searching the view, he said, "Come here. Come on. Come with me."

Too focused on not breaking down and crying in the middle of the coffee shop to argue, she stood and grabbed her purse. With a waved thank you to the barista, Ryan led her out onto the sidewalk. The fall day was sunny, bright and cool, with a clean and cutting breeze that forced a shiver through her. It chilled her overheated face and took the edge off her unease. Out here, in the sun and the wind, she could breathe a little deeper. Ryan tucked his hands into his jacket pockets and jaywalked her across the street, weaving between parked cars. Half a block up, he opened the door to a Mexican restaurant and ushered her inside.

It was empty. At eleven a.m., it had probably just opened. A hostess in a black t-shirt set down the stack of silverware she had been rolling into colorful napkins. "How can I help you?" she called as she made her way to them, from the back table where she had been working.

Ryan pointed to the side wall and called back, "Is your bar open?"

"Yep! Go right ahead!"

"Thank you!" he said, as he placed a hand on the small of Meredith's back and guided her through empty tables. A little confused, curious to see where this was going, Meredith ignored all instincts that told her she should not be drinking before noon, and with a client no less, and let it happen.

Long swoops of cut paper festival flags hung over the bar, each with intricate designs sliced into bright squares of fuchsia, lime green, and turquoise. "What do you want?" Ryan asked. "Margarita?"

What the hell was happening? How had she gotten here? For lack of anything better to do, Meredith kept her mouth shut and nodded.

When the bartender approach, with his hair stylishly slicked back and his biceps bulging out of the sleeves of his black t-shirt, Ryan ordered two margaritas, on the rocks, with salt. And something else. Or, at least Meredith thought he did. She wasn't entirely sure what was happening, because he did it all in Spanish. Which was a surprise.

He pulled out a stool for her. As she sat down, she asked, "You speak Spanish?"

"Kind of. A little." He sat down beside her. "Naomi speaks it, so I've picked some up from her over the years. Her family is all from Mexico."

"Oh." Meredith nodded, still too shaken and off-kilter to do much else. Beside her, Ryan pulled out his phone and typed a text. A few seconds later, his phone buzzed and he read the response. Typed something back. Then got another message back. On it went, in a rapid exchange. Before she could stop and remind herself that it wasn't any of her business, she asked, "Who are you texting?"

He laughed, bashful, while he kept typing on his phone. "Richelle."

"Richelle? My friend and roommate, Richelle?"

He winced and smiled. "She might have been a little worried about you. I'm just letting her know that the meeting went okay, and you did not kill anyone."

"Oh!" Too surprised, too emotionally wrung out to react properly to the strange knowledge, she just nodded. "So that's how you knew where I was going to be."

"Yeah. She and I might have done a little bit of scheming. Naomi helped too, come to think of it."

The bartender set two bright green margaritas onto the shiny wood counter in front of them, followed by a basket of tortilla chips and salsa. Ryan and Meredith both thanked him.

Meredith stared at the coarse grains of salt that lined the lip of the glass in front of her. "So you weren't the only member of the cavalry? I had a whole army behind me today?"

Ryan looked at her plainly, a sweet smile in his eyes. "Yeah. You did."

Without breaking the look, Meredith stared back. Studied him. "But you were the one who actually came with me."

Heat and truth and a swirl of strange and new things lingered between them for a long moment. Ryan nodded.

Her eyes scanned every inch of his face, searching. Why? How? She found her answers, or at least some of them, in the creases of smile lines around his eyes, in the long lashes, in the soft, full curve of his mouth. All of it was just him. This was just who he was, impossible as that seemed. Thoughtful, insightful, and kind. Clever, funny, and brave. It was just him. He was the sort of person who would see what someone needed when they didn't know how to ask for it, who would show up to a battle just to lend support, who would let her take the lead.

He was brilliant.

And for some reason, he had marked her as someone worth knowing, worth seeing, worth showing up for.

Ryan's mouth parted under the heavy weight of her stare, and he bit at his thick, pink bottom lip with the edge of his sharp, white teeth. His chest lifted as his breathing quickened, affected. He waited for her to say something, to do something.

She grabbed her drink and lifted the glass by its green, cactus-shaped stem. Expectant, she held it aloft and waited for him.

With a smile and a breath of shaky laughter, he raised his own glass and clinked it against hers. "Cheers."

"Thank you. For everything." She sipped the cold drink, and the bright pop of the lime and tequila zipped right through her, an electric tingle that chased away the rest of her lingering anxiety over Michael.

Shaky, but growing steadier by the moment, Meredith sat at the bar and talked and laughed with Ryan. He kept her distracted. He let her eat almost all of the chips. And he paid for her drink.

"You going to be okay? You need anything?" Ryan asked when they were back outside on the sidewalk. "You want to go up against him again? I'll help you egg his house, if you want."

Meredith laughed and shook her head. "No, thank you. I don't think that's quite necessary."

"Okay." Ryan shifted from foot to foot and crossed his arms over his broad chest. "Seriously, though. Do you need anything? Because I'm free all day. Richelle has to work, but I promised her I would keep you company if you wanted. If you want a distraction or a friend to hang out with for a while…"

As he trailed off, Meredith rolled her eyes and shook her head, but inside she was laughing. Ryan and Richelle both had very protective streaks, and she wasn't sure she loved the idea of their new union.

How was a stone-cold-Slytherin girl supposed to hide anything from the combined forces of two earnest, emotionally open, supportive, nagging, goddamn Hufflepuffs?

She was okay. Really. She had worked through this angst long ago, and the confrontation with Michael, unsettling and unexpected through it had been, was a relief.

But…

The whole thing had left her shaken. Ever since she had learned Michael had come by her home, she had felt like she was running a marathon to get through it. Now, at the end, she felt so wrung out her legs might give way. She didn't really want to go sit at home by herself, to be honest, and her only appointment for the day was supposed to be Ryan.

So why not keep the appointment? She laughed a little to herself as she considered it.

"Aren't you forgetting something?" she asked him with a sharp look. "We have an appointment. I blocked off my whole afternoon for you."

"Wait, really? You want to keep that? After everything you went through this morning, I thought…"

He trailed off as she shook her head, sure and precise. "I can get some work done. And anyway, I feel like I owe you big time for what you did for me today."

"Hey, you don't owe me anything." He raised his hands and shook his head. "That's not why I showed up today."

"I know." He had shown up to be supportive. To be a friend. A friend…which was what he was looking for in a romantic partner. He'd given her that label, friend, rather quickly. What had he said? That he could start feeling romantic and sexual attraction to someone only after he felt like he would be willing to fight a bear for them? Interesting. Did he know how much his intervention that morning had meant to her? She wondered. And she said, "You paid for practice dates. We're two weeks into your coaching, so I think you're ready. And you came here today so nicely dressed."

Pleased and teasing, Ryan happily brushed at the collar of his shirt.

"So let's have a practice date. A real one, that doesn't involve any of my ex-boyfriends." She shot him a look. "It will be a good chance for me to see if you've been paying attention to everything so far."

"I've been paying attention!"

"Okay." Meredith shrugged and issued a challenge. "So prove it. We've talked about conversation topics, opening up, appropriate places to go and things to do. Put it all together. Wow me with a perfect fake first date."

"That's a lot of pressure. I didn't know there would be a test today." Ryan side-eyed her, but then he paused. All scrunched up and thinking, his lips pursed in a tight pout, his face looked very serious. A light breeze picked up and fluttered his curls. He stayed unmoving, thoughtful, until he suddenly came to a decision. "Okay. I've got it. Follow me."

Chapter Eleven

For half an hour, on the way to their mystery fake-date destination, Meredith kept quiet and asked no questions about where they were going. It pained her. Ryan could tell by the smirking set of her mouth, the snarky little glimmer in her eyes, the way she kept shaking her head when she thought he wasn't looking. While they stood and talked together on the metro, she kept up conversation but eyed him skeptically. During the whole ten-minute walk from the Cleveland Park station, she talked with him but kept her eyes peeled on her surroundings, glancing at every Irish pub and Vietnamese pho place like maybe this would be their destination. Ryan kept walking at a leisurely pace along busy Connecticut Avenue, content to enjoy the nice day and the company, and near-laughing at Meredith's obvious skepticism.

She really did not like surprises. Though she kept it all in, Ryan could tell she was desperate to ask questions about where they were going.

He walked a little slower, just to keep her antsy, and smiled to himself while she huffed and looked around. Nothing to see but old brick apartment buildings with air conditioning units hanging out of every window, and rows of full, mature trees along the street, their leaves still shiny and green—almost but not quite ready to turn yellow and orange.

Within ten minutes of walking, they reached the destination he had in mind. Ryan stopped them in front of the entrance to the park, the big sign, banners, and lush, colorful landscaping popping in welcome greeting. "Ta da!"

Unpleasantly surprised, Meredith glared at the sign with her mouth agape, and then she turned to glare at him. "The zoo? You're taking me to the zoo?"

Ryan nodded.

She pretended to be annoyed, but Ryan noticed the begrudging amusement that tilted her mouth in a smile. "Okay. You're already losing major points on your choice of appropriate first date location and activities. This is not at all in line with the information I gave you on that topic."

"No, no, no!" Laughing, Ryan wagged a finger in her face. While she rolled her eyes, Ryan stepped in a little closer, his height an advantage, and he crossed his arms over his chest as he argued. "You said an ideal first date location should be somewhere inexpensive, public, low key, and where you can have a conversation. How does the zoo not meet all of those criteria?"

Very close, close enough that Ryan could see tiny, pale little freckles he'd never before noticed under her blue eyes, Meredith held her ground and laughed as she shook her head.

"You know." Ryan pointed over his shoulder at the big, vibrant display at the zoo entrance. "I actually put a lot of thought into this. Before today."

"Alright." Meredith's eyes narrowed and her mouth pursed into a tight, reluctant smile. She leaned closer. All of a sudden very close. Half a foot of cool air separated them, but Ryan could feel the aura of warmth from her body as she studied him and smirked up at him. "I might be willing to concede, so long as you put forward a compelling argument. Go ahead. Convince me."

Convince her. That he was listening.

Right.

For a second, with Meredith so close, her eyes so blue, her smirk so clever, he had forgotten what they were arguing about. The grin that slowly bloomed across his face, that squeezed his heart fast, was unconscious and unstoppable.

She was incredible. He had known that already, but...

Damn.

It was one thing to know it—to know that Meredith was brilliant and clever and cutting and funny and beautiful. It was another thing entirely to feel it, to feel the impact of all the glorious edges and curves and twists of her, pumping through his blood.

Shaky, a little dizzy, he took a breath and dove back into her game, answered her teasing challenge. "Okay. Well. For one thing, you said a first date should be inexpensive. The National Zoo is free. I can't possibly pick something more inexpensive than that." He counted off each point on his fingers as he listed them. "Two: this is very public. It's a park in the middle of the day, lots of people around. Three: low key. This is casual, not too intense, and we could leave at any time. And four: this is definitely a place where you can have a conversation! The whole thing is just talking and looking at animals."

One of Meredith's fine blonde eyebrows lifted, and so did her smirk. "What about the other point? I also said a first date spot should be a place where you can get a drink and snacks, but not a meal."

Huffy, Ryan laughed. "I'll buy you an ice cream."

In a flash, Meredith leaned back and her hand shot out into the narrow space between them. "Deal."

He shook on it and walked with her along the wide pathways into the park. "I really did think about all of your guidelines, you know. Tried to come up with good options that fit. But I hate sitting at a table, starring at the person across from me. It makes me nervous. This was something that still fit all of your suggestions, but that let us be up and moving around, doing something."

"Okay. Fine. That was thoughtful," Meredith conceded. "Do you think that was what helped over the weekend?"

"Over the weekend?"

"The hiking group?" she nudged. "When you met Stephanie?"

"Right!" He had nearly forgotten. "Yeah! Definitely. That setting worked a lot better than any of the bars or restaurants I've gone to on first dates before."

"Good. I'm glad you're starting to get the hang of what works best for you." They reached a fork in the path, and Meredith let Ryan lead the way. He knew where he wanted to take her, and thankfully she didn't question. She was too focused on work. On the client she was trying to set him up with. The client, Stephanie, who was nice and pretty and perfectly fine…

But who wasn't nearly as interesting as Meredith.

They'd had a nice time on the group hike, had talked about a bunch of books and TV shows they both liked, and it was fun. But even though Stephanie seemed warm and open and sweet, Ryan couldn't stop thinking about Meredith. Her sharp tongue, her willingness to push, her strong opinions. He was drawn to her. Couldn't stop thinking about her. And that slight prickly edge she had, that quick and biting humor, had him interested. He was hooked on her, tangled in her thorns. Stephanie was nice. Meredith was more.

Which was probably a problem.

He wasn't supposed to be so drawn to, so intrigued by her. He wasn't supposed to care for her so quickly and so personally.

"Do you feel ready for dinner with her? Do you want to talk anything through?"

"I feel fine about it. We already have some things we know we have in common, so that helps." Ryan glanced at Meredith as they walked along the main pathway through the heart of the zoo, the crowds thin and meandering on the weekday afternoon. Bright autumn sunlight glinted off the silvery wave of Meredith's long hair, and her heels clicked smartly on the pavement. The sight of her, all posh and pressed and professional, walking comfortably through this breezy, tree-lined outdoor setting, was a strange and lovely juxtaposition. He couldn't help but glance at her, his eyes lingering over the strong lines of her profile. And he couldn't stop himself from saying, "Are we supposed to talk about that, though?"

"Talk about the things I'm supposed to be coaching you on?"

"Right, but this isn't coaching, is it? I mean, isn't this supposed to be a fake date? If I'm supposed to treat this like an actual date, for practice, then I don't think I should be talking about the other women I'm casually maybe seeing." His heart sped up a little, and the words came out rushed with the little tangles of deception. It was a good point. But really, he didn't want to talk about Stephanie or anyone else he might end up dating. All he wanted was to spend the day with Meredith. Meredith, who had been through hell this morning and who needed a good day. He wanted to give it to her.

Meredith, who wouldn't be interested in him, even if he did know for sure that he was, maybe, possibly, interested in her. He was her client. She did things like this all the time. And besides, if she was interested, she wouldn't be bringing up his other potential love interests. No, he would have the date with Stephanie tomorrow. He would keep trying to follow Meredith's advice to find a serious partner.

But for today?

Maybe he wanted to pretend a little. To not think about it. To enjoy quality time with a beautiful woman and not feel so wrong-footed or complicated. To spend time with Meredith and be a friend to her on a hard day.

After a pause and a long, scrutinizing glance out of the side of her eye, Meredith nodded. "Alright. That's a good point."

Ryan smiled to himself and shushed the tiny, unimportant voice in the back of his head that insisted this was a little dishonest of him, a little misleading. Later. He could worry about that later. For now, he had the whole day with Meredith and a destination in mind.

As they kept to the main pathway through the zoo, ignoring all of the turn-offs and side paths that led to the animal exhibits, Meredith glared at him. "Ryan, we're missing all the good animals! We just walked right past the pandas!"

"We're not missing the good animals. They're in enclosures, not running wild. They'll still be there when we loop back around." He laughed and shook his head at her huffy insistence. "I know you hate surprises, but will you please just trust me for a second? We'll see all the animals, but there's somewhere in particular I want to start."

"Alright." Meredith grumbled a bit, but good-naturedly. She followed him along the path. "I haven't been here in ages. How do you know your way around?"

"I used to live a few blocks away. I would come here for runs in the morning."

When they reached the spot Ryan had in mind, he nudged Meredith along, his hand lingering on her back longer than strictly necessary. He gestured at the rocky enclave of the exhibit. "Here. This is where I wanted to start."

As Meredith's face lit up, she beamed like she was holding a stardust secret in her mouth, her smile tight and contained but no less vibrant for it. Ryan watched her and felt fond and warm. She hurried up to the side of the enclosure to look down into the deep blue pool. Simple and happy, she said, "Seals are my favorite animals."

"I know. You mentioned that last week."

"I did? No I didn't. Did I?" The lines of confusion on her forehead faded into a soft and sincere look, full of understanding. "And you remembered. And you brought me here because I had a bad day."

Her eyes were almost too blue to look at, too deep, too bright, too intense. Too beautiful. He looked anyway, and his breath went quick and thin while she stared up at him, tender and all-knowing. It ached. Voice caught, he nodded.

A tiny, trembling quirk of her bottom lip was all she betrayed, but her eyes were sad and soft. She was affected. By the morning, and by him. "You're sweet."

That was all she'd say on the matter. Before he could respond, she turned back to watch the sleek gray and brown seals swimming in elegant laps around the pool. In silence, they stood side-by-side with their thoughts and stared.

"I love their snoots," Meredith said, her voice thin and quiet, almost a whisper. "They're so long and stupid looking."

Ryan squeezed his eyes shut and snorted a laugh. "Snoots."

"Shut up. Don't make fun of me." With a sharp, pointy elbow, Meredith jabbed his side and he laughed while he shook her off. "Hey, Ryan. Would you steal one of these seals for me if I asked? Because I had a bad day?"

"Definitely." Ryan nodded as he crossed his arms over his chest. Very serious, he announced, "I'm going to need a bucket of fish and a top hat."

Both of them watched as a speckled harbor seal took a sliding leap out of the water and up onto a platform. A smile tugged at Meredith's mouth. "Why do you need to wear a top hat to steal animals from the zoo?"

"Oh, it's not for me. It would be for him." He pointed at the harbor seal, which gave a baleful, woeful honk and looked, with sad puppy-dog eyes, in the direction of where food should be. "I figure if we put him in a disguise, he can just walk right out with us. Very dapper. No one would ask questions of a gentleman in such a fine hat."

Meredith giggled. The laugh snuck out, and she bit it back with her mouth closed, but silly little hiccupping sounds of amusement shook through her. When she couldn't keep it all in, she hid her face in her hands and let them contain all of her quiet laughter. Watching her, Ryan beamed with softly burning happiness. He wanted nothing more than to make her laugh again, to see her glow.

"Come on." In a flash of wild, shaky bravery, he wrapped an arm around her shoulders. "There's an underwater viewing area."

Together, with Meredith pressed warm and tight against his side, they walked down the slope and around to the viewing area. The glass walls were tucked inside curved and wild architecture designed to look like a mermaid's grotto, and Meredith smiled as the cool dappled light through the water shifted and shimmered in the dark little hollow. She leaned in a little closer. Her arm snaked around his waist. He held her there, safe and sweet against him, and held himself still.

Silence rang and echoed in the little viewing area, and they stood together in it for a long while. Heart pounding. Head spinning in a pleasant, gentle whirlwind of possibility and new feeling. And calm. Perfectly happy and at peace. With the top of her head just within reach, with her whole body in his arms, Ryan drew in lungfuls of her. Sweet and fruity, the scent of her shampoo swirled through the cool air surrounding him, softly overpowering the salty, fishy smell of the seal exhibit. Together, they watched the water. Seals swam past the window in graceful glides, bubbles trailing out from their twitching whiskers. Meredith said nothing. Ryan didn't either. This was too lovely, too tender to be real, and he was afraid that speaking, or even thinking too much, would break it.

When Meredith did speak, a long while later, her voice was a hoarse whisper. "Hey Ryan?"

Still he said nothing, but he looked down at her and nudged.

She took a deep breath and steadied herself. "Thanks for fighting a bear with me today."

It was so easy, so natural, like breathing, to lean in a little closer and rest his forehead against the top of her head. Intimate and close, her murmured into her hair, "Anytime."

Beneath the arm wrapped around her shoulders, her breathing hitched. A tiny squeak of emotion cracked out of her throat while she held herself still and tired not to cry in the middle of the zoo. Raw and exposed, the pain of all those old wounds dragged to light by her ex was too much for her to ignore. She needed to feel it, to honor the mark it had left on her heart.

While the seals swam in effortless loops and flips through silent water before them, Ryan held onto Meredith and said nothing. It was what would help her, and he wanted to give.

"Alright." As she pulled away from him, that entire side of Ryan's body instantly chilled and missed her heat, but he stepped back to give her space. She sniffed and wiped the bit of moisture away from her eyes, careful not to smudge her mascara. It only took a moment for her to pull herself up, to slide her mask back on, and Ryan smiled a little to see it. Control and competence were powerful in her core, and Ryan liked that she was so guarded, so thoughtful in how she presented herself. But he also liked the little glimpse inside her walls, and that he had been briefly welcomed inside them. She straightened her hair and blazer. "I'm ready. What's your favorite animal? Wait. No. Don't tell me. I'm going to figure it out."

All business, on a mission, Meredith marched out of the grotto. Completely enamored, completely captivated, completely fucked, Ryan followed.

Chapter Twelve

He went on the date.

Of course, he was supposed to go on the date. Obviously. Ryan was a client in search of a compatible, long-term, serious partner, and Meredith had a professional obligation to help him find that compatible person. Exactly as she had recommended, exactly as she had hoped and planned for, Ryan had gone out to dinner with another client, Stephanie. A good match. And a good sign that they had already met, connected, and wanted to see each other again. Good. Good!

But after the day before, when Ryan had showed up to help with her ex, when he had bought her margaritas and taken her to the zoo and given her the space to talk and feel and process with someone comforting and kind by her side…well. A tiny, selfish, irrational little part of Meredith had kind of hoped that he would skip it. That he would shrug and smile with those stupid dimples, and say, *Stephanie seems great. But really, I'd rather spend more time getting to know you.*

And really, if he needed a date to his big showcase debut two weeks from now, he could do no better than Meredith. She could rock formal wear like she was born in it, and she had strong professional networking skills that would be an asset to him.

Even if it was fake.

Fake was okay. She could do fake with Ryan, to help him out. Even though that fake date with Ryan at the zoo had been the most thoughtful, the most fun, and the most intimate date she'd been on in years. It was fine. For a moment, a few times yesterday, he had looked at her and she had thought...

But no. She shook it off. Any interest she'd thought she'd seen from him, she must have imagined. Most likely, it would be too soon for him to feel that way about her, anyway. He needed time. And with the crushing deadline of this showcase, he wouldn't get it with her. If he had been interested in seeing if they could connect further, he wouldn't have gone on the date she'd set him up on. Probably.

Stupid to worry about it. In yoga pants and a plush, oversized sweater, her hair up in a bun, Meredith heaved herself up from her bed, kicked a few decorative pillows out of the way, and trudged out into the hallway. Laughter greeted her at the landing, warm and loud, drifting up the stairs along with light from the living room. The sound of Richelle's round voice and happy giggling was enough to kick Meredith in the pants and get her to stop feeling so sorry for herself, and she smiled as she stomped down the stairs. Loudly. To give her roommate some warning that someone was about to crash in on her date.

Richelle didn't mind, though, and neither did Naomi. When Meredith reached the foyer and walked past the archway that led to the living room, her bare feet and sure tread making the floor boards squeak, Richelle and Naomi both called out to her.

"Meredith! Come join us!"

"No, no!" Meredith waved them off. "I don't want to interrupt you guys. I'm just going to grab something to eat."

"We just ordered a pizza. Come have some and sit with us for a while!"

On the one hand, Meredith considered Richelle and Naomi, slouched and cozy on the couch. Both of them were dressed in glitzy club dresses, Richelle in glittery black, and Naomi in vibrant red. Naomi's gold heels and purse twinkled in a discarded pile on the floor. They looked cozy, Naomi curled up on the sofa with her legs folded under her, Richelle snuggled close. Both of them glowed happiness, as bright and shimmering as Naomi's bronze highlighter. It would be rude to interrupt.

On the other hand, that open box of pizza on the coffee table was temping.

"Oh, alright. Just for a minute." It was the smell of the pepperoni that did her in. She grabbed a greasy slice and sat down in the arm chair across from them, her foot propped up on the edge of the coffee table. "What are you two doing all dressed up and snuggling on the couch? I thought you were going to that bar with the salsa music tonight?"

"Oh, we are," Naomi said. "But the good music doesn't start for a couple more hours. You should come with us!"

Richelle's eyes and grin went wide at the suggestion. "Oh my God, yes. You should!"

"No, I don't think so." Meredith took another big, cheesy bite of pizza to avoid having to say more.

"Anyway, I'm glad I got a chance to talk to you, Meredith." Naomi sat up a little straighter, and tugged at the short hemline of her dress to keep her thighs covered. She glanced at Richelle, a question. "I wanted to ask you something."

Richelle nodded, silently urging her on.

"I mentor a group of middle school aged girls, and I was hoping you might be willing to join us for our Women Entrepreneur Day next spring."

"Seriously?" Meredith blinked and swallowed down a bite of pizza. "I would love to! Tell me more about it."

Naomi explained her work, and that she organized opportunities for the girls she mentored to meet with women business leaders, professionals, and entrepreneurs from a diversity of fields. "Each of the women will present about the work they do and answer questions, and then we'll pair each of you up with a few of the girls to help them work on a mock business idea. And you run such a cool, unique business, I think the girls will really enjoy learning from you. We'll have about ten women entrepreneurs, mostly Hispanic and Latinx women, but not all." She shrugged a little and smiled. "My mom will be there."

Touched and more than a little excited, Meredith nodded. She liked her job. Even loved it, sometimes. She was proud of what she had built and the work that she did. Most other people she told about it, other than clients, struggled to see the value. Naomi's support and validation was powerful. "Definitely count me in. That sounds fantastic."

"Your mom will be there?" Richelle asked. "What does your mom do?"

"She's a vet. She has her own clinic, up in New Jersey."

"I didn't know that! That's awesome. And she's coming here, to

DC, for Women's Entrepreneur Day this spring?"

Sly and sweet, Naomi nodded.

"Huh." Richelle and Naomi only had eyes for each other, and Meredith smiled and tried not to watch the tender moment too closely. "Will I perhaps be meeting Mama Martinez when she comes to town?"

"It's Mamita Martinez, thanks. And yeah." She flicked Richelle's shoulder with a long, painted finger nail. "You'd better."

Richelle grinned and gazed into her girlfriend's eyes, and Meredith considered sneaking out of the room, but the sappy moment didn't last long. Naomi turned back to her. "Thank you so much, Meredith. The girls are going to love you. I'll send you all the information."

Meredith had finished her pizza and she should go, she should leave them alone. But Richelle launched into a ridiculous story of what her second graders had gotten up to in last week's art class, and soon the three of them were laughing and chatting together comfortably. A little bit of tension lingered in the back of Meredith's mind, discomfort that perhaps she wasn't welcome in this private gathering, but her intuition tended to be good. She didn't feel like a third wheel. Sitting here, comfortable and cozy in the living room, just felt like being with two friends. It was enough to distract Meredith from her twisted-up feelings about Ryan.

At least it was, until Naomi turned on her. "So are you allowed to tell me how Ryan's doing with this coaching?"

"I'm allowed to tell you, yeah. I don't give out any personal information about my clients, but..." Meredith shrugged and brushed back an imaginary strand of hair. "He's doing well. He's fine. He just needed a new perspective and a little bit of a push."

Naomi nodded, accepting this, but Richelle's eyes narrowed, searching and knowing, as she studied Meredith. Though a little flush of heat rushed up her neck, Meredith kept her cool.

"And this woman he's out to dinner with tonight. She's a good one? You think she'd be a good match for him?"

"Yeah. Stephanie. She's another of my clients. She's very smart, pretty, sweet. They have a lot of the same interests. I think they'll get along well." Meredith forced a smile and tried not to sound bitter. "Clearly, they already got off to a good start, since they decided to see each other again after that group hike."

Naomi shrugged and gave a skeptical, sour look. "Eh. Maybe. I don't know. He didn't talk about her at all after they did the hiking thing, beyond just the basics that he met her. I worry he is maybe just going along with this because he feels pressure to get it right, and that he doesn't trust himself." She laughed and sat forward. "Really, I should have gone with him on the date tonight. I can always tell when he's into someone before he can."

"Interesting. Well, I guess we'll see how he feels after tonight. If you have your doubts, I'll push him a little bit in our next session, just to make sure he feels good about everything." Meredith paused. "He really didn't talk about her at all? Stephanie?"

Naomi shook her head.

And yesterday, at the zoo, he had been reluctant to talk about anything regarding his upcoming date. "Huh."

While Meredith stared down at her bare toes on the shaggy white throw rug, Naomi said, a bit cryptically, "He has been talking nonstop about you."

Meredith jolted up. Naomi feigned innocence as she picked bits of pepperoni off a slice of pizza. "Well, that's probably only natural.

We have been spending a lot of time together lately. For the coaching."

Naomi shrugged while she popped slices of pepperoni into her mouth and then put the wrecked, shredded-up piece of pizza back in the box. "Yeah, but he's not talking about the coaching. It's all...*Meredith told me the funniest story.* And, *Did you know Meredith did this,* and *Meredith can do that?* And, *I wonder if Meredith likes...*"

"Oh!" Richelle laughed, low and deep in her throat. "You think he's into her?"

Naomi shrugged. "Maybe. I'd have a better idea if I saw the two of them together."

"How do you feel about that?" Richelle asked.

"I feel like that's not really any of my business to speculate about," Meredith said, and she tried to mean it. Really, though, her head was spinning, her chest and neck suddenly flushed. "And anyway, it doesn't mean anything. If he was interested in me, why would he go on a date with someone else?"

It was a solid argument, and the ace up her sleeve that she'd hoped would shut the conversation down. But she couldn't keep a tiny tinge of bitter rejection out of her voice, and Richelle had known her too long to miss it. "Oh my God!"

Meredith tensed. "What?"

Richelle nearly pushed Naomi off the couch in her rush to sit up straight and stare at her friend, and Naomi, though ruffled, didn't seem to mind. "You like him! Whether or not he's into you, you're into him! Meredith. That's big. That's huge. You never catch feelings. Not in ages."

Meredith sighed and shook her head. "Maybe. I think maybe I'm just vulnerable right now. Because of the whole thing with…"

"With Shitlord Michael. Yeah. That makes sense." Richelle smiled sweetly. "And it's also complete garbage. You're deflecting."

"I am not deflecting!" Meredith screeched, even though she was obviously deflecting. "I just—"

Her phone buzzed in her pocket, a lifeline, and Meredith leapt up and grabbed for it.

"Oh, how convenient." Richelle rolled her eyes. "Go ahead, answer your phone, more deflecting!"

"This is not deflecting. This is—" Meredith looked down at her phone screen and stopped dead. All the wind rushed out of her sails. Dammit. So much for deflecting. "It's Ryan."

Naomi and Richelle's laugher followed her, mocking her, as she stalked out of the living room and went to take the call in the kitchen. Not because she was eagerly awaiting word from Ryan, and not because she was perversely pleased that he was calling her so early in the evening. Just because this was work. That was all. "Hey, Ryan. How'd the date go?"

"It went fine!" he said on the other end of the line. Meredith held the phone to her ear and tucked her arms in tight to her body as she leaned her hip against the edge of the kitchen counter. He sounded bright and cheerful. "It was really nice. Until I fucked it up. We decided neither of us was really feeling it, so I was just calling you to let you know that I am a failure, and despite all of your hard work, I am destined to die alone!"

Meredith snorted into the receiver. "You are not destined to die alone."

"Yeah, you're right. I'll probably get a cat. Maybe a dog. An animal companion. So when I die, they will be there to eat my eyeballs."

"Gross. Also, you are such a drama queen." Meredith laughed a little. This was unfortunate. Obviously, she wanted her techniques to work and her clients to have a successful date. But a wretched, selfish little goblin in her stomach flipped and spun in a happy dance at the news that things had not worked out between Ryan and Stephanie. "What went wrong? Do you want to talk about it?"

"Nah," Ryan said as Naomi entered the kitchen in her fancy dress and bare feet. She walked right up to Meredith. "I'll tell you about it in our next session."

Naomi brushed a hand against Meredith's arm and mouthed, Invite him over.

Meredith tensed and shook her head at Naomi, while at the same time telling Ryan, "Alright. If you're sure."

I'll help you out, Naomi mouthed. She poked Meredith's arm. So you have a better idea what's going on with him.

"I—" Meredith started to answer, not sure who she was talking to or what she wanted to say anymore.

"Yeah, I'm sure," Ryan said. From his breath, and the hum of traffic in the background, it sounded like he was walking. "I'll just go home and commiserate with Naomi."

"Naomi's here, actually. She's spending the evening with Richelle."

Naomi leaned in closer to the phone. "Hi Ryan!"

In a rush, Meredith dove in before she could think about how stupid this was. "You should come over! Join us for a while. We have pizza." She winced, but Naomi smiled and nodded while she rubbed an assuring hand up and down Meredith's arm.

"Yeah!" Naomi shouted. "Come and hang out with us, Ryan!"

"Yeah, Ryan!" That was Richelle. She yelled as she walked up and wrapped an arm around Naomi's waist. "Come hang out with us!"

"Um." Ryan paused, and Meredith held her breath. "Yeah, maybe just for a while. If you really don't mind."

Relief coursed through Meredith, and she didn't even know why. This was ridiculous. This didn't mean anything. But she smiled against herself. "I'll text you my address."

When she hung up, Richelle and Naomi both smirked.

Meredith hid her face in her hands. "Oh my God, this is a terrible idea."

"It is not!" Gentle and soothing, Naomi grabbed her wrist and pulled it down away from her face. "This is a good thing. You're kind of into him. I suspect he is kind of into you. Let's just get the two of you together in a casual, group hang-out and see how things go. We're not going to harass you guys or embarrass you. It will be fine."

"Exactly." Richelle looped her arm through Meredith's and led her back out of the kitchen. "I'm your best friend. I know you have trust issues, but you can't really think I would betray you and embarrass you in front of the cute boy, right?"

"I know. I know."

"Okay, good." Richelle smacked Meredith's ass and sent her towards the stairs, and Meredith gave a little squeak and hop.

"Now go put real pants on."

She ran upstairs and pulled a pair of jeans on, but didn't change anything else. This was silly. This wasn't a date. She didn't need to dress up or try too hard. She also did not need to be blushing right now, but she didn't have any control over that. Alone in her bedroom, she took a moment to sit on the edge of the bed, hug a throw pillow, and question all of her life choices. Alright, so yes, she maybe had a bit of a crush on this guy. And his friend seemed to think he had a bit of a crush back. And he was on his way over. To hang out. Casually. As friends.

Meredith's heart raced as she grit her jaw and sucked in long, slow breaths.

This was fine. She could navigate this.

It was only just that Richelle was right; it had been a very long time since she'd had feelings for someone. All of her dating in the past few years had been hook-ups and casual flings. Ryan was not that. What she felt for Ryan was not that.

What she felt for Ryan was…

Big. Real. Maybe a little scary. The potential of them was a grand and sweeping universe of possibility.

By the time she put on her big girl pants, finished her existential crisis, and made it back downstairs, Ryan was already knocking at the door. She let him in.

"Hey." He smiled that stupid, gorgeous, lopsided smile with the damned dimples as he stepped into her foyer. He looked around, but his brown eyes kept landing back on her. "Nice place."

"Thanks." She smirked as she looked him up and down. "Nice outfit."

"Thank you." He waved up and down at his tight jeans, the pale button-up, and the hip black blazer he wore layered on top. All of it, she had picked out during their shopping excursion. "I have this great style consultant. She works miracles."

"You're not wrong. Come in."

In the living room, Naomi and Richelle greeted Ryan as he sat down in an arm chair across from them, beside Meredith.

"How did it go tonight?" Naomi asked. "You fucked it up?"

Ryan winced and nodded. "It started off well. It was nice. Still didn't feel any sense of attraction or chemistry, but I tried to not panic about that, tried to think that that can come later, and wanted to give a good effort at actually sharing and getting to know each other. I know I have self-sabotaged a lot of past dates because I don't share anything real about myself, so I was determined to not do that this time."

Naomi and Meredith both raised their eyebrows. Naomi asked, "And then what happened?"

"And then I…" Ryan shook his head and laughed. "I kind of blurted out that my parents didn't love me."

"Oh my God. You beautiful idiot." Naomi pouted and reached out to pat Ryan's leg, and she laughed a little, but the look in her eyes was fierce, and knowing, and raw.

"I know."

"Okay. Well. That's not the worst thing. I give you points for trying." Meredith said. "But you overcorrected."

"I overcorrected. Yep! It got weird after that."

"Yeah, I'd imagine." Meredith made a mental note to check in with Stephanie and adjust her strategy for their next session, but she stopped short once she fully processed what Ryan had tried to laugh off. "Wait, your parents didn't love you?"

Eyes wide, he wagged his finger at her. "No way! No therapy. You have to finish your degree before you're allowed to psychoanalyze me."

Richelle cackled laughter. "You tell her, Ryan!"

Meredith raised both hands in defense. "Alright!"

Had they been in her office, in a session, Meredith would have pushed for more answers. Ryan was thoughtful, affectionate, and demonstrative, and if his parents were not, if they had never taught him how to share his emotions and connect with people in a healthy, trusting way, that might explain why he stumbled when talking about himself. It could be relevant to his dating situation. And more so, she wanted to know him. Wanted to know who he was and where he had come from.

But this wasn't work, they weren't alone, and Ryan hated having so much attention on himself. She knew that much. So she deflected. For him, to rescue him from the burning heat of the spotlight, she dropped it and changed the subject.

After Richelle and Naomi had both told a few more ridiculous stories about some of the crazy, funny things the kids they taught got up to, conversation turned back to Meredith and her work.

Naomi asked her, "Do you ever have any really crazy, weird clients?"

Meredith shrugged and thought about it. "Not too many. A few people with weird fetishes and kinks, but they all tend to be really nice. Mostly, the rough ones are guys who don't respect women and we have a bunch of tests to figure out how deep that disrespect goes in the beginning. I don't work with anyone I consider really crazy and weird."

"Like the tests Richelle gave Ryan when they met."

"Yeah, exactly," Meredith said while Ryan and Richelle smiled at each other.

Comfortable, Naomi leaned back against the arm of the couch and stretched her legs out across Richelle's lap. Absent-minded and sweet, on instinct, Richelle rubbed her fingers into the arch of Naomi's foot.

They looked so cozy, so at ease with each other, and so in love. Meredith glanced at Ryan and they shared a tender smile at their friends' happiness.

"How do you know if a couple is going to last in the long run?" Naomi asked.

It caught Meredith off-guard a bit. "I don't."

"You work in this field, though. Love and dating. You must have some insight."

Meredith thought about it for a moment, and watched the smirk that grew across Richelle's red lips. Ryan was staring at her too, and Meredith could feel the weight of his gaze on her, waiting for her response. "I really don't know if a couple is going to last in the long run. But I do tend to know some things, some warning signs, that mean they won't last in the long run. Like when one or both of them have really low self-esteem. That tends to be a glaring red alarm bell. People who don't know their own worth tend to tolerate too much, or they let themselves be treated badly because they're lonely. Relationships like that often end as people learn and grow and know themselves better. But I don't know how to tell if a couple will last. I don't have any tests or tricks to predict that."

All three of them nodded thoughtfully. Naomi nudged Richelle with her foot. "We've got no problem there. I already know I'm the best."

Richelle hummed her agreement. "And I am diamond quality. We match."

"You know what you should do, to test if couples are strong and solid?" Naomi pointed at Meredith. "You should challenge them to poop in front of each other. If they can't do that by the end of year one, they aren't cut out for true love. That's what I say!"

Shocked, Meredith laughed. "I am not going to advise my clients to defecate in front of each other. That's terrible dating advice. I would have no more clients!"

"Bad dating advice, maybe. But good love and relationship advice. Seriously!" Quick, a flash of glittering red and bronze, Naomi sat up and lifted onto her knees to pet and play with Richelle's hair. As she twisted a finger through a tight, black curl, she announced, "We're going to die. All of us! Like, seriously, think about that. We are going to die someday! And if you fall in love with someone, and you can't use the bathroom in front of them, either because you're not comfortable or because they think it's gross, or whatever, how the hell can you expect to die in front of them? If you can't poop in front of them now, then thirty years from now, when you get cancer, how can you trust them to change your diapers and carry you to the bathroom? How? You can't! Our human lives are short, and our mortality is a messy and undignified affair. You can't trust a love you can't poop in front of. That's what I always say."

"You always say that, huh?" Ryan smirked.

"Yes. I do." Naomi smirked back. "As of now. But it's a good point, and you know it!"

"Actually...yeah. That is a good point." Meredith had to concede to the reality of it, even though it was ridiculous. But yes, an uncomfortable truth. "I don't think I'll ever actually pass that specific advice to clients, but you do make a good argument about how people in love need to be able to see each other as actual, real people."

"Babe, have you ever used the bathroom in front of anyone?" Richelle asked.

"Yes." She pointed across the room. "Ryan!"

"That's different!" Immediately, he tried to wave her off. "That's not the same thing!"

"Yes it is! And anyway, Ryan got real up close and personal with the messiness of my mortality." She sank down with her legs out to the side of her, perched like a mermaid on a rock, with her arm wrapped around Richelle's shoulders. "He took care of me after I had surgery. My mom was supportive, and she was there for the actual hospital stay, but I couldn't ask her to take off that much time from work. And my little sister came and helped out, and she was very sweet, but she was only ten years old at the time. Ryan and I were living together, and he was my best friend, but I did not expect him to step up in such a big way. He did. He carried me around and wiped my ass and changed my bandages. Ryan's the real deal. He set the bar for me."

Ryan rolled his eyes, but his smile was soft and fond.

"Don't roll your eyes at me!"

Meredith said nothing. In silence, too warm, she sat with her thoughts and felt wrenchingly, painfully alone. She couldn't imagine someone loving her that well, treating her with such unflinching care. In the three years she had lived with Michael, including the time when she'd planned to marry him, she had never once used the bathroom in front of him. He had walked in on her while she was peeing once, and then threw a fit, scoffed, and demanded that she lock the door next time. Ridiculous. There had never been easy comfort between them, no real trust. Never, not in even the simplest moments, had she been truly and comfortably herself while with him. How could she ever have thought that he really loved her? How could she ever have thought that marrying him was a good idea?

Well. Maybe because she had been young and proud-headed, and Michael had worked hard to convince her that her own bar should be lower, that she'd never be able to be herself in a relationship, that she'd always have to try just a little bit to make herself more likeable. She hadn't yet realized that every single romance novel and romcom and love story that straight women loved to swoon over was accurate and real, and was setting women's expectations for men exactly where they should be. She hadn't yet realized that people like Ryan McKenna actually existed.

It saddened her. She had been one of those people she'd warned about—someone with not enough self-esteem. No more. Her bar was high. Sky high. And with every new detail she learned about Ryan, the more she thought he might just be able to reach it.

Even when the new details she was learning were oh-so-conveniently dropped by his best friend, in an earnest and heartfelt, but also painfully transparent attempt to talk him up and show him off.

It was working. Maybe.

Uncomfortable under Naomi's loving attention, but fond and soft all the same, Ryan turned to Richelle. "That is true. And any time you're really to take over the daily duty of wiping her ass, you are welcome to it. I would be happy to pass that mantle on to the right person."

"Hey!" Naomi shouted while Richelle threw her head back and cackled, and Ryan winced and ducked when Naomi swung out an arm in his general direction. While Naomi laughed with Richelle, Ryan turned to Meredith and caught her staring at him.

She should have looked away.

She didn't.

Heat and strange, uncertain meaning passed between them. So many questions. So many possibilities. Meredith held the gaze unblinking, a smile playing on her lips, her heart racing, until Ryan melted in a bashful grin and turned away. A little smudge of pink heat and emotion crept up the back of his neck, just above his collar.

Interesting.

Also interesting was the knowing look, the raised brow, that Naomi shot in Meredith's direction. "Alright, enough talk about my ass—which I am perfectly capable of wiping on my own, thanks very much. Are you coming out with us tonight or not?"

It took Meredith a second to realize the question was directed at her. "No? No. I don't think so, guys."

"Oh, come on!" Richelle began to needle, too. "It's going to be really fun! It's all good music, cheap drinks, and people trying to salsa dance! They give little lessons, too, so you learn a few steps. You should come! Both of you should come!"

Ryan winced. "I don't think—"

"You're coming." Naomi cut him off. "Look at you. You're all dressed up and handsome looking! You never look this fancy! It would be such a waste for you to just go home."

For a second, he glared and considered it. "I'll go if Meredith goes."

"Come on, Meredith!"

"Oh, please?" Richelle whined and batted her long eyelashes in a sweet, puppy dog look. "Come hang out with us? I know it's not your sort of thing, but I promise it will be fun. Please, Merry?"

At the old nickname, Meredith huffed a laugh and rolled her eyes. "Don't call me that."

"Merry?" Ryan asked, hint of a smirk primed and ready to go at the opportunity to make fun of her nickname. "Why Merry?"

"Like the hobbit!" Richelle shouted before Meredith could stop her. "Back in college, we were pretty inseparable, and that's what people started calling us. She's Merry and I'm Pippin!"

"Even though that so does not describe us." Meredith shuddered. "I guess it's kind of cute. I appreciate the dynamic duo aspect."

Naomi considered this. "No, you don't really give me much of a hobbit vibe. You're more of an elf, I think."

"Oh, for sure." Ryan scoffed. "Cool, composed, mysterious, blonde boss lady? You're obviously Galadriel."

Meredith slapped her own knee, and the clap was loud enough to pop over Richelle's laughter. "Thank you! Obviously! I'm glad someone gets me."

Ryan looked sweet and amused and pleased with himself, and this time he held eye contact with her.

Even when she smirked and teased. "You think I'm mysterious?"

"I..." He choked and caught himself with a laugh, but then sobered. "I think you contain oceans, yes."

The comment went right to Meredith's heart and sent it racing. The sincerity, the bashful warmth, and the crinkly-eyed smile all went right to Meredith's vulva and damn near ruined her underpants. God damn, he was cute. The attention made her flush warm all over. Poised, she clenched her jaw tight and fought against the smile that threatened to show just how pleased she was, but it glittered in her eyes, in the tight hold of her mouth. Ryan saw. She knew he did.

Naomi stood and maneuvered around the coffee table, grabbed Meredith by the arms, and pulled her up out of her chair by the extra fabric of her sweater. "Okay, well, you should come be mysterious and sexy at this bar with us. Yeah? Please?"

Meredith laughed and shook her head, but considered it. With Naomi so close, holding onto her, it was hard to say no. A club-like atmosphere was not her scene. She was already in her comfy clothes. And she kind of wanted the alone time.

But also, it would be nice to spend time with Richelle and get to know her girlfriend better.

Plus a smaller place with salsa dancing sounded way better than hundreds of drunk people grinding to random, impersonal club beats.

And...Ryan would go if she went.

Meredith tilted her head back to look up at Naomi, whose height advantage was quite noticeable at this close range. Naomi pouted and stuck her crimson-lipsticked bottom lip out while she tossed her waves of chestnut hair. Meredith rolled her eyes but started to smile. And when Naomi quickly glanced at Ryan out of the corner of her eye, then pointedly looked back to Meredith and nodded, Meredith knew she was done for.

"Alright fine." She threw up her arms. "I'll go."

"Yes! I'm picking out your outfit." Brokering no argument, Naomi marched out of the living room and up the stairs. "Richelle, we'll be right back!"

Meredith stood rooted to the spot for a second, wondering what she had gotten herself into as she looked back and forth from confident Naomi, to pouting Richelle, to amused Ryan. Ryan leaned forward and said kindly to Richelle, "You know, you can go help with the outfit selection, too. I won't be sad. You don't have to keep me company."

Immediately, Richelle brightened and leapt up off the couch, her soft afro curls bouncing. "Okay! Thanks, Ryan!" She grabbed Meredith's arm and tugged her along up the stairs.

Inside her room, where Naomi was already waiting, Richelle shut the door and asked in a dramatic stage whisper, "Okay. Yes. Right? Totally yes. I think, anyway!"

"Oh, definitely yes," Naomi said. "So much yes."

"What's yes? What are we talking about?"

"Ryan and whether or not he wants to stick you, dick you, and wife you the fuck up. Yes, by the way." While Meredith choked and barked a loud laugh, Naomi waved her off and sat comfortably on the edge of Meredith's bed. "We're not actually here to pick out your outfit."

"If you couldn't tell." Richelle sat beside Naomi on the bed and ran her hands back and forth over the silky duvet. "That was a ruse! Very clever, Naomi."

"Thanks, babe!" Naomi blew Richelle a little kiss. "No, but who am I, your mother picking out your dress for Sunday school? Of course not. You're a grown ass woman and you can dress yourself. I just wanted to make sure I got a chance to talk to you in private. I know you're nervous about how you feel for Ryan, and you weren't sure if he was on the same page or even in the same novel. He is. Hope that helps!"

Inexplicably more nervous than before, jittery and a little giddy, Meredith wrung her hands together and curled her toes against the throw rug. "Are you sure?"

"Hell, I'm sure and I barely know the guy," Richelle said. "He can't keep his eyes off of you."

Naomi nodded along. "Remember how I said I usually know he's into someone before he knows? I think that's where he is right now. You know some of his history. You know that he has felt awkward in the past, like something is wrong with him. I think he's probably feeling some really big feelings for you, but he'll be unsure of himself. If you want this, you will need to spell it out for him."

"Okay." Meredith nodded. Why was she so nervous? Why did she feel like she was thirteen and gossiping with her girlfriends about whether a cute boy liked her? Why did she feel like she was about to die of embarrassment right now? Probably because this was new and uncharted territory for her. It had been a long, long time since she'd had real feelings for someone, since she had met someone she wanted to date. Michael, plus the two or three other guys she had dated in high school and college, had pursed her, chased her, worn her down until she fell. Nothing came out of friendship; there was nothing equal about it. This thing with Ryan was terrifying because of how much control they both had. No one was falling here. This felt like stepping, like walking clear-headed and strong, directly into something big. She didn't know how to do romance like this. She had never tried before. But she wanted to. "I can—I mean, if you really think…"

"I do really think. But Meredith." She paused and stared at Meredith, hard but not unkind. "I don't think you need to hear this, but I would be a bad friend to Ryan if I didn't say it. You know he's demi. Which means you know if he's showing interest in you, then it is already important to him. It can't just be about attraction for you, because for him attraction doesn't exist on its own. Don't start this unless you see a future there. Okay? He doesn't do casual, or experimental, or phases. You know what he's looking for."

Meredith nodded. She did know. It was the same thing she wanted, though for a long time she had convinced herself she'd never find it. "A partner."

Naomi nodded.

"I know." Meredith took a breath, and her admission was quiet. "I want that too. I have feelings for him too."

"Wow. Meredith." Richelle reached out, grabbed her hand, and held it. Her pretty round eyes were soft and sincere. She knew Meredith's history and hang-ups better than anyone. While Richelle had stayed optimistic and kind as she dated over the years, ever confident that she would meet her Princess Charming someday, Meredith had grown more cynical and shrewd. Richelle had seen the trend and knew the reasons for it. "That's a big deal for you."

"I know. I know. I…" Suddenly emotional, with too many feelings all swelling up and bursting out of her at once, Meredith groaned and stamped her foot while she waved at her stupidly teary eyes.

"Now I actually do need you to help me pick out what to wear! It actually matters now! I don't know how to…I don't know! Romance! Impress the cute guy! Please help me," she whined.

Richelle giggled at the outburst and looked sweetly sympathetic, while Naomi snorted a laugh and asked, "The date coach doesn't know how to date? Isn't this what you're good at?"

"No. What I'm good at is telling people what to do. You think I know how to take my own advice?"

"Alright, come on." Richelle grabbed Naomi's hand and dragged her across the room to Meredith's closet. "Let's help her out. Don't worry, Meredith. Your lesbian fairy godmothers are here to make you look hot."

While Richelle and Naomi sorted through her closet and considered options, Meredith stood back and danced from foot to foot, her arms crossed over her chest. "God, this is so dumb," she muttered, half to herself. "This is silly. I shouldn't care! Why do I care? We're not teenagers! We're all pushing thirty!"

"Right, and thirty is when the sex is supposed to get really good, so this actually seems like higher stakes. You're not wrong to get some help." Richelle held out a navy blue cocktail dress and scrunched her face thoughtfully. "Too classy?"

"Way too classy," Naomi answered, her head buried deep in the back of Meredith's well-organized closet, full of blazers and pencil skirts in varying colors, but with few party-hot options. "And excuse me, what are you doing standing there with your ass in the wind? Get to work on your hair and make-up!"

"Alright!" Meredith ran to her dresser and dumped out the contents of her make-up bag. Tubes of liquid lipstick rolled off the shelf and onto the floor, and an eyeshadow palette popped open and sent a puff of glittery purple dust flying in a cloud.

Halfway through her mascara, with her eyes open like a dead-eyed zombie in the mirror, the applicator poised just below her lashes, she heard Naomi say, "Yeah, that would look good, but it's kind of hard to get off. I don't know. How easy do you think she wants to be?"

"Not easy at all!" Meredith jumped in to cut off whatever naughty suggestion Richelle was about to make on her behalf, and Richelle looked amused and chastised. "I just want to look nice and get his attention. I'm not planning to drag him to the bathroom and bend over in a stall, for God's sake! I don't plan on having sex with him tonight at all!"

She paused for a second, reconsidered that hard line, and then recommitted. Right. That was right. No need to rush into anything.

More calmly, while Richelle and Naomi giggled, Meredith explained to them, and to herself, "I want to talk to him about this. If we're both going to take this seriously, we should talk. Like you said, he might not even quite know how he feels right now. He might need some time to think it through. I want to respect that."

"Fair enough," Naomi said. Then, she shoved a black jumpsuit in Meredith's direction. She had bought it as a work outfit, and with a gray or white blazer over top, it looked chic and professional. Not really what she was aiming for tonight, but she didn't really own anything else! She didn't do anything else! "You're wearing this."

While Naomi and Richelle waited, Meredith considered. Without the blazer? With thin straps, a low neckline, and a silhouette that hugged her waist and booty, it would look sleek and glam. Sexy. But still with a bit of her natural cool, competent attitude that Ryan seemed to like so much. "Alright." Confidence spread through her as she smirked. "I'm wearing that."

Chapter Thirteen

Loud salsa music started up again after a pause, and a cheerful instructor shouted to the crowd, "Alright, we'll start with the basic move. Right foot on one…two…" Naomi and Richelle, each holding glasses of frozen margaritas, laughed and bumped each other's hips as they went through the motions of the lesson. No one in the small crowd was taking the steps too seriously. Off to the side of the dance floor, Ryan stood at the bar with Meredith.

"You sure you don't want to join in?" He nudged her and teased.

"No." Meredith firmly shook her head, her silky blonde hair a shining sheet that fluttered around her bare shoulders. She sipped her wine, a smile playing in her eyes, and Ryan stared enraptured as her cherry red lipstick left a mark on the rim of the glass. "No way."

"Hm." Ryan hummed deep in his throat. "Scared?"

Meredith rolled her eyes and laughed. "You're such a menace."

"It's okay. I get it." Affecting casual, Ryan leaned back and rested his elbow on the edge of the bar, his own beer collecting condensation. Warm and happy and nervous, he stared at Naomi and Richelle because looking directly at Meredith was blinding. Not like looking into the sun. More like looking into the Ark of the Covenant in the first Indiana Jones movie. In that black, figure-hugging jump suit, all sleek and sexy, Meredith looked too good to be real. He didn't know how to handle it. He rarely felt like this, rarely felt so deeply and passionately attracted to someone, and it was intimidating, unfamiliar, near-forgotten territory. He couldn't be sure, but judging by the way his heart sped up and his skin flushed warm every time he dared glance at her, he was reasonably certain that if he stared too long at her, full on, he would melt or explode. Which would not do. Meredith didn't need that. Meredith probably didn't even want that. So he held it together, pretended that he was not about to burst into flames any second, and teased her. "I mean, the basic salsa steps could not possibly be any easier. Anyone who can count to three can do that." With a wave of his hand, he gestured out to the crowd, where lines of people laughed and stepped in time to the music while the instructor shouted out the count. He glanced at Meredith. "Sorry to hear you can't count to three. It must have been difficult for you to make it this far in life."

Quick and hard, she smacked his arm and flashed a grin. "Shut up, McKenna. Obviously I can do that! I'm watching! I'm learning it! I just don't feel the need to go up there and learn it in front of everyone. But obviously, I can do that. And count." To prove her point, she moved through the basic steps, foot forward and then back, with a miniscule little shake of her hips on each movement. It looked rushed and too contained, emotionless, but correct. She rolled her eyes at him. "See?"

"Oh, look at you, dancing queen!"

"Shut up. Let's see you do it!"

"Please." He scoffed. His version of the foot work was just as correct, but smoother, more fluid. Ryan knew he was not a bad dancer. Smug, he asked, "Like this?"

"Yeah, that was okay," Meredith grumbled. "Why aren't you out there? Do you want to go dance? Don't let me hold you back!"

"No!" He rushed with a laugh and held back from explaining that there was literally nowhere in the world he would rather be. There was nothing he would rather be doing in this moment than standing at the bar with her, teasing her, watching her pinch up her face and concentrate while she pretended not to pay too much attention to the lesson from afar. Nothing. It was perfect. And it was so her—to hang back, watch from a distance, calculate, and try nothing until she could be sure she would succeed. The little thought line that crinkled across her forehead was endearing as hell. He couldn't decide if he wanted to mess with her to get it to crinkle deeper, or if he wanted to wrap her in his arms and kiss away the strain. Both. Maybe both. "I'm just messing with you, Meredith. It's fun to get a rise out of you."

Unblinking, through narrowed eyes, she glared at him and then announced, "You're lying! You want to go dance!"

"No!" He laughed again. Of course, he wouldn't have minded. Under different circumstances, he would have been out making a fool of himself, laughing with Naomi. He forced himself to look at her, and the glowing perfection of her was almost too much to bear. Those cheekbones of hers looked sharp enough to cut him in two, if her tongue didn't do the job first. "I would rather hang out with you than do anything else right now. That's the truth."

The honest confession brought a smile to her face, tight and reluctant and joyously happy, and for an instant, Ryan wondered. Could she feel the same way? About him?

Probably not. Sometimes he thought, with the way she looked at him, maybe. Possibly. But how could he know? He barely knew how to tell when someone was interested in him at the best of times. With Meredith, though? Meredith was the sort of person who had big, engaging emotions and desires, but they were hard to read from the outside. Probably, he was imagining or reading too much into things. Wishful thinking. Probably, all of her clients fell for her!

All of this, all of the big and crashing feelings he had for her, were overwhelming and strange, and he didn't know how to move forward without drowning in the depth of it. He didn't know if he should. More than anything, she needed a friend right now.

The smile faded from her face as she rolled her eyes and glared at him, but her tone was warm and teasing. Friendly. "Alright, fine. But when they actually lower the lights, bring out the DJ, and properly open up the dance floor, I'll go out there with you. Deal?"

He held out his hand, which she gripped and firmly shook. "Deal."

Comfortable on the surface, but with every organ in his body twisting in unsettled upset, Ryan leaned back against the bar and stood quietly beside Meredith. Both of them watched Naomi and Richelle, who were infectiously giggling together on the dance floor, ignoring almost everything the instructor said. A few people around them craned their necks to watch as Naomi taught Richelle how to do a spin, and a few splatters of Richelle's margarita splashed out of her glass and hit the worn wood planks of the floor, but neither of them noticed. They only had eyes, along with big, laugh-infested smiles, for each other.

"God, they're cute together."

Ryan grinned. "Yeah they are, aren't they? They seem happy."

"Nice work, setting them up."

"Thank you." With a magnanimous wave of his hand, he said, "I consider their love my greatest masterpiece."

Meredith snorted into her wine glass. "You have a lot of masterpieces, huh? Speaking of, how's all your prep going for the big showcase? We've only really talked about the dating side of it, but you have a lot of work to do, don't you?"

Ryan threw his head back and groaned. "Don't remind me."

"Going well, then?"

"It's…going. Somewhere. Hopefully to the showcase!" He shook his head. "Pretty much every moment I haven't been with you, I've been in the shop working. I have a few pieces already in stock that are good enough to display, but I have to make three or four more from scratch. Plus my regular client orders. I'm a mess."

"You can handle it." Soft and sure, Meredith smiled at him and glanced his way. "You're very capable. You can get them all done."

"I don't know." Ryan winced, although her surety in him was a lighthouse—calm, and steady, and warming. "I'm doing okay now, but when the deadline gets closer and I'm still not done? When I'm running on two hours of sleep and I have to use a circular saw? I think there is a life of piracy in my future. For one thing, I can run off to the sea and never think about this showcase again. And for another, pirates are pretty inclusive and don't mind when you're missing a hand."

Meredith hummed. "I think you missed that calling by about two hundred years."

"Dammit."

"Alright, so since piracy won't pan out. What are you making for the event?"

"Well. A few things." Ryan took a deep breath. He wasn't great with talking about himself or his work, but it was different with Meredith. A little easier, a little more genuine. "I had this really pretty pale wood that almost had a silvery look to it once I sanded it, so I'm doing a big, round bookshelf out of that. It has a crescent moon shape overlaid on one side, with the shelves set back. Almost done with that. And then I have this table that turned out really well. The wood was messed up. I like working with scraps and pieces that get discarded because they have imperfections, and then trying to work those imperfections into the piece instead of hiding them. And this one slab of wood had this huge, twisty crack that ran right down the middle. I filled that in with a turquoise colored resin, and then stained the wood so the whole thing looks like an aerial view of a river snaking through a desert." Warm and tight, his words came faster and faster until they tripped in his throat. "It's really cool, and I am rambling and this is probably really boring for you. Sorry."

Damn. Heat crept up the back of his neck and he laughed into his beer glass. Why was he so damn awkward whenever he had to actually share something about himself? She didn't want to listen to him prattling on about wood grain!

"Are you kidding me?" Wide-eyed, she stared at him. Her red lips parted, and then fell wide open in a look of shock. "Ryan! That's not boring! That sounds amazing!"

Except, maybe she did. Interest and appreciation was evident all over her face, in the high-pitched tone of her voice.

"Thank you." God, he hoped he wasn't blushing. When were they going to turn the lights down in this stupid place? Meredith's intense, blue-eyed approval was too much to bear. "I feel good about what I have so far. It's just a lot. I don't want to talk at you for three days about all the stuff I have to get done."

Was he imagining it, or had Meredith just leaned in a little closer?

Her bare arm brushed against his blazer sleeve, and he felt the touch of her only through the movement of the fabric. "It would probably be easier to just show me. Could I come see your workshop sometime?"

"Yeah." The response burst out of him on a shaky breath. "Of course. You're welcome any time."

"Really? You'll give me a tour?"

Closer. Definitely closer. She angled her body to face him and rocked forward, just barely shifted her weight, but the closeness of her was all-consuming. "Of course."

She smirked. "And you'll let me play with the power tools?"

"No," he said even though she pouted and glared, like he was no fun. The idea of Meredith in his workspace, with her cool judgement and her high standards, made him nervous. Never in a million years did he think she would be unkind about his work, but still. She was hard to please, and he respected her opinion. He gulped and swallowed down a rush of new longing, the heady desire to fly into action and give this woman everything she could dream of. He wanted to design and build a whole houseful of custom pieces, just for her. That was absurd, and he knew it. More realistically, he wanted her to visit his shop, to see the things he made. Wanted her to know him. Wanted to show that he was starting to know her, and could learn to know her so very well. Wanted that badly. Visions of pristine Meredith in her perfect business wear walking through his sawdust-covered workspace, stroking her hands along the rough materials he shaped into life, caught his breath. And there was a piece there, waiting for her. A desk he shouldn't be working on in the midst of all his other obligations, but that he kept coming back to with every spare moment. The desk he had designed especially for her, nearly finished. Actually gifting it to her felt like an enormous bridge he did not know how to cross.

"I'll tell you what. No power tools. But I'll make you a compromise." Feeling unexpectedly brave, he shifted his own weight, moved just a half step closer to her, and she tilted her head to gaze up at him with that smirk still strong on her sharp features. "If you come to my shop, I'll have a present there for you."

"Something you'll make?"

A big something, way more than anything she might expect. Already made. But the real answer was close enough. He nodded.

"Deal! I get a Ryan McKenna original, right before your big, high society debut? If I hold onto it until after the showcase, I'll be able to sell it for a billion dollars."

"That's assuming I don't completely bomb the showcase. Then, I might have to take the gift back so I have something to eat during the long, cold months of social shunning."

"Oh. I was picturing...I don't know. A keychain or something." Meredith's eyes narrowed. "The thing you're going to make for me is edible?"

"No. Not at all." Ryan stared at her, unsettled horror in his eyes. "But the showcase might be bad enough that I have no other choice."

She snorted and flicked her wrist to lightly smack his arm again. "Ryan, stop. You're ridiculous."

"And that's exactly what all the rich old people are going to think!" He was laughing and joking about it, but the showcase was a concern. The date with Stephanie had gone nowhere. And even if he hadn't messed it up, he wasn't interested in Stephanie, or anyone else. All he could think about was Meredith. Really, what he wanted was to take Meredith to this stupid showcase. As his date. As his girlfriend. He could ask. She might go with him as a friend, another fake date like the few they'd already had. But that didn't feel right. His feelings for her put them on uneven footing, and it would be disingenuous to use her friendship like that. "It's two weeks away at this point, and I have no prospects. I don't know. I think I need to resign myself to the idea that I'll be there alone and all of the old rich people will gossip about how sad and lonely I must be. Who knows? Maybe that will get me some sympathy clients?"

"I don't think it's going to be as bad as you think it's going to be. But…" Meredith paused and looked down at her drink. She held herself steady, in thought, considering something. "Ryan. What if…"

"Alright everyone!" A loud voice crashed over the speakers, interrupting Meredith and causing both of them to flinch. The lights popped and plunged the bar into darkness, which alleviated half a second later when swirling dancefloor lights and green lasers chased each other across the room. Everyone from the dance lesson gave a shout and a cheer, while a DJ announced, "Let's get the party started so you can all try out your new moves! I want to see you on this dance floor!"

More cheers and hoots were drowned out as the music started up, a fast and fun Latin club beat. Ryan squinted when a laser flashed over his eyes and he looked at Meredith.

She looked back at him, considered him. Whatever she'd been

about to say was gone, drowned out by the bar's sudden transformation. With a sly grin, she threw back her wine glass and drained the rest of it, and then thunked it back down on the bar top. "Alright. I shook on it. Time to make good on that deal. Let's go, dancing queen."

Before Ryan could do more than laugh, Meredith had grabbed him by the wrist. At first, her grip was harsh and demanding, but as he rushed to catch up with her, it gentled. At the edge of the small but rowdy crowd, Meredith's hand slipped a little lower and gripped his in a proper hold. She didn't look back. She kept her eyes trained on the task before them, a little dancing bounce in her step, focused on pushing through the swell to reach Naomi and Richelle. Ryan's heart raced as she held his hand and led them into the chaos. He followed gladly.

"Woo!" Richelle threw up her arms when she saw them approach through the crowd. "You finally joined us!"

Richelle grabbed onto Meredith and Naomi reached for Ryan, and that was the end of the hand holding. He felt the loss like hunger. "You two looked great during the lessons! You were getting all fancy with the twirls!"

"You know me!" Naomi laughed and grabbed Ryan's hand so he could spin her in a ballroom twirl, her tumble of hair cascading in a whirl out behind her. In heels, Naomi was the same height as he was, and he stretched his arm high to make sure she had room for a good and proper spin. "This girl gets fancy when she has tequila!"

"You're always fancy!"

"Babe!" Richelle sashayed closer to Naomi. "Can we try to dance properly now? I think I got the hang of it and I want to test it out!"

"Sí, mi reina!" Naomi twirled away from Ryan and into Richelle's arms.

As the two of them held each other's hands and jumped into a lively salsa, laughing and squealing with each step, Meredith slid in close to Ryan and stood up on her tip toes to ask, "What did Naomi just say to Richelle?"

Ryan leaned down to holler near her ear, "Mi reina means my queen."

"Oh my God!" Meredith shouted and groaned. "They are stupid cute."

"So stupid cute."

"Alright, come on!" Meredith grabbed his arm again. "Dance with me!"

He let her drag him into an approximation of a salsa dance, both of them laughing and watching Richelle and Naomi for advice. Most everyone around them on the dance floor was freely dancing, while incorporating a few newly-learned salsa steps into their moves, and Meredith quickly broke from the classic pattern. And she looked damn gorgeous while doing it. With every drop of her hips to the baseline, every shimmy of her pale shoulders, Ryan missed a step and lost the beat.

He wanted her. Badly. It was new, and staggering, and painful. He hid it well, shoved it down, and focused on having fun with his friend.

Laughing, he admonished her and said, "I don't remember them teaching any of those moves in the lessons!"

"Go with the flow, Ryan! Don't be such a control freak!" She grinned and flipped her hair in a wild, messy tumble.

It took him a second to realize that she was mocking herself.

Meredith did not often go with the flow, or let loose at all.

She caught his eye, laughing and bright and happy, and this private, privileged sight of a rarely-seen facet of her took his breath right out of him.

And it made him joyously, blindingly reckless.

Grinning ear to ear, he grabbed her by the arm and tugged her in closer. Not touching. But together. Linked. "Alright Hartman, let's see what you've got!"

Her face morphed into a battle glare. "Oh, you do not know what you just did. You'd better brace yourself, McKenna." She planted a hand on his chest and shoved him back to give herself space. Took a breath. And plunged into an aggressive and impressive Running Man, right in the middle of the bar.

Ryan threw his head back and laughed, and watched enthralled at her furious challenge. He'd have to be blind not to notice how perfect her tits and ass looked, bouncing around like that as she expertly executed the cheesy 90's dance move, but what really caught him was her face. She looked so serious, so angry, like she was snarling and out for blood, a crazed hardness in her eyes.

Behind him, Richelle shrieked and cackled. "Meredith! Oh my God, I haven't seen you do that since sophomore year of college!"

Meredith kept it up for another second, but then stopped and cocked her head in Ryan's direction. The fury on her face cracked with a smile she tried to hide. "Well? What do you have to say to that?"

"What do I have to say to that? How can I complete with that? That was—" He bluffed just long enough to let her start gloating, and then slid into an embarrassingly good rendition of The Carlton. She wanted cheesy 90's? He could keep up with cheesy 90's! Arms swinging with the ridiculous and jolly two-step, while Naomi and Richelle laughed and cheered him on in the background, Ryan pinned Meredith with his own battle gaze. "Oh! How do you like that! You want to play?"

"Decent moves, McKenna. But you're going down!"

And just like that, they were in a dance-off.

Richelle and Naomi got into it, each of them going in turns or sometimes pairs, back and forth with challenges and jeers. Naomi brought her best Whip/Nae Nae to the game, and Richelle busted out a surprising flapper-girl Charleston. Ryan scored a few more points with some of the moves from Thriller, and Naomi taught everyone how to Floss. But the crown, without doubt, went to Meredith and Richelle. Giggling, her hair a mess, Meredith grabbed Richelle's arm and murmured something into her ear. Richelle immediately gasped, laughed, and agreed. Side by side, they performed a perfect replica of the painfully awkward dance sequence from Napoleon Dynamite, while Ryan and Naomi stood back and laughed their heads off, half amused, half in shock that they knew all the choreography.

When it was done, Meredith hid her face in her hands and shook with laughter, and Richelle wrapped her arms around her. Together, they doubled over and rocked back and forth, dancing and laughing. "I can't believe we still remembered that!"

Naomi yelled, "Remembered it? I can't believe you knew that whole thing to begin with!"

As Meredith waved a hand in front of her face, eyes glittering, she explained, "It was a pledge challenge, when we joined our sorority! The two of us got together in Richelle's dorm room and spent hours learning it in freshman year!"

As they both straightened up, Richelle tugged Meredith into a proper hug, and then pulled back and looked at her with happy, heavy meaning. "I have not seen you like this in a long time."

"I know. Sorry. I used to be fun!"

"Not what I meant." Richelle bopped Meredith's arm. "But it's nice to see you cutting loose and being silly again."

Meredith nodded. Ryan wasn't sure if he and Naomi were supposed to hear such a private exchange, but he listened to every word. "I feel lighter, I think. I didn't realize I was still carrying so much of it."

Her ex. Carrying so much of the pain he had caused her, the damage he'd done to her sense of self. The realization sobered Ryan, especially having witnessed just how much Meredith had needed that final severing.

It was an honor, to see her like this. To be trusted enough and wanted enough to have earned this side of her.

His heart surged with aching fondness for her, and a deep need to protect this side of her, to protect her light and joy. She didn't need protecting. But he wanted to be tender with her all the same. He would be, if she wanted that too. God, would he ever be.

While Richelle and Meredith spoke quietly together, Naomi glared at him thoughtfully and yelled over the loud music, "Why the hell don't we have a best friend choreographed dance routine?"

Ryan pouted and considered the fair question. "Work on it next weekend?"

Brusque and sure, Naomi nodded. "Work on it next weekend."

Richelle finished saying something to Meredith, patted her hair, and then set her loose. Right away, she turned on Ryan. Both arms held out in question and challenge, she pinned him with a look. "So? What do you say to that?"

"You are the champions!" he shouted, and Naomi echoed the cry, both of them bowing down to the ridiculous brilliance of Meredith and Richelle. "We accept our defeat!"

"Good." She grinned at Naomi and Richelle, but then zeroed in on Ryan and grabbed him by the arm once more. "Now come buy me a drink, you menace. I cannot believe you just made me do the freaking Napoleon Dynamite dance in front of a whole bar full of people."

"Made you? No way!" Although even as he defended himself, he knew there was some truth to it. Meredith liked a challenge—couldn't back down from one, really, and he had egged her into a competition. She also liked to win. It was inevitable, once he'd pushed her buttons, that she would pull out all the stops she needed to seize glory. "I did not make you. You did all that on your own!"

She grumbled and laughed while he shouted their order to the bartender, and then passed her a fresh wine glass. She fanned her face while she took a sip. "Want to go out on the patio? Get some air?"

She blinked, surprised, but then nodded. "Yeah. That sounds perfect."

This time, he led the way through the crowd, and her hand stayed pressed against the small of his back so they didn't get separated.

Outside, the cool night air hit like a slap and made him realize he had been warmer than he'd noticed. The loud music and sounds of the club faded to a muffled rumble, distorted and strange, through the buffer of the door. Close clusters of trees and shrubs ringed the small, brick patio and provided an oasis that felt separate from the city just beyond them, though the quaint and classy Georgetown streets were largely quiet this time of night. It was private. No one else had made their way outside. Ryan led Meredith over to a tall, wrought iron cocktail table so they could set their drinks down.

Underneath a string of fairy lights that set the dark shadows dancing, Meredith looked otherworldly. Golden.

"Thanks. This was a good idea." Eyes soft and certain, she stared at him. The look was a mystery. Unreadable. Unblinking. He would give anything to know what was going through her head, but he was content to stand beside her and enjoy the night, content to have her eyes on him, even if nothing else. "And thanks for the dance-off."

"You having fun?"

"Yeah." She let herself smile, a slow melting of her mouth, as she looked him up and down. "You're pretty good company."

"You're not half bad yourself."

She took a sip of her wine and carefully set it down. Her eyes focused on the dark tabletop and she ran her finger back and forth over the edge of the glass, a nervous little tap. "I meant to say earlier. Before the music came on and interrupted…"

"Oh, right. Yeah. You were saying something about the showcase?"

"Yeah. I was." She nodded to herself, a deliberation, and then drew in a breath and braced her shoulders. Intent and focused, she lifted her eyes and looked at him. "I would like to go with you to the showcase. As your date. If you want me to, that is."

"Oh." For a brief moment, Ryan froze. He wanted to agree, wanted to scream that yes, dear God, of course he wanted her to go with him! The outburst and the short-lived flash of excitement that nearly prompted it died in his chest and left a shaky, uncomfortable disappointment. "That's really nice of you. But I can't. I don't think that's a great idea."

"Oh." Her face fell, hardened with confusion. "Why not?"

"I…" This was awkward. Painful. He exhaled long and slow and tried to get his bearings. It was no use lying or trying to pretend it was something else. She was a friend to him, and she was going through a particularly rough time where she especially needed people to be good friends to her. He owed her honesty. Even though it felt like walking across the National Mall in his underwear. Even though he stumbled and rushed through the confession. "I kind of accidentally fell for you. I have feelings for you."

Her red lips parted. "You…"

"I'm so sorry. I know you don't need this right now, with everything you have going on. And I'm sure this is an annoying thing you have to deal with from clients all the time, and I hate doing that to you. But I care about you, and I owe you the truth. I would love to take you to that showcase." Humorless and rough, he laughed. "Hell, I'd love to take you anywhere you wanted to go with me. But I can't do the fake date thing anymore, even as friends. Because it's a lie, on my end. I don't want to abuse your kindness or manipulate you."

In silence, Meredith stared down at the uneven red bricks below their feet and processed every embarrassing thing he had just vomited out onto her. "You have feelings for me. I thought…" Carefully, she shook her head and cleared her throat. "I thought you needed time for things like that."

"I do!" And he had. His feelings for Meredith, his attraction to her, definitely had not sprung up overnight. Nothing for him happened at first sight, and it was only after he really saw the depth of her, after she let him stand beside her while she faced something awful, that his attraction to her started to bloom. But their unique situation had some unexpected quirks that meant his emotions and attraction had moved faster for Meredith than they had for anyone in the past. "But funny thing about the coaching and the fake dating: they were situations that kind of forced and built intimacy really fast. We sped right through that phase."

Smiling, distant, she nodded. "Yeah, we kind of did, didn't we?"

It was too warm. Or maybe too cold. Ryan couldn't decide. He shifted back and forth from foot to foot, uncomfortable and anxious, and nervous dread tickled the back of his throat. "I'm sorry. I'm really sorry." The words gushed out of him. He needed her to understand: he wasn't asking anything or making demands of her. He was trying to be respectful. This was his problem, and he wasn't asking her to solve it for him. "If you need me to stop coming to you for coaching, I can. I would completely understand. I don't want to put you into an uncomfortable situation, or--"

"Ryan." Sharp and sudden, she cut him off.

He paused. Tensed.

Up and down, her eyes raked and skimmed along the lines of his body. As one corner of her mouth lifted in a smirk, Ryan's heart beat faster. "You have feelings for me?"

"Yeah. I do."

She stepped a little closer. And then closer, still. Slow. Deliberate. Her every move was calculated and intentional. "And you're attracted to me?"

Air trembled through his chest with every quick, unsteady breath he took, and the heat of her flushed through his whole body, up and down his spine, into his groin. He couldn't speak. Could only look down at her calm, considering face and nod. Yes.

In a flash of plush red lips and sharp white teeth, her smirk widened into a coyote-clever grin. "Good."

She grabbed his face with both hands, lifted up, and pulled him down into a kiss.

For half a second, Ryan froze. It took him so by surprise when Meredith's mouth pressed against his that his brain shut down, incapable of thought.

Then she shifted against him, her lips incredibly soft and sure, her body incredibly close.

And Ryan properly woke the fuck up.

Insistent and needy, he stepped closer and drove their bodies tighter together. Both of his hands sprang into action, with one arm snaking around her waist to tug her closer, and the other hand lifting to cup her face. When he yielded, when he met the kiss she'd given him, she whimpered.

That tiny little sound zapped through him like lightning, igniting every part of him and attuning him to Meredith—nothing but Meredith. He melted into her. Her soft lips teasing and sucking on his own, the swell of her breasts pressing against his chest, the scent of her citrus-y perfume swirling through his senses. All of her. A rush of feeling, of fondness and disbelief and desire all twisted up in one massive swell, rose through him, and he had to pull away to catch his breath. Panting, still holding her close, he whispered, "Meredith…fuck," into the silk of her hair.

And then kissed her again.

As his tongue flicked at the seam of her mouth, seeking more, needing to taste, Meredith groaned low in the back of her throat. She opened for him. Let him inside. She was so soft, and she tasted sweet, and he couldn't get enough of her. As their tongues met and flicked together, as he kissed deeper, she teased him and pulled her tongue back, let him follow into her mouth…

Where she stopped being so sweet. He should have known.

It caught him off guard when Meredith sucked him with a pull he could feel tugging directly from his tongue right down to his cock. It throbbed. Already half hard, he groaned and canted his hips on instinct. She pressed back, her own body roiling with energy, seeking out contact with him while she ran a hand down his back. He stroked her arms, the bare skin of her shoulders, and shifted to nudge his thigh in between her own. A breathy whine snuck out of her throat as he sucked on her bottom lip, and she wrapped both arms around his neck while she rocked her hips. He held her by the waist with both hands, to brace her, to give her leverage, so she could take whatever she wanted, whatever she needed. He wanted to give it to her, to give her everything. She deepened her kiss and swallowed the sound of his groan as she ground down against his thigh, and then—

"Shit!" Meredith hissed in a whisper against his mouth as she jumped back from him like she'd been stung. Confused, bewildered, too fucking horny to think straight, Ryan blinked and shook his head…

Just as another group joined them on the patio. Ringing laughter and the sour scent of cigarette smoke crashed over their private courtyard and shocked Ryan back to his senses. A group of four women and two men, all smiling and with hair messy from dancing, chatted loudly as they made their way to one of the other tables. No one looked at them or paid them any attention.

Thank God.

Ryan worked hard to fight down the wide, shit-eating grin that threatened to crack over his face as he watched their oblivious progress. But Meredith had her back to the group. Face scrunched up and pink, she barely held back her laugher, and her whole body shook with tense, silent giggles. Just looking at her, so happy and embarrassed, with her cheeks and her chest flushed, Ryan had to look away so he didn't crack up.

They had made out.

They had almost just gotten caught making out, like a couple of teenagers. Meredith—calm, composed, in-control Meredith—had been about to ride his damn thigh, right here on the patio of a bar.

He giggled to himself and pressed a hand to his face to cover his stupidly squinting eyes. Damn, he was a lucky son of a bitch! What a night!

It took a moment to get their laughter hidden and under control, but neither of them could stop smiling. Meredith bit the insides of her cheeks, sucked them in until her mouth was in a tight purse, in an effort to hide her giddy happiness, but still Ryan could see the smile all over her face. It glittered in her bright blue eyes.

He reached out, grabbed her hand, and held it gently.

She took a sip of her neglected wine, shuddered, and shook her hair back off her shoulders. "Right. So, I was asking you out. When I offered to go to the showcase with you, I meant for that to be a real date. Not a fake one." She grinned to herself. "Sorry I wasn't clear."

"I'm not sorry. I really liked the way you chose to get your point across when I misunderstood." Bashful, he glanced at her and started chuckling again, and so did she, so he stepped in closer to her side and wrapped an arm loosely around her shoulders. It was casual, and affectionate, and intimate, and she tucked into the warmth against his side. "If you want to communicate other things to me with that method, it would be fine by me."

"I think I will." She glanced up at him and said in a rush, "I really like you. If that wasn't obvious. I have feelings for you, too."

Ryan had to look away, or else he might float right off the surface of the earth. He glanced up at the courtyard and stared for a second at the swoop of fairy lights in the trees above them, letting his eyes go soft. His heart beat a brave and stubborn rhythm in his chest. "I really like you too."

"Good." Meredith nudged him. "You'd better."

Ryan snorted a laugh and dared a glance back at her. "Why did you seem so surprised when I told you how I feel about you?"

"Because I was surprised. I thought there was a chance you were starting to develop feelings for me, but I didn't think you were further along than that. My plan was to tell you how I felt, maybe talk about it, and then give you some space to think about it." She shrugged, and her face softened. "I didn't want to push you or rush you at all. I know you need time. I know it's been a bit hard for you."

It was such a small thing, really. So basic. But that Meredith knew him so well, that she had thought things through like this, brought a tight little burr of prickly-sweet emotion into his chest. With her, he felt seen, and understood, and respected. He was demisexual. He knew that now. He was somewhere in the gray area surrounding the asexuality spectrum, and the way he experienced sexual attraction was a bit different for him than it was for most people. He knew that neglecting that part of himself, denying that aspect of his sexuality and trying to force himself into a different mold, had been the real source of his dating woes. Little by little, he was learning to embrace that part of himself.

And Meredith was right there with him.

The thing that had once made Ryan feel so off, so out of step with everyone else, was something Meredith saw and understood and met without hesitation. Not something to overcome, but something to respect. She didn't demand instant attraction, or instant chemistry, or instant answers. She saw him. And she liked him.

That easy care from her, that effortless and unflinching respect for his terms even though they were different from most, was validating in a way he hadn't quite known he needed. It prickled at something warm and dear behind his eyes, and he blinked to chase it away.

He was falling for her hard. He cared for her so much.

And he wanted her so much. It had taken him a bit of time, but now that the attraction and chemistry clicked into place on his end, it did so with wild abandon. He was ferociously, painfully, desperately attracted to her. To every bit of her, to everything about her, mind, body, and soul.

"Thank you. That means a lot to me. But I don't need time to think about it." His voice was deeper, huskier, and she could hear the desire and feeling heavy in it. Her lips parted as he tightened his grip on her, as he dug and massaged his fingers into the meat of her hip. "I'm already here. I'm with you."

"Good. I'm glad," she murmured. "Now what?"

Slowly, he pressed a line of breathy, teasing kisses along the line of her neck and down onto her shoulder while a tiny, almost inaudible whimper sounded in the back of her throat. "Now? Anything you want. Do you want to get out of here?"

A lazy, slow grin widened Meredith's mouth as she glanced at him. "Yes."

Ryan reflected it. With her, his whole body thrummed with excitement, with anticipation and desire for all the new ways he would soon know her, all the new parts of her he would soon discover. But she was a comfort, too. Safe and steady, an adventure and a thrill, all at once. Because he knew her, understood her, trusted her. And because of that, he felt confident. Even though propositioning someone, inviting someone home for sex, was not something he had done in years, it came easy with her, and only gave him a twinge of hesitation. "Your place or mine?"

"That depends."

"On what?"

Meredith's perfect red mouth pursed in an amused pinch, her eyebrows lifting. "On where Naomi and Richelle plan to spend the night tonight."

"Good point. We should go to whoever's house they are not going to go to."

She smirked. "We'll have to ask them. Which means they're going to know what we're doing. And they'll be insufferable about it."

Ryan grimaced. It was true. Naomi would tease him to no end; already tonight, she'd been shooting him more than a few knowing, smug looks. But then he ran his eyes up and down the sleek, perfect lines of Meredith's figure—her long legs, the curves of her breasts and ass and hips, the smirk on her wickedly clever mouth, and that quickly made him bold. "Worth it. Come on."

He grabbed her hand, and she laughed while he dragged her back into the bar.

Chapter Fourteen

As Ryan led her into his house, Meredith's mind was racing. Her heart, too, for that matter, in an excited and fluttery, stupid sort of way. But mostly her mind.

They were about to have sex.

It had been a long time. A long time since she'd had sex at all, having all but given up on getting any kind of real satisfaction from generic hook-ups on Tinder. An even longer time since she'd had sex with someone she liked. Someone who liked her. Someone who made her feel good about herself.

Actually, come to think of it, if she was being really, painfully, brutally honest with herself…she wasn't entirely sure she'd ever had sex like that.

She'd thought she had. At the time, she'd thought she had been having sex like that with a few people. But the benefit of growth, of hindsight, changed the way she looked at her past experiences. Always in the past, with every man she'd ever been with, she felt as if she had to play a role in the bedroom. The role of whatever her partner wanted, or the role of what she was supposed to be.

That, or with hook-ups, she kept her walls up and kept it devoid of any intimacy, separate from her emotions or her personality.

She did not want that with Ryan. She wanted more. She wanted him, and them, and everything.

But she didn't quite know how to have sex like that. She didn't quite know how to break free of that false narrative men had built around her sexual self: that she was pleasant and soft, that she existed for their pleasure and their benefit. None of that was true, but she'd allowed past partners to push her into that accommodating mold. With Ryan, though? She didn't want to squeeze herself into that false role. She wanted her to be her, and him to be him. Authentic and together.

But she'd never had that with anyone.

It was a bit terrifying and far too vulnerable.

This was a hell of a time to be thinking about it. As Ryan led her into the foyer and smiled, all shy and dimpled, as he took her coat and hung it in the hall closet, Meredith smiled back, and her body shivered with the cold air, with his presence, with wanting.

But her mind raced ahead in spiraling, dizzying loops at a thousand miles a second.

She was about to have sex with Ryan. And also, at this same moment, she had come to the stark and intimidating realization that maybe, possibly, she had never actually had good sex in the entirety of her almost-thirty years on Earth. That it had always been unsatisfying on some deeper, unexplored level. That she didn't know how to be herself.

"So, this is my place. Well, my place and Naomi's place. This is where we live. Do you want a tour?" Ryan asked in a rush, and then grinned and answered his own question before Meredith could respond. "I'm going to give you a tour. Because I'm a little nervous, and I don't want to just…I don't know. Throw myself at you? Right away? I mean, I do. But that's bad manners. So. Tour!"

"A tour sounds great." Meredith laughed, but inwardly sighed with relief. It took him saying it out loud, actually handing her the word to ascribe to her own emotions, but once he admitted his own nerves, she realized she was in the same place. Nervous. A little.

About the sex. And about the fact that she'd maybe never had it in a way that really, truly made her feel good about herself. Except with her vibrator, obviously. That was uncomplicated.

The rest was messy. A lot to untangle.

Probably, she should have gone to therapy for this years ago. Except she couldn't go to therapy, because she was the one who was supposed to know all about therapy, and that was like admitting weakness. Maybe. It was messy!

"Living room." With a flourish of his hands, Ryan presented the room. He pointed. "Horrible couch that we hate but won't get rid of."

Meredith nodded as she took it all in. Clean and cozy. Like a cabin, but modern. All of the furniture, other than the horrible couch, was done in light wood. Abstract, colorful paintings on the walls. Bare wooden floorboards. It was nice. Meredith chewed on her lip until it hurt.

Was she supposed to tell Ryan all of this? Did he need to know her baggage?

Could she get her mind to stop racing and whirling long enough to get the words out if she wanted to speak them?

And Ryan. Ryan was so damn sweet and kind. This had happened fast. Not wildly fast—they'd been dancing around this and getting to know each other for weeks now. But it was only just this evening that Meredith had let herself entertain the possibility of a relationship with him. It had been a long time since she had entertained the possibility of a relationship with anyone. And now here she was, in his house, with him looking at her like she was the moon and stars, and they were about to have sex—probably good sex! Because he liked her. He just liked her.

It was simple.

And yet, that felt just as complicated and messy as the rest of it, because sometimes Meredith didn't think there was much about her that was particularly likeable. Other people had often agreed.

She was an acquired taste, and she didn't quite know if she could handle the disappointment she'd feel if he suddenly realized she was too much for him. It had been a long time since she'd dared open her heart for anyone, since she'd met anyone she even wanted to believe in, and Ryan—

"Hey." Gentle and soft, Ryan reached out and touched her shoulder, a warm and fleeting stroke of his calloused hand on her bare skin. "Where are you right now?"

She glanced around, confused, and flashed him a smile that felt more confident than it was. "Your living room?"

"I meant your head. Is everything okay? If this is too fast, or if this isn't what you want, I completely understand. We don't have to do anything."

Her answer was unreserved, a clear certainty that stood strong and undeniable though her mind raced with other hesitancies. "This is what I want."

Sex. Him. All of it.

Soft and tender, he smiled. "Me too."

"Okay." She could do this. She wanted this. And he wanted her. Meredith took a breath and held it until she was sure she was projecting nothing but confidence. "So what's wrong?"

"Nothing." Lopsided, one side of his mouth lifted. The right side. When he was being cheeky or teasing, he only smiled with the right side of his face. She had noticed. She liked it more than she was willing to say out loud. He took a step towards her and then poked her shoulder. "I just thought something might be wrong because you went all quiet. You haven't stopped bossing me around, or telling me what to do since the day I met you."

Meredith smirked, though her mouth tightened and threatened to widen into a more genuine smile.

He liked her.

Everything about her.

The storm in her mind calmed a little as Ryan watched her, as he looked at her with unabashed fondness. She was nervous. She wanted to be careful with her own heart, and to be gentle with his. All of that, yes.

But he was nervous, too. Because this was new and unusual for him. Because it had been a long time. Because this could never be simple for him, and he would undoubtedly have a whole tangle of emotions tumbling through him right now, too. And because all of a sudden, for the first time since he had met her, she wasn't taking the lead. Already, he was nervous, and her quiet panic had thrown him off.

That last one, at least, she could definitely do something about.

She approached him carefully, and he shifted to let her into his strong arms. As they kissed, slow and warm, he tightened his grip on her. One arm around her back, the other stroking up and down her side. He sighed and opened for her when she teased his lips with her tongue, and he pressed his whole body closer.

She pulled away and smiled at the softly dazed look in his pretty brown eyes, at the way his lips stayed parted and panting, eager for her. Wicked and careful, she grinned. "You thought there was something wrong because I wasn't telling you what to do?"

He laughed and held her close. The heat of him, and the firm press of his tall, muscled frame zapped tingling sparks of anticipation up and down her spine. The scent of him filled her every breath, fresh and clean and masculine. She drank him in while he smiled and laughed off her teasing attention. "A little bit, yeah."

"Hmm." Eyes sharp, Meredith studied his face. The happy, focused creases around his eyes, the languid, charming tilt of his mouth. And God, did he have a perfect mouth. Plush and kissable. She wanted it everywhere. She wanted him everywhere. And he felt the same way about her. Her mouth lifted in a smirk and her eyes tightened.

He liked her. She didn't quite know how to be herself in bed because no one had ever really liked her enough to want the real her. Only a fantasy, or a watered-down version. But not Ryan. Ryan liked her. Her footing might be shaky, and she might not quite know what to do. But she was safe with him. She could be herself with him.

Her confident, bossy, in control self.

He was nervous and didn't want to throw himself at her? That was fine. But she had no qualms about throwing herself at him.

And he wanted to be told what to do? Also fine. Telling people what to do was Meredith's goddamn forte.

With just a hint of teeth, she mouthed kisses along his jawline and felt him melt against her. He was tall. Tall enough that she had to lift up on her toes to reach his ear. She sucked on his ear lobe, pinched it gently with her teeth and tugged it, all the while building up the tension. All the while feeling his breathing hitch faster, in and out of his chest.

All the while working up the nerve.

Ryan liked that she was bossy and opinionated. He liked that she took charge of things and held tight to control. He liked that she was competent.

More than that: Ryan liked her. Liked her. Wanted her. Very specifically, her, and everything he knew about her. She repeated it in her mind, like a mantra to center herself.

Her heart thundered against her rib cage. It was a great struggle, and also the single most powerful breath of her life, to murmur into his ear, "Get on your knees."

He froze. His breathing quickened, shallow and shaky. When she pulled back to look up at him, a quiet question in her eyes, his face fell into shock. He had been teasing. This was not what he had expected.

As his eyes glazed over, his lashes fluttering in surprise, he stared at her and whispered, "Fuck."

And then he dropped to the floor. On his knees, with all of his strength on offer at her feet, he gazed up at her with lust-blown eyes. His pupils were so wide she could barely see a sliver of his brown irises. "Like this?"

She flashed him a grin, her teeth digging into her bottom lip. The sight of him there, on his knees for her, with his broad shoulders and his strong thighs and his perfect curls—wearing clothes she had picked out, no less!—did something to her. Something powerful. Her mind calmed, but her heart sped up and her pulse raced up and down her body. "I don't know. You tell me. You were the one who wanted me boss you around."

"This is not exactly what I had in mind." Shaky and breathy, he laughed. The smile lit his whole face, and that honest, open happiness was her favorite look on him. "I should know by now not to underestimate you."

"That would be wise." She took a step back, put some distance between them. The old floorboards creaked under her weight as she kicked off her heels. "Is this okay?"

"Fuck yes. What do you want me to do?"

"For now?" Her gaze was intense, deliberate, a challenge. "Just watch."

"Fuck, I like you." The confession burst out of him on a breath. He looked happy and raw and open, completely vulnerable to her and thrilled by that fact. His mouth quirked in a smile, but he stayed put, like she asked, and watched her from a distance. "I like you so fucking much."

"I know you do." It warmed her to hear it said outright, so plainly, as was his style. She knew. She wouldn't be doing this, wouldn't be acting like this with him, if she didn't know. But still, she liked hearing it. "I like you too, Ryan."

He stared, unabashed and appreciative, eager, as she slid the straps of her jumpsuit down off her shoulders.

His mouth fell open, a perfect pout of his lips, when she pushed the top down over her chest and exposed her breasts. She'd not worn a bra, and the stiff fabric of the outfit dragged along her nipples, already firm and too sensitive, as she slid it down her slender body. She kept going. Slowly. All the while, his eyes darted down inch by inch to see each new stretch of skin she laid bare for him, and then quickly flicked back up to watch her face. "Oh my God," he murmured under his breath, thin and desperate. A thick and definite bulge strained against the front of his jeans, but he didn't move. He stayed still and watched her, stared at her, drank in the sight of her.

Her own breath was shaky and unsteady. Lust burned through her. So did nerves. And so did something stronger, something strange and powerful and intoxicating, as this gorgeously strong, kind, perfect man waited on his knees for her and watched her every move.

She slid the elastic waist of the jumpsuit down over the curve of her ass and then slowly stepped out of the legs. Ryan watched. His breathing hitched. As she hooked her thumbs into the line of her blue cotton panties, she hesitated for only a second, but the sweet, needy pleasure in Ryan's eyes gave her courage. She slid them off and watched as his hand twitched, as he pressed his palm hard against the bulge in his jeans, desperate to relieve some of the pressure building there. Without breaking eye contact, she tossed her underwear aside and kicked to swipe away the jumpsuit on the floor.

She stood before him.

It was the most naked she had ever been.

Every other time she'd gone to bed with someone, they wanted her to put something on—a schoolgirl costume, or a sweeter personality. Her compliance and innocent yielding had been just as much a costume as the plaid skirt and knee-high socks her ex had wanted her to wear, though at the time she hadn't recognized she was wearing it.

Ryan was the first person who had ever wanted to see her stripped down completely bare.

And right now, while he squeezed at his aching cock through the layers of his clothing, while he panted for breath and stared into her eyes, he looked like he wanted her so badly he might die from it.

As the cool air in the living room hit her body, Meredith ran her hands up and down her sides, along her hips, across her stomach. Ryan followed the motion like a cat watching a fish tank. "Like what you see?"

He nodded.

Good. She approached him, her bare feet strong and sure on the hardwood, and he craned his neck to look up at her as she drew closer. When she was within reach, in front of him, he lifted his hands to her sides and stroked her skin, up to her waist and then back down to her thighs. Hungry and needy, he pressed hot, open mouthed kisses along her stomach. Each one sent a shiver running through her. She shifted involuntarily, widened the set of her legs to appease the wet, throbbing need growing between them. Ryan groaned against her skin, nipped biting kisses on her hip that pricked and had her gasping, tensing, for just an instant before he chased away the sting with sweet, quick licks.

Every nerve ending in her body was primed and twitching, sensitive and ready to fire, ready to be touched and stroked and kissed into oblivion. But Ryan, fully clothed and worshipfully kissing and touching her naked body, was too pretty a sight to give up just yet. She wanted to take her time. His big hands dragged across her abdomen, the callouses on his palms scraping her in a rough and tender claiming as he cupped her breast. Her mouth fell open. Her breathing quickened. She wanted to throw her head back and moan. She didn't. That would make it all end too quickly. Her whole core clenched tight as she held herself together, held back her reaction, stayed in control. At least on the surface. Inside, she burned. She ran her fingers through his hair, let them tangle in his soft curls.

Down the line of her nose, she watched as he massaged and ran his hands over her breasts, heat and need building everywhere in her body while he kept kissing along her sides and ribcage. His skin tone was a few shades darker than her own, and the contrast of his tan with her pale ivory was soft and lovely. Breathless, she watched as his big, thick fingers delicately teased and pinched her pink nipple.

He squeezed. Sucked a fierce kiss onto her side.

The electricity of it shot through her, caught her off guard, and she did throw her head back. A whimper slipped from her tight throat. The muscles in her thighs twitched as her hips tried to rock forward, towards the heat of him.

Ryan chuckled, a huff of breath against her skin that she felt more than heard.

He dipped lower. Kissed and bit at the meat of her thighs, inching closer to exactly where she wanted him with every hot press of his mouth. Need nearly overtook her as he nudged into the space between her thighs. He hesitated. Pressed forward, the barest brush of his nose and mouth against the thatch of her pubic hair. And then he pulled back and looked up at her, his hands braced on the outside of each of her thighs, a question clear and longing in his eyes.

She nodded.

Unhesitating, he dove forward to press kisses against the mound of her vulva, to slip further down and flick his tongue between the folds of her. Meredith panted. Tensed in anticipation. And then caught herself saying, "Wait."

Not because she didn't want what he was offering.

Just because he'd never be able to eat her out properly from that angle.

He froze and pulled away as she lifted one foot and slowly applied pressure to his chest, pushing him. He got it. Quickly. The elbows of that nice black blazer she'd picked out for him were going to get dusty, but he leaned back and lowered himself down until he was lying, ready and waiting for her, on the living room floor.

Naked and wet, she stood above him, stared down at the lust and need evident all over his face, at the thick ridge straining to get out of his jeans, and she licked her lips. "Undo your belt. And unzip."

He did, watching her all the while. Exactly what she had asked, and no more. A wet spot of pre-come stained the front of his gray boxers in the bunched-up area of fabric where his cock pushed out between the tines of the zipper. She had to fight not to smile proudly at the sight of it—or, at the almost sight of it. Poor thing. He was probably aching.

"In case you need to touch yourself," she explained with a smirk as she lowered herself to her knees beside him.

Ryan tensed. His breathing quickened, and Meredith watched the quick rise and fall of his stomach. But he smirked back when she paused. "You going to keep me waiting all night, Hartman?"

"You're a menace, McKenna." She laughed and rolled her eyes. And then—without thinking about it, because she knew she would get shy if she stopped for a second to think about it—she hoisted one leg over him and straddled his face.

Ryan gasped and then groaned. His hot breath huffed over her damp and sensitive clit, and he immediately craned upwards to reach for her. She cut him and his soon-to-be-stiff neck a break and lowered herself down another inch. All of the muscles in her thighs and core worked to hold her up in the right spot, to keep from crushing him.

"God, yes. Fuck, Meredith, you are so fucking hot." His tongue flicked out and went to work.

Meredith did not hold back her reactions any more.

With sure, long licks with the flat of his tongue, he worked her clit. Kissed it. Wrapped his lips around it and sucked, hard, hard enough that she saw stars. As she threw her head back and moaned his name, her hips rocked forward and she rode his face, desperate for more. He gave it to her. While groaning and smacking his lips like she was the best thing he had ever tasted, he firmed his tongue to a point and drove it into her pussy with deep and sure thrusts before he pulled back to lick and suck on her clit. Again. And again. Meredith whimpered. Writhed. Ground down harder onto his mouth, onto the rough stubble on his cheeks that burned her inner thighs.

Each attack on her clit had her tense and moaning, nearly sobbing, holding her breath as her pleasure built, as she forgot how to say anything but his name, over and over again, on repeat. "Ryan! Oh, fuck. Ryan!" And each dive of his tongue into her hole had her squirming and panting and begging for more, a desperate need to be filled by him. To be fucked by him. His tongue inside her was a tease.

And then he'd mouth her clit again and she'd forget about anything else.

She didn't want it to ever end. And also, she desperately wanted to come. Her hands twitched and flinched as they itched to move towards her body on instinct, ready to take control. But she held back and gave him all the power. Trusted him to take care of her and to give her what she needed.

He braced her up with one hand, his fingers digging into her ribcage as he held her in place. His other arm moved. Her mouth slack and wide, she glanced back in a lust-soaked daze and followed the line of his arm, stared at where his hand disappeared into his boxers. In hard, furious jerks, the thick, pink tip of his prick peeking out from under the elastic, he fisted and worked himself while licking and groaning into her.

"Fuck, Ryan…" Thin and high, her voice squeaked out as her body gave. She threw one arm out to brace herself, and then the other, barely held herself aloft over him. Desperate, close, so, so close, she twisted her fingers into his hair and shoved herself against his mouth. "Ryan, please. Fuck. Make me come. Please make me come!"

His tongue swirled circles around her clit, and his mouth worked with the right amount of friction, the right amount of suction. Fuck, he was good at this. He sucked like her clit was a straw and he was determined to get the last bit of milkshake out of a glass, and his tongue worked in rough flicks, his mouth all over her, everywhere, and…and…

There. Finally. Finally. She nearly sobbed.

Her release crashed over her, wracked her whole body. She rode the waves of it, rocking against his mouth with abandon as her fingertips clenched and clawed at the hardwood floor. She let out a high-pitched, keeling whine in the shape of his name, the only thing she had left. "Ryan!"

He groaned as he finished her, wrung every last second of her orgasm out of her, until suddenly the feeling flipped on a knife's edge and it was too much. She gasped, hissed a breath, and pulled away, climbed off of him. Her legs were shaky underneath her. She sat her bare ass down on the floor and shook with relief, with pleasure, with too-bright emotion as she caught her breath.

He sat up and lunged for her. With his jeans hanging open, his eyes blown wide, he grabbed her and pulled her close to his chest, where she shook and breathed and clung to him. "I've got you, Meredith. I've got you."

She was floating. She was burning.

She had just had the best motherfucking orgasm of her entire goddamn life, given to her by a man who adored her, and wanted her, and respected her as much as she adored, and wanted, and respected him.

And she was not even close to done with him. No way.

She pulled back and looked him over. His hair was a wreck from her grasping fingers running through it, and his clothes were disheveled and rumpled. Slick, glossy moisture gleamed on his chin and all over his perfect, kiss-swollen mouth. His clever pink tongue darted out and licked some of it away, and he wiped the rest off of his face with the back of his hand. "How was that? Was that good?"

Was he seriously asking?

The deep, hot kiss she gave him was a good enough response as any. Wet and slick, the bitter tang of her own taste lingering in his mouth, they kissed with open mouths and hungry tongues. Her hand worked its way down his body, sliding along the buttons of his shirt, until she reached his cock. Through the fabric of his boxers, she gave him a squeeze and a stroke that quickly had him groaning. He shoved his hips forward, driving into her touch, and she slipped her hand inside his boxers to give him more. Kissing, with his hands tangled up in her hair, she cupped the silky soft head of his cock and rocked it in her palm, before she decided there was a better way to do this.

"Off. Off, off, off." She shoved at his blazer, and he pulled away to scrambled out of it while she lifted up on her knees and undid the buttons of his shirt. Together, they pushed that away too. Her jaw went slack at the sight of him bare-chested. Perfect. Absolutely fucking perfect. His torso was a thing of beauty, gorgeously broad, and muscled, and golden, and she might just drop dead on the floor if she didn't get to see him completely naked right this second. She grabbed his jeans and tugged. "These too. All of it."

He lifted up to strip them off, and his underwear along with them. He paused while she stared at him.

Perfect. All of it.

That taught stomach, those strong thighs dusted with hair, those broad shoulders. That bashful look on his face as she stared at him like she wanted to eat him alive, even though he didn't move, he let her look to her heart's content.

And that cock. Damn, that cock. Thick and proud, it jutted out from his mess of dark brown curls, all dusky pink and leaking. She wanted it. Wanted to gag herself on it, impale herself on it, or both.

She bit her lip and smiled at him.

"Come here." He pulled her close. Up on their knees, Ryan pressed their bodies together. Her breasts squashed against the hard muscles of his chest, and his thick cock rested tight and snug between their stomachs. Meredith ran both hands down along his back while they kissed, while he rocked against her and pressed them tighter together in rhythmic thrusts. He whispered into her neck, in between kisses, "I want you."

"I want you too."

"Downstairs." She kissed him and sucked on his lower lip, let her hand wander down into the space between their bodies to wrap around his firm length. "We have to…oh, God." In between groans, in fits and starts, Ryan managed to get his words out. Meredith didn't make it easy for him, though. She tugged him in long strokes. Squeezed him. Rubbed her thumb over the slit. "Condoms! They're downstairs."

Meredith paused and shot him a look. Honestly, who did he think she was? Smirking, she reached for the purse she'd discarded on the floor and dug through it in search of the little foil-wrapped square she knew was in there. When she found it, she held it in front of his face and raised one eyebrow. "What have I ever done to make you think I'm not the kind of woman who would bring condoms?"

Ryan blinked while he stared at the blue foil, and then grinned at her. "God, I like you. I like you so fucking much."

"That's what you keep saying." She nipped at his jaw and smacked his ass. He yelped and flinched and laughed. "Now get your dick in me, McKenna."

"Yes, mam." He laughed, his hands shaking, while he ripped open the condom and rolled it onto himself. "How do you want it?"

"I want to see you." She kissed him. "Beyond that? I'm open to any position I'm physically flexible enough to pull off."

He quirked his head to one side. "That sounds like a challenge."

"Might be." She shrugged and shot him a teasing smile. "Maybe not right now."

"Cool, so I'll have you swing upside down from the ceiling some other time."

"Like some sort of vampire?" Meredith laughed. "Right. I forgot. Your attraction to supernatural women."

He grinned and laughed against her chest as he lowered his head and kissed along the slope of her breasts. His tongue flicked at one of her nipples before he sucked it. She whimpered and petted his hair, but the bright smile didn't entirely fade from her face. He pulled away long enough to say, "It was werewolves, actually," before he switched sides and gave her other breast the same attention.

"And Sasquatch." Meredith gasped and arched her back. "Don't forget. You did tell me that you would fuck a Sasquatch."

He bit her nipple. Just a nip, quick and sharp. She swore, but also laughed and swatted him upside the head. "I did not say that. You deliberately misunderstood."

"Okay, sure, whatever you say…"

"Hey Meredith?" He kissed her. Flicked his tongue into her mouth. One of his hands slid down her body and prodded in between her legs. His thick finger dipped into her entrance, and she spread her legs wider to let him finger her and tease her. Her hands splayed across his chest, and she toyed with his pebbled, brown nipples. "If you got cursed by a witch and turned into a Sasquatch, I would still want to be with you."

"Aw, you sap." She fluttered her eyelashes at him. "You say the sweetest things."

"And I would definitely still want to fuck you."

"Such a dream, you are."

"Even if you were covered in hair like a crazed wildebeest."

"And a poet!"

"Even if you were really smelly and liked to haunt the dreams of hikers in the Pacific Northwest."

"Oh, Ryan!" She threw her head back and laughed, though his fingers in her wet pussy had her writhing. His cock stood ready and wrapped between them. "Take me now!"

He grinned and kissed her.

She let him. And then pushed him back. "No, seriously. Take me now."

He laughed and nodded, pulled his fingers out from between her legs, and rested both hands on her hips. His breath was shaky. He didn't quite meet her eye.

She knew him. It was a pleasant discovery, that she knew how to read him, that she knew his hang-ups and uncertainties, that she could see them plainly on his face. It was a sweeter sort of pleasure, to realize that she really was learning him, that she was on a path to knowing him well.

Even though that look on his face, the energy he radiated, was not what she had expected in this moment.

"Hey, wait." She grabbed his arm and stroked it, her other hand still pressed against his chest. "Are you still nervous?"

"I—" He caught himself, smiled a little, and nodded. "Yeah."

She paused and felt for him at the sight of the dear, uncertain hesitancy in his eyes. He'd been so sure, so fevered and intense while eating her out. But now, on the cusp of having her for himself, of actually getting to come, he hesitated. She cupped his cheek, and he leaned into it, his stubble grazing her palm. "Ryan."

"It's just that it's been a long time. And also, I haven't had very many first times. And you...you matter so much to me. I want to get this right. I want to be right for you."

It stopped Meredith's breath. Aching, tender fondness squeezed her heart at the admission. Her face scrunched up in an emotional, painfully sweet smile. "I like you. I like you so fucking much."

It squinted his eyes. "I like you too."

"Come here." Meredith took his hand and tugged him along, pulled him to her as she laid down on the floor. Her body prone and ready for him, she opened her legs to make room, and he kneeled in between them, braced himself over her. She craned her neck and kissed him. "I've got you, Ryan. Come on."

Legs spread wide and hitched up, she gripped the base of his cock and guided him to her entrance. The thick, blunt tip of him nudged up against her and then slowly pushed in. She gasped as he filled her. "That's it. Yes. God, yes. That's so good."

He paused and held himself still once he bottomed out, deep inside her. The fit was tight, the girth of him stretching her with a slight and satisfying burn. She needed a second. So did he. Above her, Ryan's forehead was tense with lines, but his eyes were focused on her. "Okay?"

She nodded. "You?"

"Yeah. God, yeah."

"Better than any Sasquatch you've ever been with, I hope." Demon spawn that she was, she couldn't help herself. But, in her defense, he liked it when she teased him.

He snorted in her face as he pulled out and then rocked back in. "How are you making me laugh right now? Now who's the menace?"

"Still you, if you're not going to fuck me properly." She hooked her ankles around the backs of his thighs, just under his ass, and urged him forward. He did not disappoint.

As he picked up the pace and found his rhythm, Meredith arched her back off the stiff floor and groaned each time he slammed into her. Hard. And insistent. And devoted. He kissed her with messy passion, each kiss wetter and looser than the last as he started to lose himself in her. He groaned her name and fucked harder when she sucked on his neck, when she dug her fingers into the meat of his flexing ass. Each stroke filled her, fucked her, shoved the breath out of her, shoved the thoughts right out of her head, until all she could think was, "Ryan! Oh, fuck, yes, Ryan!"

He was close. Sweat popped along his hairline and he panted hard, his face twisting up as he chased his orgasm. Needy and eager, she helped him along. When he kissed her, she tempted him with flicks of her tongue until he did what she wanted, until he pressed into her mouth. Inside, trapped where she wanted him, while his hips pistoned in and out of her, she sucked on his tongue hard enough to claim it, and then caught his lower lip as he pulled away.

It was enough to tip him over. With a groan, he threw his head back and spilled inside her. Meredith watched the pleasure and release wash over his face, watched his jaw go slack, watched his eyes go soft. Watched him come. She fucked him through it, her pussy burning, wet, and tender, and as soon as he was spent, she yanked him down into a kiss.

He collapsed onto her, nearly his whole weight pressing her into the floor. Nothing about it—his weight, his body, his strength pinning her down—felt trapping or restrictive or oppressive. It felt like a gift. Like an honor. He was vulnerable. Shaking, trembling as he caught his breath, as he softened inside her. She held him through it, stroked his back, and murmured into his hair, just like he had done for her after her own orgasm had left her wrecked, "I've got you, Ryan. I've got you."

He lifted up enough to kiss her, to cup her cheek and press his face to hers.

Tangled up together, arms wrapped around each other, they breathed and held each other as the night air cooled their damp, bare bodies.

She was going to fall in love with him. The thought hit her with sudden clarity, a deep and unavoidable truth. She was going to fall in love with him, and there was nothing about it that made her want to stop.

Chapter Fifteen

Memories of the night before resonated through every muscle in Ryan's body as he slowly woke the next morning. He didn't have to blink or shake himself to remember; he didn't have a moment of confusion when he opened his eyes and saw another person in bed with him—for the first time in quite a while. It was all there with him: every memory, every moment, Meredith. As present and real in his mind, in his body, as she was present and real bundled up in the duvet beside him.

He blinked a few times to clear his eyes, the bright morning sunlight illuminating the silvery-gold of Meredith's hair where it was tossed over her face. Still asleep on her stomach, she had her arms wrapped around the pillow, the blankets pulled up around her in a nest so that only the top of her head and her tangle of hair was visible. Beneath the covers, one of her legs bent at a strange angle, and her cold foot rested against his shin. He cleared his dry throat and rubbed sleep out of his eyes, and for a long moment, in the still and quiet morning, he watched her sleep.

And then he smiled to himself.

Everything in him ached to reach out and touch her. Simply.

Without any deeper or more demanding longing. He had a strong and pressing urge to stroke her hair back from her face, to run his knuckles along her cheekbone. To be close to her. To feel her.

He didn't, because that might wake her up. It was early still. The neon green shapes of the clock on his bedside table informed him that it was only half past seven in the morning, and they'd had a late night. Ryan was an early riser. Always had been. And really, it was no wonder his inner alarm was forcing him awake at this early hour on a weekend; the looming deadline of the showcase crept ever closer and filled him with a dreadful, buzzing need to do things, to keep moving, to get all of the work done. He would go into the shop later today. He'd have to.

But for now?

It was early. It was chilly. And Meredith needed to sleep.

All good reasons to stay in bed and not disturb her.

Even though the need to touch her was strong, he contented himself with the strange connected press of her foot on his leg as he shifted and reached for his phone.

Wide awake, he quietly kept himself busy by her side while she slept on. He checked social media—Facebook and Instagram. He had a notification that he had been tagged in a photo, a candid shot he didn't realize Naomi had taken. Against a darkened background, strange and distorted flashes of laser light blurring the edges of the image, the picture was of him and Meredith cackling laughter on the dance floor. Wildly warm and fond, Ryan stared at it for a long moment. Meredith's nose was scrunched up, her head thrown back and her hair golden and blazing. He looked stupidly happy too, grinning so much his eyes were squinted shut. It was a brilliant memento, and he would have to thank Naomi for sneaking it later. She had added the caption, *"When you send your BFF out for dating advice but it turns out his coach has hella moves."* He double tapped the image to like it. Naomi had also posted a new selfie of her and Richelle from the night before, arms around each other and making kissy faces at the camera. Adorable. Ryan liked the post, and then added a comment with three heart-eyes emojis.

And still, Meredith softly snored into the pillow beside him.

His heart might burst. It really, truly might just beat right out of his chest if he thought too much about how good this was, how right it all felt.

So he checked the news. Then different news. Meredith shifted and sniffed, and Ryan watched her movements, but she still didn't wake, so he went to Buzzfeed and took a quiz to see what kind of dog breed he was based on what desserts he chose, and then another one to see where he should travel based on his favorite Harry Potter characters. (Pitbull, and Greece, respectively.) And Meredith still slept. So he opened the Kindle app and started reading a book Naomi had been trying to get him to read for ages, a YA fantasy that all of the girls in her mentor group were obsessed with, and it actually ended up being really good, so he didn't notice Meredith had quietly woken up until, voice thick with sleep, she muttered, "Did you make this?"

He blinked and whipped his head to the side to look at her, confused by the question. Still on her stomach, with her eyes squinty and puffy, she glared at the headboard. "Oh." He laughed. "Yeah. I did."

Her glare deepened. She sniffed. And she mumbled, "It's really pretty."

"Thank you."

He gave her a moment. As she stretched and twisted her body

around, she woke up slowly. Last night's mascara smudged under her eyelids, and she rubbed at her face with her whole hand. Ryan watched the sleepy, rumpled, messy morning version of her and felt like the damn Grinch—his heart grew three sizes with every little thing she did, every little stretch and grumble, until he felt so damn fond that the heavy, beating muscle might just burst out of his chest. She was perfect.

Through a massive yawn that she covered with her elbow, her arm blocking half of her face, she asked, "What time is it?"

"Almost eight-thirty." When she turned towards him, her face soft on the pillow, he did what he had wanted to do for an hour already and reached out to brush her hair back behind her ear. She leaned into it with her eyes closed, like a cat pressing into pets. "How did you sleep?"

"Good." She blinked a few times and then huffed a laugh. "Sorry. I'm useless until I've had coffee."

"I can make you coffee!" He turned over and shifted under the blankets so they were both on their sides, facing each other. She looked back at him with the same soft fondness he radiated. Gently, he brushed a fingertip down the center of her face, along her forehead and nose, until he reached her mouth and she pecked him with a kiss. "Breakfast, too. What do you want?"

She sighed and shrugged and nuzzled closer to him. When her legs nudged against his, he shifted and let her tangle them together, and she stroked up and down his chest. Voice thick and gravelly, she said, "I really want your dick in me again, but I think I'm too sleepy to move that much."

Ryan snorted a laugh and tossed his phone clean off the bed. It clattered to the floor while he wrapped an arm around her waist and tugged her bare, languid body closer to his. She tucked into him, melted against him, and let him kiss along her neck and shoulder. "I can do all the work."

Tempted, she rocked her hips towards him. All of her warm and soft skin against him, touching him from chest to foot beneath the cozy blankets, already had him eager. Against her stomach, while she wriggled and nuzzled closer to him, his cock swelled thicker by the second. She felt it and pushed into it, which only made him harder. "I don't know. I haven't brushed my teeth yet…"

"I don't know why you think I'd care about that." He ran his hand down along her side, across her back, over the curve of her hip. She rocked her hips again, trapped his growing erection between their bodies and squeezed it there for a breath until she unclenched and released him. "I already told you I would still want to fuck you even if you were a Sasquatch."

A thoughtful hum rumbled in the back of her throat. "And they don't even brush their teeth at all. Ever."

"Exactly."

Slow and lazy, she grinned. "Alright, then."

Just as slow and lazy, he kissed her. Sucking and soft, he pressed her lips open and tasted her while their bodies rubbed together under the blankets. Her morning breath was stale and sour, and he knew his was too, but if it didn't matter to Meredith, then it didn't matter to him either. He kissed her deeply, and let his hands wander while he did it, down her stomach, until he reached the crease between her legs. She hummed into his mouth and shifted her angle, lifted her top thigh, so he could touch her.

Eyes soft and drowsy, she sank deeper into the pillows as he fingered her. While he rubbed tight little circles against her clit, she hummed and let her eyes sink shut. Completely relaxed.

Completely uninhibited.

As Ryan's heart sped up, as he watched the way her tongue darted out, the way the rosy pink flush bloomed across her cheeks and chest, he could not decide which version of Meredith he was more turned on by: the one last night who took charge, threw him on the ground, and rode his face until she came, or the one this morning who sank into the mattress and let him take care of her every need.

The answer, obviously, was both of them. All of them, all of her, every her.

The pressure in his groin built and intensified with every second, and every little moan or flutter of her eyelashes pulsed through his blood, directly into his cock. He wanted her. Badly. But he could play with her a while longer.

As his fingers dipped deeper, Meredith's mouth fell open and she sighed. He pushed inside her gently, one finger only, careful not to be too rough in case she was sore. They'd fucked twice last night, once on the floor of the living room, and then again in his bed before they fell asleep together. In and out in an easy glide, his thumb still rubbing at her clit, he worked her with his hand until she was dripping and moaning.

She was more than ready. And so was he.

He pushed back the blankets to sit up, and Meredith shivered as her bare torso was exposed to the chill air in his bedroom. While he grabbed a condom from the bedside table and put it on, wincing at the rush of relief he got just from the brush of his own hand, Meredith stayed melted. Drowsy. Leisurely. She watched him roll the condom down his shaft, and she slipped a hand down between her own legs to keep doing what Ryan had started for her. The sight throbbed through him, a fierce and furious pulse.

Jesus, if he watched her like this any longer, he might just come untouched.

Back on his side, he tugged the blankets back up and cocooned them together. He nudged her hip. Kissed her. "If you turn over onto your other side, I can keep playing with your clit while I'm inside you."

Meredith turned over. Quickly. Still relaxed and sleepy, but more quickly than she'd done anything else this morning.

When Ryan laughed, she turned to grin and flirt with him over her shoulder.

Her smooth, perfect back pressed flush against his chest, their bodies tucked tightly together, Meredith rolled her hips forward and lifted one thigh while Ryan pushed into her. Her tight, wet heat surrounded him, and he groaned and pressed kisses onto her neck and shoulder and back. And, as promised, he tucked his hand down her front and worked his fingers between her legs.

There was nothing rushed or frantic about it, nothing desperate or needy. It was comfortable and slow and achingly tender. Both of them wanted to come. Both of them knew they would get there. There was no rush. And with Meredith all over him, all around him, with his cock deep and warm inside her, Ryan almost didn't need to move.

Almost. He did. With slow and shallow thrusts, he fucked her sweetly, and held her close. Each slide inside her surged through him, the pleasure building up slowly along his spine, deep in his balls. He wouldn't last much longer. He sucked on her neck and kept his pace, let himself get lost in just how fucking good she made him feel, but he also rubbed her harder. Faster. More deliberate. He would come soon, but he would make sure she came first.

Hips writhing, she pushed back to take him deeper every time he thrust in, her ass a soft and pleasant cushion against his lower abs, and then she rocked forward on every outstroke to grind her clit against his hand. She tensed. Her breathing quickened, each breath gasping in, holding tight in her core, and then hitching out. She was close. He could feel it through her whole body. He worked her. Worked himself. Tried to wait, but his own breathing quickened along with hers.

When she came, it was with her whole body. In one instant tense and quivering, poised and ready for it, and then the next, roiling and writhing as her orgasm rocked through her like electricity through a live wire. She groaned. Moaned his name. The tight ring of muscle at her entrance squeezed him tighter in clenching rhythm.

And that was enough to send him over.

His own orgasm punched him gently, a swell of pleasure that built and then spilled out of him. When it was done, he held her close and breathed in the scent of her.

This was perfect. This was everything he had ever wanted, or the beginnings of it, anyway. On the cusp of a future with Meredith, he felt dizzy, and staggered, and brave. This close, soft comfort, this raw and undemanding intimacy, was the sweetest thing that had ever belonged to him. He squeezed his eyes shut and wrapped his arm tighter around her waist as he slowly caught his breath, as she caught hers.

More than he'd ever wanted anything before, he wanted to be a home to her. He wanted her to be the same to him. Wanted it from a deep and lonely part of him that instinctively saw her as an equal, a match, a partner, and rang out with hesitant joy at their growing closeness.

"Alright," he murmured into her hair once he had found his way back to himself, once they had both calmed and relaxed, once he felt sure he could speak without vomiting up a million sappy, heartfelt, and embarrassing confessions. His softening cock had nearly slipped out of her, and he really should get the condom off and get them both cleaned up, but he lingered, not quite ready to pull away from the heat of her. "You want that coffee now?"

She nodded.

"Breakfast too?"

She twisted to glance at him over her shoulder. "I have been told that you make a top-notch Nutella crepe."

"I do." He laughed, and then winced and hissed as he pulled his too-sensitive cock the rest of the way out of her. He grabbed tissues and passed her a few, and then took the condom off before it could leak and make a mess all over the sheets. He sat up and let the blankets fall to his lap, leaving his chest bare as he stretched. Meredith stared at him. "You want them in here? Breakfast in bed?"

With a thoughtful pout, she considered this and then shook her head. Her hair was a tangled wreck, the fine blonde strands sticking out in several directions. She sat herself up, let the blanket fall, and stretched her arms wide in a way that thrust her chest forward, which meant it was Ryan's turn to stare. Meredith had the most perfect tits in all the world; pert, round handfuls that he planned to spend a lot more time getting to know, up close and personal, just as soon as they had the time. "Nah." He blinked. Looked away from her chest just in time to catch the smirk on her face, which meant she had caught him ogling her. "I need to go get washed up and pee so I don't end up with a UTI."

"Ah, the joys of having a vagina." He snorted a laugh and shook his head as he pulled on a pair of boxers. Then, remembering Naomi's declaration from the night before, about love and intimacy in relationships, he turned and waggled his eyebrows at her. "Can I watch?"

She glared at him. "Not during our first date! How easy do you think I am?"

"I think this is our fourth date, actually." At his dresser, he yanked out two t-shirts, one of which he tossed to her so she wouldn't have to choose between prancing through his house naked, or putting last night's clothes back on. Although, he wouldn't have minded had she wanted to choose the former, it was chilly, and the latter would be uncomfortable. She caught the gray t-shirt and pulled it over her head. She was not a tiny or petite woman, but the shirt was huge on her, and it hung off her frame in a soft and loose draping of fabric that just barely covered her bare ass. "Our first date was when you took me shopping. Second was coffee with your ex. Third was the zoo. Last night going into this morning is our fourth date."

"Hm." She studied him and raised a teasing eyebrow. "I'll think about it after the fifth one."

"Deal."

When Meredith joined him upstairs in the kitchen, he shoved a mug of coffee into her grateful, grabbing hands. She groaned into it and drank it down while he finished making breakfast for them. She sat at his kitchen table in his t-shirt and her underpants, one knee bent to prop her foot up on the chair while she watched his every move. It kept Ryan in a state of fuzzy excitability, and he burnt one of the crepes because he couldn't stop himself from glancing back at her every minute.

With the first bite, Meredith shook her head and glared at him, dead-eyed and terribly serious. "These are insane. This is so good."

The praise and approval from her sent a little zip of happiness up his spine, and he struggled not to smile too much.

They ate together in the quiet, with silly and simple conversation. Ryan felt like he was flying, and at the same time like the wide sky Meredith gave him was as safe and comforting as home. Every little quirk of her mouth, every tilt of her head, every movement of her hands, he watched with soft focus, observing and learning. He wanted to know her. Every bit of her. He wanted to know her past. Her future. Everything. It filled him, the deep and pressing need to know and be known.

It was this need to know her, and nothing more—nothing claiming or complicated, nothing possessive or jealous—that had him asking, at a quiet moment in their conversation, "Any chance you want to tell me what was going through your head last night?"

She paused and quirked an eyebrow. "That you're smoking hot?"

"Thank you. Back at you." They shared a moment of lingering, smirking eye contact, full with meaning as memories of the past few hours crashed through Ryan's mind on repeat. There was, though, the flashing bit of memory from the beginning, the moment of uncertainty Meredith had shown when he first brought her home. Meredith was a deep thinker, and a deep feeler. She contained oceans. And she didn't willingly let many people see below her sleek and glimmering surface. Ryan wanted to. If she was willing, if she would let him, he wanted to know all of the depths of her. And he wanted to know why she had hesitated last night, what had gone through her mind. "Actually, I meant right at the beginning, when we first got back to the house. You seemed a little distant. Like you were working through something in your head."

Long and soft, she sighed into her coffee cup and then set it down on the kitchen table. It sat, waiting, beside her empty plate, only a few streaks of chocolate remaining after she'd scraped up the crumbs with her fork. Her lips parted on a breath. Her eyes glazed and she gazed at a spot over his head. With her hair up in a messy blonde bun, wearing his too-large t-shirt, her legs naked and prickled with fine goose bumps in the chill, she looked bare. Vulnerable.

Maybe she didn't want to be. It was a big deal, really, for Meredith to strip back all of her walls and layers, all of her blazers, and business sense, and composure, to sit here with him like this. He had pushed. He didn't want to push. Truly. He just wanted to know everything about her, simply because he was beginning to suspect that she was the single most interesting and worth-knowing person in all the universe. But he didn't want to push. "Sorry. That's not my business. We don't have to—"

"I…my…" She cut him off, stuttered through the beginnings of her answer, and then cut herself off with a wave of her hand in front of her face, to clear the air. Ryan waited, poised, every muscle in his body tense. "It's stupid. But I got a little nervous."

He nodded. That was what he had suspected. And that was alright. He certainly had been too, though not for the same reasons. Unlike him, Meredith was not demi and therefore unlikely to be staggered by the unexpected ferocity of her own sexual attraction.
Something else had been on her mind, making her nervous. "About me? About us?"

"No. God, no. Not at all. Not that. Just…"

A hint of relief breathed through him at her certainty. He stayed quiet. Let her work through it. Let her find the words. Gave her space to convert her feelings into articulate thoughts. That space, that boundary, was something he, himself needed often. Far too frequently, people in his life had demanded immediacy. Immediate reactions, immediate understanding, immediate responses. Immediate feeling and immediate translation of those feelings into words. He certainly wasn't about to rush her for answers, for things she wasn't ready to share.

It took her a moment. She answered with a laugh, though she stared down at her hand on the tabletop. "I got a little too in my head because I realized that I had never sex with someone who wanted me to be me. Completely me."

"Oh." It stopped his heart dead. Completely dead. And then while his heart was dead, the defiant little thrust of her jaw, the tense way she taped her fingertips on the table and avoided quite looking at him, squeezed it until it surged back to life to ache and hurt for her. On instinct, he grabbed her fidgeting hand and held it. "Meredith, that's…"

"Not true anymore!" she said brightly, through a forced chipper grin.

"No, definitely not true anymore." He squeezed her hand. "As I have told you quite a few times now—"

"You like me. Yeah, I know." That softened her fake smile into something small and real. "I know I'm a bit much, though. I have always been a little much for the people I've dated. I don't really know how to be soft and tender."

It sounded like a warning.

They hadn't talked yet about what this was, where it was going. He knew what he felt for her, knew what it meant, and knew that she understood and respected that. But she was warning him. Letting him know that she did not consider herself easy to date—easy to know, easy to like, easy to love—and he might want to pull back. It was a thorn. An attempt at defense.

Blindly, more than a little angry at everyone in her past who had forced her into such awful lies, he shoved his way through.

"That's…I don't…Meredith." Everything he felt for her caught in his throat, choking him, as it all clamored to climb out of him and make her see just how fucking brilliant he thought she was. He paused. She let him. "You are not too much. Not for me. Not for anyone. Anyone who accused you of being too much? That's on them. Not on you. And okay, so you don't know how to be soft, and sweet, and mushy. I'm not asking you to be."

"I know, I know. But I want to be. With you. I think. But I don't really know how to do relationships, Ryan. I have changed so much as a person since the last time I was in one, and I don't quite know how to be myself and navigate…" She squeezed his hand. "This. I'm not saying I don't want to. Because I do. I want this. I'm not trying to pull away right now."

Ryan nodded and sat with it for a second. He didn't know much about how things had been between Meredith and her ex, but he had seen enough and heard enough to know that he had tried to break her. That man had not liked her, had not liked the actual woman and had only wanted a day-dreamed reworking of her. He had wanted her to be softer, smaller. It made sense, that Meredith would have some things to work through if that was the bulk of her dating experiences. That was the last relationship she had been in, and she had built an entirely new life for herself since then. She had also built a lot of walls around herself since then. He got it. He understood. "This is kind of weird, new territory for you."

"Yeah. Exactly." She bit her lip and said, quiet but sure, "Be patient with me. I hope you can be. That's all I'm asking."

He nodded.

Everything he wanted to say, should say, caught up in a tangled, pressing knot in his chest. Her confession, her hesitation, pulled it out of him. He wanted her to know that he understood. And he wanted her to know, at least a little bit, exactly why he understood. It wasn't something he talked about often or with just anyone, and it wasn't something he liked to dwell on. But he wanted to be known by her as much as he wanted to know her. "My parents are not good people."

Quiet, urging him to continue talking, to get the spiky, writhing pressure out of his chest, she drew her eyebrows together and nodded.

So he did. The admission lacked big emotions—he'd felt his way through all of those years ago and it didn't hurt him much anymore. But it was uncomfortable. "My dad has an awful temper. My mom does too. Bitter. Resentful. Things were pretty unstable, growing up." He sniffed and shifted in his seat while he tried not to linger or get caught up in memories—all the times his dad had swung at him and his mom had snarled and rolled her eyes and told him he deserved it; all the times they had gotten into screaming fights throwing plates across the kitchen; all the times teenage Ryan had retreated out to the barn and outbuildings on his family's property and sat out there for hours, working and messing around with tools just to avoid the unpredictable wrath of his father, the emotionless blame of his mother. Meredith lightly dragged her fingernails over the back of his hand, and he said, "I don't talk to them anymore. I very much believe in boundaries, these days. You need to take things slow and take care of yourself? I get that. I do too. And I'm definitely not going to pull away from you or drop this just because you need some extra time to adjust to things, or because it's not going to be exactly like it would be with someone else."

Eyes sharp, all-seeing, and terribly blue, Meredith pinned him with an uncompromising look, held his hand, and nodded. She got him. He got her. They were going to do this. This thing, this whole big, uncertain future of them stretched out wide and wild and welcoming before them.

"Thank you. And any time you want me to go slash your parents' tires and egg their windows and leave flaming dog poop on their porch, I'd be happy to do that."

"Only if I get to do the same to your shitty, abusive ex-boyfriend." He snorted a half laugh. "And thank you, but I couldn't let you do that. Mostly because Naomi has been ready to brawl with them for years, and she'd be pretty hurt if I held her back but let you go for it."

"She could come! We could do it together, like a bonding ritual. Richelle could go with you, Naomi could come with me."

"We'd all be best friends by the end of the day."

"Exactly."

Laughing, Ryan shook his head. "Alright. I really hate to run off, but I have to get some work done today." He stood up from the table and grabbed both of their dishes to wash. In a rush, before he could think it through too much or make himself nervous, he said, "I was wondering, though, if maybe you'd like to come with me to the shop. So I can show you what I'm working on."

"Yes! I would love that! I really want to see the work you do." Meredith nudged him away from the sink with her hip and took over washing the dishes. He let her, but grabbed a towel and dried while she flashed him a cheeky grin. "And anyway, I think I was promised a present! I know how busy you are prepping for the showcase, and I don't want to get in your way, so I will give you the option of a raincheck if you don't have time to make it today."

"It's already made." He cleared his throat and stared down at the rough towel in his hand as he dried out the inside of a coffee cup. "Actually. I already made it."

"What? Seriously?" Smirking and pleased, she nudged him again. "What is it? What did you make for me?"

"I…uh…" Damn. Was it weirder to tell her in advance? Or to just take her to the shop and show her? He should tell her, he decided. Definitely tell her. Meredith had told him early on that she did not like surprises. But still, either way, he felt weird about it. It was extra. It was over the top. He had started making heavy office furniture for this woman the day he met her, well before he had even started to realize he was attracted to her, that he cared about her. That was weird. But it was something he had wanted to do. For her. Without expectations or deeper, hidden meaning, he thought of something nice he wanted to do for her, and he did it. Now, in hindsight, he may have done a bit too much, too soon. "It's a desk."

Meredith stilled. Water poured from the sink tap and cascaded off the spatula she was in the middle of washing, but nothing else about her moved. A film of soapy bubbles covered her elegant hands. Eyes pinched closed, she turned her head to look at him and then blinked wide. "A desk. You made me a desk?"

Embarrassed and on the spot, feeling very called out, Ryan squeezed his eyes shut, nodded, and tried not to laugh. "Yeah. I did."

A long, wheezing snort hissed out of Meredith's nose and she bit back a wide grin. "Damn, kid! You've got it bad for me, huh? You're in deep!"

Ryan chose to ignore her claim, since it was too obviously true to be worth arguing, and instead chose to focus on the fact that she was laughing and teasing about it. Her tone was warm and full of laughter, and that melted away most of his nerves. "Kid? Who are you calling kid?"

"You are two years younger than me."

"Okay, oh ancient one." Ryan winced and held up a hand to protect himself when Meredith flicked the clean spatula and sent a splatter of water droplets towards his face. "Keep it up and just see if I don't build you more surprise furniture!"

"You know those birds? Weavers?" As she turned off the tap and wiped her hands on a towel, she grinned and leaned her hip against the edge of the counter. "The males spend a bunch of time building a nice little house for their girlfriends. That's you. You're a silly bird."

She tried to bury it in an insult, but Ryan missed nothing. That word caught him like a hook yanking his attention. It grabbed him and wrapped him up tight in a million bright, happy feelings. Smug, he leaned in a little closer to her. "Oh, so you're my girlfriend now?"

"Well, you see." Meredith inched closer to him, a smirk playing on her lips, in the bright blue of her eyes. She pressed a hand to his bare chest, and he leaned into the touch just slightly while she looked up at him and teased. "The male weaver birds build the houses. Then, the females inspect them, and if they don't like the house, they trash it. They rip it apart, and demand the male make a new one. A better one. So I guess what I'm saying is… I might be your girlfriend, but…" She lifted up onto her toes to pop a quick, flirty kiss on his cheek before she pulled back and glared. "It better be a damn good desk, McKenna."

He huffed a laugh and wrapped his arms around her waist to tug her in closer. "If you hate it, I will happily give you the sledgehammer while I start a new design."

Gentle laughter hitched and shivered through Meredith's body. He felt it in her chest as she pressed against his, as he grabbed handfuls of the soft t-shirt she wore and held her close. As he kissed her, the curve of her smile against his mouth was a treasure.

"Thank you." She pulled back and gazed up at him, a sincere and vulnerable openness softening her features. "For the desk."

"You haven't even seen it yet."

"I don't need to see it to know how much it means to me. And I'm sure that since you designed it, it will be exactly the sort of thing I would like. I saw that about you the first time I met you; that you're insightful, that you notice things and see people. Thank you." One corner of her mouth lifted in a smile that was sweet, and fond, and sad. She whispered, "Thank you for seeing me."

It struck a certain chord in Ryan, the one that had long felt out of tune. Part of him had long felt lonely, out of step, sure something was just a little bit wrong with him. Meredith saw otherwise, right from the start. She cut to the heart of who he was and what he needed. She was kind with his uncertainties, but unwavering and firm too, and helped him see the value and validity in the parts of himself he'd always worried were ill-fitted. That chord in him wasn't out of tune at all, and Meredith sang its harmony.

He wanted to be the same to her. He hoped he was. Meredith had been lonely, too. She had felt out-of-step or out-of-tune or broken for a while now, too, for all of her own reasons, with all of her tangled past. They could be good for each other, right for each other.

He wrapped his arms around her whole body, held her close, and pressed a kiss into her hair. "Thank you for seeing me too."

Chapter Sixteen

Meredith glanced at the clock on the wall across from her desk. Her old, ugly, soon-to-be-replaced desk. Ryan still needed some time to put the finishing touches on her new, custom-designed desk. It was gorgeous, and no amount of teasing in the world could cover up just how much she genuinely loved the piece he had made for her. When she saw it in his workshop the other day, it had taken the breath right out of her. No one had ever done something like that for her, for one thing. And for another, the desk Ryan had designed was exactly to her tastes—sleek, light, modern, and minimal, with just a few details and flourishes. Already, he knew her well.

Just thinking about it yanked a smile onto her face.

"Okay, I really do have to go," Ryan said on the other end of the phone line. "I want to try to get this table finished before you come by this evening. You do still want to come by this evening, right?"

"Yes. Definitely. To drag you out and make you get something to eat, if nothing else."

With only a week left until his big showcase, Ryan had been

spending nearly every moment at his shop, building, and sanding, and perfecting all of the new work he planned to display. Nearly every moment. He'd managed to sneak in more than a few moments with Meredith, and they'd seen each other almost every day over the past week. Even if he couldn't spare more than an hour for dinner before getting back to it, Meredith felt a silly, giddy sort of warmth just being around him.

"Have a good rest of your day. Hope your client meetings go well."

"Thanks. You too. Don't cut any limbs off."

"I'll do my best!"

She rolled her eyes and laughed as she disconnected the call and set her phone down.

She had a boyfriend. A really good, sweet, crazy-hot boyfriend. It was quite a change.

In the still and sunny quiet of her office, Meredith sat tall in her chair, folded her hands in front of her, and thrummed with energy. She took a deep breath to calm and center it.

Twenty more minutes until her next client meeting. She tapped her fingers on the desk—the ugly, old desk—and then picked her phone back up. Plenty of time to check email and get caught up on everything. As she scrolled through her overflowing inbox, she ticked checkmarks down the whole column to delete most everything. Spam. Political blasts. Coupons. Nothing real, names she didn't recognize—

Until one name she did.

Frozen, with a sudden and instinctive chill, her finger hovered over an email from Dr. Michael Wilson.

Michael had email her.

Had reached out to her again.

She swallowed thickly, her throat gone dry.

After their meeting at the coffee shop, when she had given him her old engagement ring and a piece of her mind, she had thought for sure it would be the last she heard from him.

But now, an email. Subject line: *Meredith – Concerned for you.*

She could delete it. Probably, she should just delete it.

She opened it before she could talk herself out of it.

Quick and tripping, her eyes scanned the message. He had attached a photo. A screenshot from her Instagram account. Why hadn't she set that damn account to private? He didn't follow her, she knew that much. But he'd been checking up on her, as evidenced by the photo he had found of her and Ryan out on the dancefloor last week. She loved that picture. When she saw it that first morning, after she had woken up in Ryan's bed, she had stared at it for a long and tender moment.

Michael's screenshot included Naomi's caption: *"When you send your BFF out for dating advice but it turns out his coach has hella moves."*

That caption.

Which made it pretty obvious that she had met Ryan through her business.

That he had started out as a client.

Her stomach sank and twisted with something hot and sick and writhing as she read the rest of the email.

Concerned for you...

Weren't acting like your best self when we...

Sad to see how self-destructive you...

Knew there was something strange about...

All of it, simpering criticism and manipulative insult, wrapped up in false concern for her.

Heat flared through her cheeks, her chest. She tugged at her neckline. It was hot in here. Hard to get a full breath.

Had he just written to insult her? She could take an insult.

Why couldn't she breathe? Why was it so god damn hot in here?

Because he wouldn't write just to insult and demean her. There was more. There was a hit coming, a hit disguised as something else, just like all of his hits used to be—the metaphorical ones, and the physical ones. She braced herself, grit her jaw, held steady.

And then, at the end of the email: *I find it ironic and rather pitiful, Meredith, that after all the heinous things you accused me of (a few weeks ago, and at the end of our relationship) that you would engage in this kind of behavior. For all the vitriol you spewed about how I have had relationships with a couple of my interns, you must know that dating a client is a far more egregious and unforgiveable breach of ethics. As someone who once cared for you, and as a professional established in the field you still hope to enter, I suggest that it would behoove you to end your current relationship and proceed carefully. I do not imagine the faculty at any graduate program in the area would be much impressed by your professionalism were they to discover you're in the habit of sleeping with your clients.*

Meredith's head spun.

She couldn't breathe.

She had completely forgotten how to breathe, and she held tight to every last drop of oxygen trapped within her chest.

I do not imagine the faculty at any graduate program in the area would be much impressed by your professionalism were they to discover you're in the habit of sleeping with your clients.

I do not imagine the faculty at any graduate program in the area…

Any graduate program in the area…

"Fuck." In a hitching gasp, the word burst out of her. She sucked in a new breath to replace the precious one she had lost and held it just as tightly. Heat flamed in her face. Her heart skipped and sped. "Fuck."

It was a threat. Meredith knew a threat when she saw one, and this was a threat. A threat to do what he wanted, or else he would make sure that every professor in every grad program she might ever think of applying to in the DMV region would hear that she had a reputation for fucking her patients.

It didn't matter that her relationship with Ryan wasn't like that. Obviously, it wasn't like that. She wasn't a therapist! He wasn't a patient!

But she had met him through work. He had signed a contract with her and paid for her help.

Jesus, she had been dating him for a week and she hadn't even thought to refund the money he paid her. Dammit. That was unprofessional. Unethical. Gross.

And if anyone found out…if Michael decided he really did want that one last little bit of control over her, if he chatted with his psychologist friends who held adjunct teaching positions in MA programs throughout the city...

He could ruin her.

She would never be able to go back to grad school if he interfered like that. His reputation was too big, and his word would mean too much.

She would be ruined. Her future would be ruined.

Desperate, she gasped and gulped for air and pressed a hand to her face to cover her eyes.

That bastard.

That son of a bitch.

She wanted to go back to grad school. In a deep and urgent way she hadn't felt before, with immediacy and greedy need, she wanted it. She had put it off. She had been afraid.

Now that Michael was threatening to take it away?

She wanted it. Needed it.

Footsteps thunked up the staircase outside her office door, and she scrambled to wipe the moisture away from her eyes, to clear the thick emotion from her throat.

When Mr. Benson knocked, she stood to welcome him with a bright smile. "Hey, Jack! Good to see you! Come on in. How did the date go this weekend?"

"Great, Meredith. Really, really great." As he crossed the room and sat himself down in one of the chairs across the desk from her, Jack Benson was beaming. It loosened the knot in her chest a little, just enough to comfortably breathe. "You are a miracle worker. Seriously. I never thought I'd find a connection with someone so quickly, but he is just..." He laughed. "Wow."

"Good, I'm so happy for you." Although stiff, the words came out with an approximation of appropriate tone and emotion. It was unfortunate. Unfortunate that she couldn't muster up the joy and satisfaction he deserved. Mr. Benson had been one of the good ones, one of the clients she loved helping, and his coaching sessions led him to the promising start of a new relationship. Later, she could feel happy for him. For now, she just needed to get through the meeting intact. "So tell me all about it! Is there anything moving in this next phase of things that worries you?"

For the next hour and a half, she pushed through. Faked smiles. Said what she was supposed to say. Managed it well.

For ten minutes after Jack left her office, she stared down at the phone in her hand and re-read Michael's email over and over again, on a loop, until the words blended together in an infuriating, awful tangle.

She couldn't let this happen. Couldn't. Could not.

She didn't have much choice, did she? No. Not really. Not for the moment, anyway. Maybe later. Maybe after some time. But not now. Ryan would understand.

He would have to.

Spine stiff, heart aching, she got into her car and drove over to Ryan's shop.

As soon as she stepped inside the storefront, her stomach twisted in violent rejection. She pushed through it. The little bell tinkled above the door, and the front room full of all of the gorgeous furniture, sculptures, doors, and displays Ryan had created greeted her. Each piece was unique and special, with devotion and creativity and craftsmanship evident in every shape, every grain. From the first second she had walked into this place last week, she had fallen in love with it.

Fallen in love with this bit of him.

Ryan was nowhere to be seen, and a loud humming buzzed from the back room.

Meredith braced herself and navigated her way along the creaky old floors, in between a set of tall bookshelves, past a whimsical little kitchenette dining table, and through the door that led to Ryan's workspace.

He was turned away from her as he sanded the plank laid out on his workbench, his back strong and broad. With the loud hum of the sander whizzing and echoing through the whole workshop, he hadn't heard her come in. He thought he was alone.

Unmoving, barely breathing, she watched him for a long moment. It was a stolen glimpse, a little look at his purest self, at who he was in solitude. Devoted. Strong. Attentive. Creative. A lovely moment.

She watched him until she felt like crying.

Which was foolish.

Because this wasn't a forever sort of situation. It was unfortunate. But not forever, and they would handle it.

Still. It felt like loss. Especially once she looked past him at all of the pieces he had already completed for the showcase—the moon-shaped bookcase polished until it seemed to luminesce, the strange and craggy table with its turquoise river, and half a dozen others. Each of them, done with such skill.

Very much so, she had wanted to stand by his side, to keep him comfortable and grounded, to watch him with pride at the event next week.

That was no longer an option. Thick and heavy, the realization choked her and clogged her throat.

But she walked around the perimeter of the space, her heels clicking harshly on the bare concrete floor, until she was in his line of sight. She waved.

The grin that cracked across his face at the sight of her broke her heart. He nodded at her to acknowledge her presence, but then took another moment to finish up. When he switched off the sander, the silence rang heavy and shrill in Meredith's ears, the sudden absence of sound jarring after such noise. Ryan wiped sweat and saw dust off his face with the back of his sleeve and flashed her a crinkly-eyed sunrise of a smile as he approached, as he leaned down, as he kissed her. "Hey. You're early. Or am I late? Either way, it's good to see you."

He moved to kiss her again.

She placed a firm hand on his chest and held him in place. "Ryan. We need to talk."

"Okay." He took a step back. "Is everything alright?"

How to answer that question? No. To put it simply. Everything was not alright. But it would be. In time, once she figured this out, everything would be okay. She just needed the space and the time to figure out how to fix this before her bastard ex could ruin everything.

Instead of answering his question, though, she drew in a deep, steadying breath and said, "I need to slow things down. With us, I mean. I need to pump the brakes a little bit."

"Okay." His response was immediate and unquestioning, a full acceptance of her needs. "That's fine. I get it. Whatever you need."

That kindness, so unassuming, broke her heart a little more. "I don't want to. I care about you a lot. I just…I need…"

"Hey. Meredith." He took one of her hands. She hadn't realized she had balled them both into fists until he caught one and gently pried her fingers away from her stinging palm. "I care about you too. Whatever you need is fine by me. I did promise you I could be patient. I meant that."

It took a lot of effort to meet his eyes. His sweet brown eyes, so full of tender understanding. She ached, looking at him. "Thank you."

"Is everything okay? You seem pretty upset right now, even though you were fine on the phone earlier. Did something happen?"

"I just… realized that I have been pretty unprofessional. Dating you like this. While you were still technically my client. And if someone found out…" Shaky and upset, not quite sure how to explain, she pulled out her phone, opened up the email, and passed it to him. "Here. Read it for yourself."

As Ryan read through Michael's condescending, insulting, threatening email, his eyebrows knit close together and a deep scowl carved lines in his forehead and around his mouth. He handed back the phone. "Wow."

Meredith sniffed and pulled herself up, straightened her back. Committed. "He's threatening me. Threatening to sabotage my grad school chances."

Ryan stared down at the ground and nodded to himself. "And you're going to let him get away with it?"

She stilled. "I'm not letting him do anything."

"But you are giving him the power here."

"I'm not giving him anything. He doesn't need me to give him power." Sharp, biting, she snapped, "He already has it. He knows every professional in my field. He's well-established. One wrong word from him, and I'd be ruined before I could even try."

Annoyed, Ryan scoffed. He shook his head. "That's bull shit. I don't believe that for a second. Just because you hurt his pride the other day? He gets off on keeping you under his thumb! He's trying to sabotage your happiness just because he can, and he's scared you into helping him do it!"

She snapped. Not outward. Inward. Ryan's admonition shut her down cold, shut down all of her emotions, and brought up every single one of her walls.

Unfortunate.

With him, she hadn't thought she needed them.

But the second he pushed too far, all of her defenses flew back into place. She hissed, "That is not fair. You want me to sacrifice my entire career for you? My future?"

"No, Meredith! I want you to stand up for yourself, to stand up to him! To be free of him!"

"You think I'm not doing that? This is me standing up for myself, Ryan. He could ruin me. I cannot let that happen. I thought you would understand. I thought you would think it was reasonable, for me to slow down, to back off a little bit until I could get this under control. You said you would be patient with me." She bit her lip. Too hard. Until it hurt, and then more. It was either that or cry in front of him, and that was absolutely not an option. Not now.

"Apparently that was a lie."

"Meredith, that's not true." He backed off, held both hands up in surrender. "If you need space, fine. You need to slow down? Absolutely. Whatever you need. I just don't think that this is you choosing this. This is him choosing for you and making demands he has no right to make. That makes me angry at him. And it also makes me sad for you."

"Fuck you, Ryan," she snarled. That was enough. No more. She couldn't hold it together for much more of this. She turned on one heel. "I don't need your pity."

He called after her as she marched out of his workshop, "You can't let him rule your life, Meredith. You can't keep making decisions based on what that jerk did to you years ago!"

A volcano of emotion, of reaction erupted from somewhere deep within her. It was rage and pain and broken glass, the fire she'd used to forge the shattered pieces of herself back together. Something beyond her. Something entirely her. Too raw. Too true. Too real. She whirled back, hair flying, and hissed, "Everything I am is based on what that jerk did to me years ago! Everything!"

A breath gasped back into her emptied, vulnerable body and filled the vacuum in her lungs. It shook. Hitched. Burned. Her lower lip trembled. She pressed a hand to her mouth, too late to contain the emotion, too late to push the awful words back in.

Maybe she didn't want to.

Maybe Ryan needed to know, to really know, if he was ever really going to understand her.

It was the most tangled and uncomfortable truth of her life. It was a truth she never admitted out loud, or to anyone but her deepest self.

But it was truth nonetheless.

Ryan wanted to know her? Here she was, the awful truth of her: Michael Wilson made her. The abuse, and manipulation, and gaslighting, and isolation, and pain, and degradation she endured while she was with him was the most formative and shaping experience of her life. Also formative was how quietly, how subtly it had all happened; the frog in the pot, slowly boiling. Slowly letting itself die. That had been her. He had tricked her, goaded her, shaped her, groomed her, until she had become a willing and active agent in her own torment. She hated that. Hated that she had given him the power, the control. That experience hardened and purified her into who she was today, a diamond born from awful, crushing pressure.

She liked who she was, yes. And also she knew she, like so many women, was a product of what was done to her.

So many women spend the rest of their lives working through damage that was done to them in a bedroom. So many women become who they are because trauma shoved their personality and outlook in a new direction. Meredith knew that about herself. She liked herself. And she knew she could never extract the parts of herself born out of trauma from the memory of that trauma. It was too tangled. Women were tangled webs of their own experiences. Pride was a long string, and at the other end was shame. Strength was knotted together with suffering. Each of them, a journey. Ending the influence of something like that was not so simply done.

Breaking free of it was not so simply done.

She gulped and sucked air in through her nose, holding tight to rein back in the lost tendrils of her control. Bit by bit, while Ryan stood rooted to his spot and watched her with tender, hurting, loving eyes, she contained it all. Straightened her back. And wiped all trace of the outburst from her face, from her body. Without another word, she turned away again and crossed the rest of the big, empty workshop, her heels clicking on the concrete, whirls of sawdust swirling at her feet with every step away.

"Meredith."

His tone made her pause. Sad, and sweet, and sincere. She looked back.

Ryan look at her. Really looked at her, deeply, and with emotion radiating off of him, readable and easy. He hurt for her. Not out of pity. He hurt because she hurt. "For what it's worth? I don't think there is a single goddam thing he could say to anyone, at any school that would keep you out. Your competence, and talent, and drive are evident in everything you say and do, and everyone around you can see it. You're too brilliant for anyone to stop."

He meant it. Every word. He really believed it.

She knew it was true. It had been a while since someone else had believed in her like that, though. Since someone else had liked her.

Or, at least, she thought she knew it was true…

If she knew she was too brilliant for anyone to stop, then why was she so worried Michael could stop her with a simple word?

Her bottom lip quivered. Emotion crept up through cracks in her defenses and seeped to her outsides. Ryan's belief in her was staggering, and real, and sky high, even when she was furious with him. Even when she was ending things.

If she stayed here one more second, if she said one more word in response, she would start to cry. It was the last thing she wanted.

Instead, she forced a whispered goodbye. "Good luck at the showcase."

His face fell a little further, a little sadder, and he nodded. Heartbroken.

She left.

And though she held it together the whole way out, all the way back to her car, as soon as she stepped out the door a dark and anxious misery gripped her.

As the cool wind hit her face and the tears began to leak, she wondered if maybe it wouldn't have been so bad to let him see her like this. To let the walls down. She'd thought the last thing she wanted was to cry in front of him, to show weakness.

But really, as soon as her feet hit the pavement outside, she knew it wasn't true. Really, the last thing she wanted was to walk away and leave him hurting alone.

She did it anyway.

Chapter Seventeen

"I don't know he was right, or if I was." Dull and tired, Meredith stared at the blank wall behind the TV in her living room and clutched a mostly-melted, uneaten carton of ice cream. It chilled her fingertips until they ached, numb, and she did nothing to warm them. "And I don't know what would be worse."

"Really?" With her own bowl of ice cream, mostly eaten, Richelle sat beside Meredith on the couch. Both in their pajamas, bundled up in hoodies and socks, they sat side by side in sympathetic hurt. It was late. Richelle had to work in the morning, and she was already ready for bed. A pretty green silk scarf wrapped around her head to protect her curls, all make-up stripped off, and a tired heaviness in her brown eyes, she stayed by Meredith's side anyway. It had been the same with them, every break-up since freshman year of college. There hadn't been many. Each had gone through a few, and the other had provided ice cream and a shoulder to cry on, sometimes a bit of tough love along with commiseration. Gently, Richelle nudged. "I think it's pretty obvious which one would be worse. If you're right, it means old dick-brain really can ruin you. That you really do have to live with that shadow for the rest of forever, and there's nothing you can do about it. But if Ryan's right…you can fix it."

"Yeah I guess that's true," Meredith whispered as she considered the possibility. When she had received the email from Michael, it had sucked the breath right out of her. She hated having no control. She hated the powerlessness of it, and she felt shaky and desperate with the need to get a handle on the situation. Even now, hours later, her stomach twisted with sour clenching, unsettled and anxious, because it all felt so uncontrollable. But that was only if her first instinct was right. If Ryan was right, that she could stand up for herself and put a stop to this, then this was not an out of control situation. That perspective turned this into something she could get a handle on, something she could grip and drive. "It would be better if he's right."

Richelle stared at her hard and kind. The rest of their small house was silent and warm around them, the living room heavy with shadows cast by the dim overhead light. All of it drilled into Meredith.

"Do you think he was right?" Her voice hitched. "Am I sabotaging my own happiness here?"

Sweet and tender, Richelle wiggled closer on the couch until their sides were squashed together. The rich, sweet scent of shea butter filled Meredith's breath as Richelle snuggled up and pressed their heads together. "Yes. I think you fucked it up pretty royally."

The harsh truth, delivered gently, thudded into Meredith. A thin, miserable whine snuck out of her throat. "Maybe. But what if I'm right? What if he really is about to ruin all my chances at grad school, about to ruin my future? What if—" It struck her, suddenly, how it all sounded. What if, what if, what if…Nothing but a bunch of what ifs. She didn't sound reasonable or rational. She didn't sound in control. She sounded afraid. That was all. Just afraid. She had done what she had done, reacted how she had reacted, made the choices she had made not because any of it was the best thing to do, or the right thing to do. She had done it all because she had been afraid. She had done it all because years ago, some jerk had done bad things to her and had trained her to fear him. Even now, years later, much stronger, his training and conditioning lingered in her bones, in her instincts. He insinuated threats. She jumped to fix it. To please him. That had been how things went in their relationship. Even now, even with so much distance, even with such deep disdain for him and absolutely no care for what he wanted or how he felt, that pattern of behavior held on instinct.

On a deep, shaky breath, aching and miserable, Meredith admitted, "I think Ryan might have been right."

"Of course he was right! Meredith. Babe. I'm sorry. I don't want to make you hurt worse. But if you had come to me first? I would have told you the same thing Ryan told you. That threat to keep you out of grad school was completely unfounded, and it only has weight if you give it weight." She pulled back and sat up, forced Meredith to look at her. "You panicked. It's okay. It happens sometimes. But you panicked, and you let that drive how you reacted, but that doesn't mean your first reaction was right. You have the power over what happens here. No one can hold you back. No one can stop you from trying to define your own health and happiness. The only person who has the power to do that is you."

"You think I'm holding myself back and stopping myself from being happy?"

"Yeah." Richelle smiled. "Sorry. But you asked. So...yeah. You gave up on dating, even though you never gave yourself a chance to find a real partner after Michael. You talk all the time about when you'll go back to grad school…but you haven't applied or made any moves towards that in years. You whine and act like you're embarrassed about your job, even though I know you like it and you're proud of yourself. It's like you won't even let yourself just be happy about this thing you've built because you're afraid of how people will perceive it."

Meredith winced. "Wow. Please. Don't hold back…"

"Sorry, Merry. But I know you prefer me to be honest. You want me to push you when you need a push. Well, here it is." A little harder than strictly necessary, Richelle nudged her shoulder. "There's a push. I suspect that was what Ryan was trying to do earlier, too."

She winced again, because that was probably true. This had not been the first time Ryan had tried to push her when she needed a push. Early on, when he first found out she was meeting up with her ex, he had pushed. A little too much. And tonight, he had pushed. A little too much. Meredith wasn't quite sure why she had felt a need to defend against it, when with Richelle she could handle the vulnerability. Maybe it was because this thing with Ryan was still so new, and she hadn't quite learned how to feel fully safe with him. Maybe it was because his instincts were good, but he hadn't quite learned how to love her in all of her complicated specificity yet. Maybe both. Probably both. Both were symptoms of their newness, things that would settle as they learned each other.

And, unfortunately, Meredith didn't know anymore if they would ever get the chance. After her outburst? After her very sharp and sudden severing of everything they had worked to grow? She wasn't quite sure how to mend it.

Just like she wasn't quite sure how to enact what Richelle was saying.

It was true, of course.

All of it was true. Meredith wasn't so shielded that truth could never penetrate. She had held back her own happiness. She had stopped herself from going after things she wanted. She had forced cynicism and kept her expectations low as a defense mechanism, to keep herself from getting hurt again.

Meredith liked herself. Liked the life she had built. But how much better could it be if she really, truly let herself heal? After Michael, she had been so committed to running, to moving forward, to building, to proving she was better, to proving she could get through it. Maybe she hadn't devoted enough time to her own healing. Maybe all those walls and towers she'd built for herself were pressing on an unhealed bruise she'd ignored for too long. How many things had been like that?

Richelle kissed her on the head, and then stood up and told her, "You have to work for your happiness, Merry. No one is going to give it to you. I know you know that. But I think maybe you haven't really been ready to feel it."

Because she had been afraid.

"Love you, Pippin." She called after her best friend, the one who had seen her through everything. "Thanks for knocking some sense into me."

Richelle grinned. "Anytime. Now go to sleep. Or stay up all night and fix it."

"How? How do I fix it?"

"You're smart!" Richelle's footsteps trudged heavy up their creaking staircase, and she called down from the second floor,

"You'll figure it out."

Once Richelle was gone and Meredith was alone in the living room with nothing for company but a tub of melted cookie dough ice cream, she sighed and grumbled. "Fix it. How the fuck am I supposed to fix it?"

She didn't know where to start. All of the uncomfortable, bitter truths Richelle brought into the light settled into her. Ryan had been right. Richelle had been right. She had panicked. Michael was nothing. His threat was empty and stupid, and there was nothing he could really do to hurt her, to hold her back, unless she let him.

For a long while, she sat with that. Sat with the weight of it. The clarity helped, but it also gave her a new unease. She had panicked and made a bad decision out of fear. With a few hours distance, the anxiety pulled back and was replaced by a deep embarrassment. She was embarrassed that she reacted that way, that she had capitulated so quickly, that she had let herself get caught up in the drowning swirl of that old pattern.

She should have ignored the damn email. She should have stood up to him.

She should have stood up for her own happiness.

Because she was happy. Truly. She liked herself. She liked the work she did and the business she had built from the ground up, however much she might complain about certain parts of it. She liked the boyfriend she'd found, and the possibility of love that was bubbling into existence between them.

She liked all of that.

And she wanted more.

She wanted a brilliant love with an equal partner. She wanted an amazing, meaningful career.

And she wanted to go back to grad school. Wanted it badly. Wanted it with a driving force that was more like destiny than decision. It was what she had to do, the path she had to take.

And yet, she had never once reapplied, all these years.

Old professors and colleagues reached out to her once in a while, and she had let those connections slip. Because she had been embarrassed.

Because she had been afraid.

Because what if Michael had been right, that she couldn't do it without him?

That was what had held her back from so much. The reason why she had held herself back from so much.

What if he had broken her too badly, made her into someone hard to love?

What if deep down, everyone was like him? What if she gave up control and started a relationship, and it turned out just the same?

What if…what if…what if…what if…

It was a lot of fear. A lot of what ifs. Each of them sounded and echoed in her head.

And each of them was bullshit. A thought planted there years ago by someone who had hurt her, someone who had wanted her to be small and afraid and convinced she was nothing without him. Thoughts that had no place in the glorious towers and spires of her being, thoughts that were an insidious attack from the outside that had somehow gotten trapped within the fortress of her.

No more.

She wanted them out.

She wanted to reach for things. All along, she knew she was capable. Everyone who met her knew it. But it was time for her to do more than just know it. It was time for her to feel it. It was time for her to feel like the person she knew she was, to feel like the person Ryan saw instantly the very moment he met her.

And she knew exactly what step one needed to be. She had been panicked and afraid that Michael would be able to destroy her grad school chances with a single word? She had to prove him wrong, prove that his opinion of her meant nothing when stacked against the staggering proof of her own competence.

Before she could talk herself out of it, Meredith leapt up from the couch and sprinted upstairs, empty bowls and melting ice cream containers left abandoned on the coffee table. It was late. Probably too late to be sending emails to old professors, but trembling drive, now awoken within her, no longer wanted to wait another second. So she dragged her laptop out of her bag, plopped down on the bed, and got to work. Professor Bunting's email address popped up immediately when Meredith entered it, along with the reminders of messages her old teacher had sent, checking in. A year ago was the last time. And Meredith, riddled with anxiety over how little progress she had felt like she had to share, had let the email sit and fester. She had never responded. It lingered in her inbox, waiting. A year was a long time to go between emails, but she wouldn't let discomfort stop her.

It took twenty minutes to get the wording right, but she didn't let herself obsess over every detail. It didn't have to be complicated. In a rush of nerves, she clicked the send button. And that was that.

Tucked in between the pleasantries and greetings, she had included an action. Her first step back.

I'm interested in going back to school and I'm trying to determine the best path forward. Would you be available to discuss how I might reapply, and how I might best prepare to balance the demands of the program while working?

It took longer than normal to fall asleep that night. Anxiety over the email and how it would be received zipped little sparks through her core.

And still, there was Ryan. Her unease. Her regret. Her fear and confusion. She had handled things badly. Had she handled them so badly that there was no going back? No fixing it? All beginnings were fragile and tentative things. Was this hit she'd delivered too much?

She didn't know.

But she knew it was a secondary concern. She needed to sort her own self, her own foundations, out first.

Still, she couldn't stop thinking about Ryan. About how he had pushed—how he had tried to help, and she had bristled against it. About how hurt and sad he had seemed at the whole situation. Especially when she had told him she would not be by his side for the showcase.

In the morning, she woke up groggy. But when she grabbed her phone off the bedside table and yanked it down into the nest of pillows and blankets with her, an email alert on her home screen jolted her suddenly and vividly awake.

Professor Bunting had already responded. *So good to hear from you…Would love to catch up…Come by my office…*

Are you free today? I have some time this afternoon.

Today.

She wanted to meet today. It was all so fast. Much faster than she had anticipated, and the invitation caught her off guard. On instinct, she considered saying she wasn't free, just to give herself time to prepare a little more. But no. She didn't want to wait. She didn't want to sit with the worry. Heart in her throat, Meredith typed back a response and agreed to meet at one p.m.

Which gave her a few hours to get ready. And a few hours to obsessively worry and run through everything she wanted to say, to ask.

That afternoon, as she stepped out of the Foggy Bottom metro station and out onto the streets that held the urban campus of George Washington University, a strange wave of emotion welled up within her, and it took the edge off all the worry, all the nerves, all the fear. It had been a while since she had walked these streets. It was a part of town she had avoided for a few years. GW was a city campus, all of the buildings that made up the school seamlessly incorporated into the bustling fabric of the neighborhood. Business offices and bike shares across the street from the enormous block library, restaurants and grocery stores tucked in between dorms and housing. All of it that strange and uniquely DC blend of architectural styles: half gorgeous old brick townhouses and remodeled Georgian mansions, half hideous and massive chunky concrete block buildings left over from the awful Brutalist wave in the 70's, all with a few more columns than strictly necessary.

Memories didn't come flooding back as she walked through it for the first time since she dropped out. It was less conscious than that. Without thinking about it, without checking for directions or stopping to check her path, her body knew the way. Like muscle memory. As she tucked her hands into the pockets of her unbuttoned coat, her heels sure and steady on the brick sidewalk, all of it felt pleasantly and strangely right.

Like she had never left. Like she had just walked this road for the last time a week ago. Like it was all second nature, where she was meant to be, and the path was ingrained and ready for her.

It was the same as she made her way through the halls of the psychology department, where she had taken classes that one semester. The musty scent of the old building was an immediate recognition, and she let it calm her as she breathed it in. Welcoming. Familiar. Ready for her.

And she was not the same idealistic, naïve girl she had been the first time around. She was a grown woman, sure of herself and her value, and she was ready for this. Nothing could stop her or derail her this time around.

All of the worry that had tumbled through her for the past twelve hours fell away, and by the time she knocked on her old professor's office door, it was with a smile and a steady heart.

"Meredith Hartman!" Professor Bunting looked the same, and that made Meredith smile even more. Pleasant, plump, and petite, with a tuft of frizzy gray hair, the little woman had always looked like she might be more at home hosting a baking show than running a master's program. That was her disguise. Meredith recognized it better now, saw its value. She stood up from her desk and waved a boisterous arm in welcome. "Come in, come in! It's so good to see you!"

Professor Bunting had one of the sharpest minds Meredith had ever encountered. Deep intelligence and cleverness were not traits exclusive to men or masculinity, but many people—Meredith included—made the mistake of underestimating this woman when they first met her. It was a mistake Meredith had quickly rectified.

Her Theories in Clinical Mental Health Counseling class was the toughest *A* Meredith had ever earned, and she walked away from that one class feeling like she had learned more there, from this one remarkably competent woman, than she had in her entire undergrad program.

Meredith sat down at the desk, the cluttered little room pleasantly claustrophobic with huge, teetering stacks of books and piles of paper. After a few minutes of pleasantries, Professor Bunting folded both hands on the edge of the desk, leaned forward, and peered with a sharp smile. "I can't tell you how pleased I was to get your email. I think it's wonderful that you're coming back to the program."

"Oh." Meredith smiled. "You're too kind."

"No, I mean it. You were a fantastic student, Meredith. I was so sorry to see you leave after that first semester." She sat back, shifted in her seat a bit. "I don't mean to pry…"

Meredith tensed, but kept her face polite and plain. Guarded, while trying to give off the impression that she was an open book. "Please! Pry away!"

"Well. I was aware…" She waved a hand and gave Meredith a sardonic smile. "I also don't mean to imply that the whole department was gossiping behind your back. But we were all aware of the circumstances, your engagement to Dr. Wilson."

Whatever Meredith had expected, it had not been this. Was there nowhere she could go to get away from him? His influence? The worry and panic from yesterday clenched her stomach, but she refused to give it any quarter. "Of course. It would have been hard for you to miss. I remember meeting you and a few of the other professors here before I even started at this school. Dr. Wilson was…" She cleared her throat. This was the crux of all of her worries, wasn't it? And here it was, the truth, and both of them acknowledging it. "He is well-connected. He knows just about every psychology professional in this city."

"That's right. I do remember meeting you, back when you were still in undergrad. Wilson would take you to local psychology professional events. I'm sure it was some good networking for you, but…well." She paused.

Meredith's forced smile stayed in place, though it was with some difficulty.

Professor Bunting did not lower her voice. Didn't shy away from the confession. It was said plainly, out in the open. But there was a kindness, a warmth to the creases around her eyes that hadn't been there a moment before. "I was not the only one who was a bit uncomfortable with the way Dr. Wilson paraded you around like you were some prized poodle."

Startled, a breath of thin laughter burst out of Meredith's throat.

"And the way he talked to you…" She shrugged and shook her head. "You were so young. But you were an adult. And I didn't know you well."

It was so unexpected, so far from anything Meredith had planned to discuss with her old teacher, that she sat immobile and shocked into silence for a beat too long while a cloud moved across the window and shifted the light atop the cluttered desk.

She saw. She saw something was wrong, back then. She had noticed.

It burned a lonely, warm hole in Meredith's chest.

No one back then had seemed to notice. Michael had dragged her around to dozens of events, surrounded her with people two or three times her own age, cut her off from all of her friends, treated her badly in public. And everyone had acted like it was normal.

It was nice. Nice to know she had been seen. Nice to know that someone else had been rooting for her on the sidelines of the worst time in her life.

"It was a long time ago." When she spoke, her voice came out as pleasant and poised as she hoped it would. Just as fake and guarded as she wanted to be. She paused. And forced herself to add something a little more real, to share something a little deeper. "At the time, I didn't see anything wrong with it. I do feel uncomfortable, looking back on it now, though."

"I should have said something. I should have stepped in." Professor Bunting shocked her once again with the blunt and sure admission. So unhesitating, with an ownership she didn't need to take on, she found the girl Meredith had once been, the woman she had become, and validated her pain. So simply. Meredith's chest and throat tightened and clouded, but Professor Bunting went on. "I just can't help but think that I should have been a better mentor to you. Academically…and personally. Woman to woman. I think you needed allies back then, and I'm sorry I wasn't a better one."

"Thank you for saying that. Thank you. Really. I…" Meredith cut herself off, sniffed away an upsell of emotion, and pulled herself back together. No crying. Not in front of anyone. Even though this conversation touched her deeply, made her feel seen and understood. It was the sort of thing she never would have listened to at twenty-two but needed to hear now. For the sake of her present self. Her past self. And her future self. "Thank you for saying that. It means a lot to me. But there is no need for you to apologize. I got through it. And I ended up where I needed to."

A sly, knowing smile tightened Professor Bunting's eyes. She understood. She saw the depth of everything Meredith's evasive words contained—the subtle admission that there had been more beneath the surface, that the discomfort she had noticed back then had indeed been a warning sign of something worse. She nodded. "As we women do."

"Exactly."

"Alright, tell me more about you! What have you been up to these past few years?"

"Well." Shaky, a little nervous, Meredith took a breath and announced, "I run my own business."

"Fantastic! You always were driven. Tell me more about it."

So she did. Proudly. For so long, she had avoided talking to anyone from her old life about this. She had been terrified for Michael to find out, until Ryan reminded her it was something to be proud of. Richelle had been right; she was sometimes embarrassed of her work, too worried about how the haughty and lofty professionals in her old life might perceive it. But that was foolish. She knew what she did had value. She liked the work. She liked helping people—good people who needed a bit of help celebrating aspects of their identities that sometimes made them feel alone or out of step with the modern dating culture. People like Mr. Benson. Or like all of the older divorcees she worked with. Or like the guys who genuinely wanted to try to be better people, to learn how to give more to the people they loved.

Or people like Ryan.

Ryan, who had come to embrace his demisexuality as a strength and a core part of him that needed to be respected while dating. Ryan, who was good, and kind, and funny, and competent, who had a lot of love to give and just needed a bit of a push.

She had been happy, very happy, to give him that push.

If only she had reacted with such welcoming grace and good humor when he had tried to do the same for her. Ryan had not been the only one of the two of them who had recently needed a push.

She swallowed down the sadness, the shame she felt at how she had reacted to Ryan. For the moment. Only for the moment. That would come next. Later.

First, herself. Grad school. Her future. Her foundation.

Professor Bunting listened and nodded along while Meredith explained her business, the services she provided to clients, and the ways she had used psychology and sociology to help people solve a problem that was holding back the happiness in their lives.

She didn't even have a chance to finish before Professor Bunting smacked a sharp hand down on the desk and interrupted with a shout of, "Meredith, that is incredible!"

"Thank you! It's been quite a journey. Never a dull day."

Professor Bunting asked a few more questions, and Meredith was heartened to realize that she seemed genuinely interested and impressed. Another validation that she didn't exactly need, per se, but that felt nice anyway.

"Now," she asked after picking Meredith's brain about the psychology behind her coaching, "You intend to keep working through the program, yes?"

Meredith nodded. "It's not my long-term plan, but I'm not quite ready to set it down just yet. Plus, I won't be able to afford to stop working. Finances drove me out the first time, and I won't let that happen again. I would prefer to keep my job through the two years of classes even though I know it will be a challenge."

"Oh, yes, for certain. But one I'm sure you can handle. I'll be honest; it's not easy to work full time while in this program. But I know how dedicated you are. And since you own your own business, you get to set your own hours, yes? You choose when you take clients?"

"Yes, exactly. So it shouldn't be a problem to schedule my client meetings around my classes."

"That's what I do! That's what many of our professors do. A lot of us are adjuncts, and we take patients through a variety of hospitals and clinics in addition to teaching and research." She winked. "If I can handle it, I know you can too."

"Thank you." The conversation had turned to school so quickly, driven there by the professor before Meredith could steer it in her own way, and she was a little caught off guard. The whole meeting had her reeling. Gently. It felt like a shake-up, and a needed one at that. She was hesitant to ask, "So you do think it's worth it for me to come back, then? You think there's still a place for me here?"

"Meredith. Of course there is." Confident and kind, she stretched and lifted up out of her chair to reach across the desk and pat the back of Meredith's hand. "Of course there is. Yes. You will have to reapply. You might have to retake a few classes and work out with administration whether any of your old credits will carry. But if you're ready to come back? Then we are ready to have you back."

It was like a whole hurricane worth of clouds she didn't realize she had been carrying lifted. Meredith grinned and nodded. "I am ready to come back."

"Good." Professor Bunting rattled off a rapid-fire list of details Meredith would need, including the application deadline for the fall semester. It was fast approaching, but Meredith knew she could get it done in time. "Make sure when you write your statement of purpose, you talk about your business. The work you have been doing is relevant and impressive, and it will go a long way towards showing the admissions committee that you are ready to get deeper into this field. And please put me down as a reference. I remember well what kind of student you were. So driven, so thoughtful, such a talented writer. You led every class discussion with your insights, and you often considered angles other students missed. And you always had a way of making people feel respected, even when you disagreed with them. All marks of a good therapist. It would be my pleasure to write you a letter of recommendation."

"Thank you so much, Professor Bunting," Meredith said as she stood up from the desk and held out her hand. "I promise, I won't let you down again."

Professor Bunting peered at her and studied her with a curious look. A knowing smile, a clever tilt to her head. She reached out both hands and gripped Meredith—not in the handshake she had been expecting, but in something more tender, more feminine. "You didn't the first time."

She didn't cry. But it was a near thing.

And when she walked back through the streets of the campus, the sun bright and the wind cold and clear, she felt set to rights. Accomplished. Validated. Strong.

This had been taunting her for far too long.

For years, she had been going at full tilt, so determined to prove herself. And she had done all of that. She was proud. But in what direction had she been going?

None. No direction at all. She had climbed, and built, and forged, and worked. But it had been a long time since she had directed it deliberately, in pursuit of something worthy. It had been a long time since she had let herself have goals, since she had acted towards her own ambition. Everything she had done in the past few years was useful and meaningful and real.

And now it would be even more so, as she aligned it all towards the goal she had once so nearly lost.

She lingered for a while on campus, strolled briskly through the park where she used to eat lunch between classes and stopped in one of the little student shops to grab a coffee. It warmed her hands as she walked back to the metro.

It would take a few months to get an answer, but Meredith would make it back here. She knew it with a calm and burning certainty. As she left, she knew she would be back soon.

She kept smiling to herself the whole way home on the metro. With that settled, with the determination to go back to school and start moving towards the career she wanted once more, Meredith felt freer than she had in a long while.

The people who cared for her most had been right about her own worth and had helped her see it in the midst of a scary, dizzying moment. Richelle had been right, that she had been holding herself back. And Ryan had definitely been right—there was nothing in the world that her bastard ex could have possibly said to hold her back. She was strong enough on her own, and her competence was evident in everything she did. Ryan had seen it immediately. It was what he liked most about her. And it was what she liked most about herself. She was a competent, smart, boss of a woman, made of glorious towers and soaring spires…and with as good a foundation as anyone. A foundation that would only get stronger the more she worked on it and tended it. She had stalled and spun in circles for a while, but now she was on track. She was going after what she wanted.

And with grad school settled, more than anything else, she wanted Ryan.

Wanted to be with him. Quite simply. Wanted to have him as a partner, a friend, a lover, all of the above. Wanted to learn how to love him right and open up enough to let him learn how to do the same for her.

She didn't need him.

But she wanted him.

And she wanted to be there for him this weekend, to stand beside him and support him at the big showcase debut he was so worried about and working so hard to prepare for.

But she had said, pretty clearly, that she was no longer willing to go with him. She had said a lot of things that she now regretted, that she knew were wrong, unnecessary, and defensive. He might not want to see her again. It had been a pretty harsh exchange. Ryan seemed to like her sharp edges…but that might have been too sharp.

That thought did melt the smile off her face, and she stared at the dingy carpet floor of the metro for a long while as the train screeched around a bend in the tunnel. She braced herself against the barely-controlled tilt of momentum and thought through how to make it right.

Chapter Eighteen

The banquet hall was chaos, and as he and Naomi directed each piece into place, Ryan tried to keep his head from spinning. Antsy, tingling anxiety prickled over him like ants across his skin. With very conscious and deliberate effort that was only making things worse, he tried not to sweat in his suit.

The suit Meredith had picked out for him.

That reminder brought another uncomfortable surge of sad emotion into his chest, and he shook it off.

"The armoire goes behind the dining table, not in front!" Distracted, he caught the mistake the loading crew was about to make to his display. The poor guy helping them halted and heaved against the arm of the heavy dolly, but he didn't complain as he swiveled to get the massive, sturdy piece of furniture into its correct place. Ryan told him, "Sorry. Thank you!"

"And I want that at a forty-five-degree angle to the bookshelf. With at least two feet of space between them." In her glittering high heels and her elegant, slinky black gown, Naomi pushed past

Ryan to go direct the proceedings to her precise liking.

Which left Ryan to deal with portly, red-in-the-face Mr. Anderson as he approached Ryan's stall. "Mr. McKenna! Thank you again for joining us. Everything you brought looks magnificent. I know our members are going to be quite impressed with your craftsmanship."

"Thank you so much, sir." Ryan shook the man's hand and tried to sound sincere. "I really appreciate the opportunity and I'm happy to be here."

It was only half a lie.

He did appreciate the opportunity.

He was not happy to be there.

After a few weeks of cramming, back-breaking work, Ryan had completed four new pieces he was happy with, and he had adjusted a few others he already had in stock in the store. It had taken him right up until the last second—he had still been in his shop that afternoon, putting a final stain on the armoire—but he was pleased with every piece he had created for this event.

And it was shaping up to be quite an event. At a swanky, elegant hotel near Embassy Row, all of the featured artisans were given display space throughout a beautiful, grand ballroom. High overhead, a crystal chandelier cast glittering gold light on the proceedings, and the black and white tiled floor gleamed. The spicy-sweet smell of crab cakes and other canapes lingered as the wait staff set up the buffet and finalized food prep. A string quartet warmed up over in one corner, and the music floated pleasantly through the bustling room as all of the featured vendors set up their spaces. Each had been assigned a team of helpers to unload and place their wares.

Ryan was pretty sure his poor team was wishing they had been assigned to the guy a few spots down who made custom pocket watches. But none of them complained as they pushed and heaved and got all of his heavy, wooden furniture into exactly the spots Naomi wanted.

All of it was beautiful, elegant, totally not his scene, and about to get much worse as soon as all the wealthy Richards and Muffys entered in an hour.

He wished Meredith were here.

He couldn't stop thinking about her, in spite of everything else going on.

He had fucked up. He hadn't heard from her since their big blow-up over her ex a week ago, and the whole encounter left Ryan feeling unsettled and wrong. He knew he should reach out to her, he should apologize for how he had reacted, should apologize for pushing and making demands that were not his to make. Meredith had been scared, and he should have had empathy for that.

But she had also made it clear that she needed space.

So he gave her space.

Even though the need to talk to her, to reach out to her, to be there for her if she needed support, lived inside his stomach and spine all week long.

As he put the finishing touches on the pieces he had talked to her about in the bar that night, he thought of her.

As Naomi talked him through his pitch and practiced what he would say to potential clients, he relied on Meredith's coaching to help him share a little about himself without freezing, and he thought of her.

As he dressed in the fitted blue suit she had picked out for him, the one she had specifically selected because he was nervous and she knew he would be uncomfortable in a full tux, he thought of her.

A hand pressed against his back, and he jolted enough to realize that instead of setting up his own event, he had been staring morosely at the shadowy dark panes of the far windows. "Hi. Yeah. What's up? What do we need?"

"What do we need? Alcohol, probably." Naomi smirked, but her smiled gentled. "You doing okay?"

"Yeah." He took a deep breath and nodded. Swallowed down a thin buzz of panic. "Yeah, I'm okay. Nervous. But it will be okay. You helped me practice, and the coaching helped, so I think I'll be okay with all of the small talk and the soft sales. It's just nerve-wracking."

"I know." She patted his shoulder. Behind her, the loading team heaved and lifted the long, turquoise-inlaid dining table into place. "You're going to hate it. But I'll be here to help you, and it's going to be fine. And everyone is going to love your work."

"Thank you. I don't know what I would do without you. Be on fire, probably."

Smug, Naomi shrugged and nodded. She was gorgeous and glittering in her evening attire, the dress sleek and open-backed, tall and glamorous in her silvery heels. With her hair pinned in victory curls and cascading down, she looked like a statuesque, silver screen movie star from the forties. And she was calm. On top of things. Ready. Ryan shook his head. "I don't know what I was thinking. I should have just asked you to come with me to this thing from the start."

"Hm." Noncommittal, Naomi shrugged again, neither agreeing nor disagreeing. This was not exactly her scene either, even though she could forcibly turn her confidence up to eleven and dazzle any crowd. It took a toll, though. She'd have a lot of eyes on her, and it was impossible to guarantee they'd all be friendly. But she was here anyway, ultra-glammed-up and ready to rock. It was how she lived her life. "Maybe. But I know what you were hoping for. I'm not entirely sure why you did ask me to come, though."

Music started up again, and the thin, sweet notes of a violin rose above the thick murmur of the bustling crowd, all preparing around them. "What do you mean?"

Slick and superior, Naomi looked away from him. "I still think you should have apologized."

To Meredith. Everything, every thought, every conversation, came back to Meredith. "She needed space. I'm trying to give it to her."

"Maybe. But that kind of seems like a cop-out." She glanced at him and then away again. "I'm probably not supposed to tell you this, but Richelle told me that Meredith said she messed up. That she regretted handling things like that."

"What? Seriously?" Ryan's pulse quickened, all of a sudden panicky and unsure. "Why didn't she reach out to me, then? I thought she needed space. That's why I haven't tried to talk to her. If she doesn't like how things turned out, then why hasn't she told me so?"

"I don't know, Ryan! I'm not your secret double agent, and I'm not going to have my girlfriend spy for you."

Ryan rolled his eyes and huffed. This was ridiculous. And Naomi was right. He shouldn't be digging for information or using Naomi like that. Before he could say so, though, and tell her she was right, as always, one of the help staff called for their attention. "Where does this one go?"

"I want that in the center, just behind where he's going to be speaking," Naomi told the guy, and then said back to Ryan, "It's such a highlight piece, right? I think it should be centered. We're going to center it."

Ryan nodded. Naomi knew what she was doing. She darted off to direct the piece into place—the one door he had brought, one that he had on display already in his shop. It was a cherry wood piece, dark, and carved with intricate whorls of pattern. It would be a good backdrop for him to speak in front of. And with the blue of his not-too-formal suit? It would look nice, he had to admit. The whole display was fantastic, a perfect showcasing of his style and his talents, and he would match it. Even though Meredith had barely known anything about what he did at that point, she had perfectly matched and coordinated his look so he would seamlessly reflect the tone of his display.

She had known him, seen him well, right from the start.

It panged hurt in his chest.

So, too, did Naomi's admission that Meredith regretted the fight. Had she been sitting at home worrying? Maybe he should have reached out sooner.

"Yes, that's perfect. Let's angle that one out a bit so it's facing directly forward. Perfect!" Naomi's voice was sure and confident as she set the last details into place, and Ryan only half listened to her. Until she snapped at him. "Excuse me? What are you still doing here?"

He blinked. "What? What do you mean, what am I doing here?"

"I mean why are you still standing there looking all sullen and gloomy? I just told you that Meredith said she regretted how things went between you two."

"Yeah… And I've been giving her space, because that's what she wanted. That's what she asked for."

"Mm-hmm. And…?"

"And…she's been worried about it, apparently. But she hasn't reached out to me."

Naomi was patient with him, like he was one of the students she mentored. She nodded and urged him along, to think it through. "Uh-huh."

"And that means…" Ryan shook his head. Thought about Meredith. Thought about all of the fear and worry she'd had over losing control of her life to someone who had threatened to derail it. Thought about how she had lost her own tight grip on control when she had come to his workshop to talk about it, how she had admitted things, painful things, that maybe she wasn't quite ready for him to know. It would make her feel vulnerable. She hated feeling vulnerable, and though Ryan wanted to be someone she felt safe with, he knew that would take time. And he thought about who she was as a person: so confident and competent when in her comfort zone, but so careful outside of it. At the salsa dance lessons, she had held herself back, watched from afar, until she knew she could get it right. She didn't like making mistakes in front of anyone. So. She had lost control over something. She felt vulnerable. And she was out of her comfort zone, and therefore likely to be more cautious and unsure.

And Naomi wanted him to think through all of this right now, because…?

It clicked. He got it. He understood her, and he got it. He had thought she needed space. But really, she needed him. She needed reassurance and support, and action that proved he was still on her side. She needed him to step up and be there for her in a moment when she felt too vulnerable to ask. "She wants to talk, to make things right, but she doesn't know how to start."

"Yep," Naomi said sure and blunt, and she popped the *p* hard. "That is the impression that both Richelle and I have."

With deep and unflinching certainty, the truth of what he had to do filled him. "I have to go. I have to go talk to her." Now. Now, now, now. He couldn't put this off for another second. Meredith wanted to talk to him, wanted to reach out…but didn't know how. All week, since the fight, she had been his one thought. Everything came back to her. He had to come back to her. Had to set this right, had to be by her side and have her by his in return. Had to. It was all he could think about, all he could focus on, and it filled him like a mission. But there wasn't much time. His heart raced and his hands shook as he pulled his phone out of his jacket pocket and checked the time. Just over an hour before the event started. Antsy, eager, he shifted from foot to foot and held himself back from running out the door. "I'm so sorry. Naomi, I am so, so sorry. But I have to go. I have to go talk to her now. I have to fix this now."

"I know you do. I know what matters here." It calmed him. She grabbed his hand and gripped it, maybe to hold him in place, to keep him from tearing off. "It's an hour and fifteen minutes until this thing starts. You get back before then. I will finish setting everything up. I will cover for you if you don't make it back in time, but…well." She laughed and glared at him. "You really don't want me to try to bullshit my way through explaining differences in quality wood grain to a bunch of rich white people."

He laughed and grinned and pulled her into a crushing hug. "I'll be back!"

It took fifteen minutes to Uber over to Meredith's house, and his mind raced the whole time.

She was worried about her professionalism while dating him? That one was easy to fix! Easy. He should have done it earlier.

She felt too vulnerable? She didn't know how to control this? That was okay. He felt the same way. They would figure it out together, united.

Her ex was threatening her, trying to drive them apart? That, they could figure out together too, united.

He had pushed when he shouldn't have. He would learn. She had lashed out when she shouldn't have. She would learn, too. She had a painful past that needed to be respected and understood? That was okay. So did he, in some ways. He had things, parts of his identity that needed to be understood and respected, too. Already, Meredith had proved she would do that for him. He would learn her well enough to do that for her in return. They had a lot of learning and growing to do together, and they could do it. United. As partners.

But to get there, one of them had to take the first step towards apologizing, opening things up, talking it all out. That, he could do. Might as well be him. He only wished he had realized earlier in the week what he needed to do, so Meredith wouldn't have to suffer through the uncertainty.

In the cool air of the fast-fading evening, indigo shadows stretching long across the pavement, Ryan jogged up the pathway and the front steps to Meredith's house. Before he could stop to think, before he had properly put together what he wanted to say, his knuckles were already rapping on the door.

When the door creaked open, a gust of light and warmth poured out of the townhouse. And there was Meredith. Perfect, beautiful, and put-together, she stood in the doorway, wrapped in a long black coat, and she startled when she saw him. "Ryan. What are you doing here? You're supposed to be at the showcase."

"I know. I know. But really? I'm supposed to be here. Right here. With you." It all rushed out of him, his voice tripping and shaky. "Because I have some important things I need to say to you."

"Okay." Her face remained stoic and unreadable, completely smooth. The shimmer of her eye make-up and the highlight on her cheeks caught the light from the foyer lamp above her. She did not move to let him in. "What do you need to say?"

"Well. I just left the showcase because this is really important to me. I came over here to tell you…" He took a deep breath and pointed at her. "To tell you that you're fired."

She blinked. "I'm fired."

"Yes. You are so, so fired. I'm firing you." The teasing smirk that lifted his voice did not go unnoticed, and Meredith was not unaffected. "I don't want you to be my date coach anymore."

One corner of her mouth, her lips painted a soft dusky rose color, quirked up. Amused. "Okay. So I'm fired. You left the showcase to tell me that?"

"That, and…" He softened. He had to get this right. Had to get the right words for his feelings. "I'm sorry. I'm sorry for how I reacted last week. You were scared. You were going through something big and threatening, and I had no business trying to tell you what to do or how to feel."

Her lips parted. Softened. "Ryan…"

"Oh, I've got a lot more!" He chuckled and gestured to the floor behind her. "You might want to take a seat. This is going to go on for a minute or two. I very much want to hear whatever you have to say, and I want to talk this out and have a discussion. But could you let me monologue for a minute first? This is important to me, one of the most important things I've ever done, and I need to make sure I say all of this right."

Quiet and still, she nodded.

"Okay." It was terrifying. Nerve-wracking. But also, not. "This whole week, I have not been able to stop thinking about you. You are going through something rough. I want to be there by your side through it. And the showcase is a big, looming thing I've been so nervous about, and when I got there all I could think about was you. How much I wanted you there with me, by my side. And I know it hasn't been very long, that this thing between us is still new, but I feel that way about everything. Whatever you're going through, whatever I'm going through, good or bad…I want to share it with you. I want to be your partner, Meredith. I know you have a sensitive past, and that I'll need to learn how to love you with some extra care because of that. I've got some of my own sensitivities that you'll have to learn. But I want to, Meredith. I'm already falling in love with you. I know you want to slow things down, you need me to be patient. That's fine. I want to be with you, and I'm hoping you still want to be with me. And that we can try to get this back…on…um…back on…" He glanced down. His eyes caught on the intense sparkle of her strappy, formal heels. It startled him so much that he paused, faded to a stop. His eyes narrowed, confused, as he put together the details he had noticed but not quite understood the first time around: the elegant make-up, the coat, the fancy shoes. Before he could stop himself, he asked, "Why are you all dressed up? Did I stop you from going somewhere? I'm sorry, I—"

Her smile was tiny and sweet, a little teasing, as she slowly popped open the three thick buttons of her black pea coat and held it open to show off a silvery-gray formal dress. "I was on my way to the showcase."

"To the showcase?" Ryan asked, shocked dumb. "To my showcase?"

"Yeah. To your showcase. I did promise you I would be there." For the first time since she had opened the door, Meredith moved. She took a step towards him and reached out. Took his hand. Squeezed it. All while Ryan's brain raced to catch up. "I want to be by your side, too. For this big thing. For the next big thing. And for all the small things in between."

His heart clenched tight in sweet, tender, loving emotion, and the happiness that blossomed through him was pure and warm and steadfast. He should have known. Meredith had hesitancies and she thought things through, yes, but she was not the sort of person who would sit at home worrying, without a plan. He had his plan, come up with on a whim and directed by his heart. She had her own plan, thoughtful and considered, equally driven by her heart. And after a week of miscommunication and distance, they had both chosen to run for each other, to take the first step. It was perfect. He closed his eyes to hold it all in, and a soft laugh escaped him on a breath. "Meredith."

"And I'm sorry, too. I lashed out at you, even though you were saying something I needed to hear." She squeezed his hand again. Stepped in closer. "You were right. What you said that day was right, and I needed that wake-up call you gave me. For so long, I have been holding myself back for fear of disappointment, or fear I'd fail again or get hurt again. I don't want to do that anymore. I am ambitious, and I want to start acting like it. So I'm going to go back to grad school. And I'm going to date you. And God help anyone who thinks they can stop me."

Ryan laughed silently at that, kept it held tight in his smile, and his eyes squinted while he looked down at her. Meredith. Amazing, brilliant Meredith. Who wanted to be with him.

"Oh. And for the record?" Close to him, very close, she pressed a hand to his chest and let herself lean in a little closer, a little tighter, a little warmer. Her blue eyes sparkled as she looked up at him, and his breath caught in his chest. "I'm falling in love with you, too. Thanks for being brave enough to say it first."

Too much emotion all swirling through him in dizzying happiness, he couldn't contain it. Both of his hands lifted and gently cupped the sides of her face. Scared, and delicate, and blazingly happy, he managed to ask, "Can I?"

"Yes. Please, yes."

The kiss turned his bones into mush. It melted his brain. It left him dizzy and hot and throbbing all over. She wrapped her arms around his neck and pressed her body flush to his, and he held on and kissed her with everything he had, everything he was worth. Soft at first, she groaned into his mouth as it deepened, and he braced a firm hand against the small of her back to press and hold her up against him.

When they pulled apart, neither went far. Ryan felt shaky. Overcome. He pressed his forehead to hers and held them together, a warm refuge against the chill, while the misty clouds of their breath ghosted around them. He had never felt like this. Not once. Not with anyone. Never had he felt such a deep, instinctive desire to be as close as possible to someone, and then closer still. Not in a needy, possessive way that abolished and destroyed boundaries of self. It was a wanting, a longing, to exist with this woman, whole and complete, side-by-side. To take on the world with her. To have with her the partner, the friend, the lover who would walk beside him in the journey of life.

It was new. All of this was new, and maybe too early to tell. But with Meredith in his arms, Ryan felt a bright and burning star's-worth of certainty that they were taking those first steps together.

He kissed her one more time, quick and sweet, and then pulled away. He didn't let go of her, though. Not fully. His thumb stroked along the edge of her cheekbone, and his fingers brushed the elegant knot of hair she had pinned in an up-do behind one ear. She was beautiful, and more than ready for the showcase. The showcase, which he really should get back to. Instead, he lingered for a while. "You're going back to grad school?"

She laughed and rolled her eyes at him, but she nodded. "Yeah. I met with an old professor, and I've been working on my application all week."

"That's fantastic." They had not talked about it much, but Ryan had known from the beginning that grad school was one of Meredith's big goals, that she'd had to divert away from her dream years ago and was working her way back to it. She would get there. He had no doubt that another diploma would soon hang on her office wall. "Seriously, Meredith. That's awesome. I'm so happy for you."

"Thank you. I'm looking forward to it. I'll tell you all about it later."

"Yeah." After the showcase. That he really needed to get back to. He stood on her front step, unmoving, and nodded. "Later."

"It's freezing in here!" From deeper in the house, unseen, Richelle shouted at them. "Are you two dumbasses planning to stand in the doorway with the cold coming in all night? Want to pick a side and shut the door? In or out, people! In or out!"

Meredith and Ryan both winced and shared an embarrassed look. The whole time, they had been standing there with the door open, while the outside got colder and darker by the second. "Sorry, Richelle!" Meredith shouted over her shoulder. "We're about to leave. We have to get to the showcase."

"You should meet up with us after, Richelle!" They had no plans, but the idea came to Ryan on a whim and it seemed like a perfect one. Already, Meredith and Naomi would be with him at the showcase, the two most important women in his life bracing either side of him while he fought through the unpleasantness. Richelle should join, too. It seemed very likely that the four of them would be spending a lot of time together from now on, and Ryan wanted to better know the woman who was so important to Meredith, and who was quickly becoming so important to Naomi. "We could go out for a drink after it's done!"

"Good idea, Ryan, but Naomi already beat you to it. She texted and told me to meet you guys at a place in Dupont. I'll see you in a few hours!"

"Okay, bye Richelle!" Meredith called as she made up her mind and stepped outside to join Ryan. She gripped his hand tight in her own. "We'll see you soon!"

"Bye! Good luck tonight, Ryan!" She called out as Meredith was shutting the door. "I'm sure you'll be amazing!"

It was kind.

And with Meredith there, as well as Naomi, Ryan felt ready for it. Ready to face it. So long as he had Meredith's hand in his own, Ryan felt like he could face anything.

Still, though, he teased, "Are you sure we have to go? We could skip it. Naomi could probably handle it fine."

Meredith scoffed and laughed and rolled her eyes and she opened an app on her phone and summoned a car for them. "You're not going to do that to Naomi."

"No, of course I'm not going to do that to Naomi." He took a breath. Looked at Meredith. In her misty gray gown, with her silvery hair pinned up, she looked ethereal and otherworldly. Elegant, and strong, and sharp, the colors of her all ivory and titanium. She could do anything. And with her by his side, he could too. "Actually, I don't feel so bad about it. I know all of the pieces I made are some of my best. I'm really proud of them. Naomi's got the display and all of the organizing on lock. And you're going to be there." He smiled. She looked up from her phone screen and smiled back. "With you there, the rest of it feels a lot less intimidating."

As she tucked her phone back into her small clutch purse, she nodded and gave him an appraising, considering look. "Naomi has your back. And so do I."

It made him grin, a sweet thing he couldn't contain. "And I have yours."

"I know you do." She kissed him again, and then she tugged his hand and led him down the walkway, under the shade of the street trees and onto the curb to wait for the Uber. "Now come on. We have a lot to accomplish tonight. I've got goals. I will not rest until you've got at least a dozen new client orders. And I am absolutely going to get you a write-up in the local paper."

"You're going to—what? How are you going to get an article written about me?"

"One of the guests there tonight owns the paper. I'm going to dazzle him with my sparking wit and plunging neckline, and then I'll talk you up so much, he won't be able to refuse. He'll think it was his idea."

Ryan stopped on the sidewalk and shook his head. "Someone there tonight owns the paper? How do you know that?"

Simply, matter-of-fact, Meredith shrugged one shoulder and said, "He's on the guest list."

"How did you get the guest list?"

"I contacted the event organizers and asked for it."

Ryan blinked and shook his head. His mouth slowly fell open in bewildered amusement. "And you recognized the name of the guy who owns the local paper?"

"No, of course not. I researched."

"Him?"

"No, not just him." She scoffed at him and raised an eyebrow. "I researched everyone."

"What? When?"

"This week."

"I thought you applied to grad school this week!"

The dark golden glow of the streetlight above them caught the sharp angles of her cheekbones and cast her in severe, artful shadows. A car drove past, its headlights gleaming off the shine of her gown. She glared at him and pinned him with a sharp, condescending look, one of her eyebrows lifted. "Come on, McKenna, keep up. This boss-ass bitch can multi-task like a motherfucker."

A laugh snorted out of Ryan's nose and his shoulders shook as he grabbed her by the hips and tugged them together. "And she can swear like a sailor, apparently."

"Mm-hmm." Meredith smirked up at him. "And she can fuck better than any Sasquatch, werewolf, or other preternatural being of myth and legend."

"Oh, definitely! Way better." The air between them shook with the breath of their laughter as Ryan leaned down and pressed a kiss to her lips. "You are so damn cool. I like you so much. Thank you for doing so much to help me with this showcase. Seriously, I don't know what I would have done without you to do all that research for me, and to coach me, and to talk me up when I was nervous. You even dressed me!"

Teasing, but with a hot and hungry gleam in her eye, she looked him up and down. "And you do look damn fine in formalwear, McKenna."

"Speak for yourself, Hartman. You are smoking hot."

A car pulled up alongside the curb and stopped just beyond where they stood. Meredith glanced at the license plate to make sure it was the right car while exhaust billowed from the tailpipe and filled the air with the greasy scent of city smog. "Alright." Chivalrous and grand, she held out her arm to escort him, and he placed his hand daintily in the crook of her elbow. "Let's get you to this showcase. All you have to do is stand there, look handsome, and act charming. Meanwhile, Naomi and I are going to circle and then sneak in to attack from both sides, hit them with a one-two punch. They'll never see us coming. We'll do all the hard work for you."

"God, I like you," Ryan said as he opened the door of the car and held out a hand for her so she could slide into the backseat without stepping on the hem of her gown. "I like you so fucking much."

She grinned up at him. "I like you too, Ryan."

As they drove across the city, lights streaking in the glass of the windows, Ryan held Meredith's hand and wondered if maybe he had lied to her a moment ago. He'd said he was falling in love with her. It was entirely possible that he was already there.

A grin bloomed across his face, and he found it hard to tamp it down so she wouldn't notice. He snuck a glance at her pale profile, at the clever, cutting lines of her cheekbones and nose, at the curving shell of her ear. Seeing her beside him, all dressed up and ready to fight a bear with him, only made him smile more.

He respected her, admired her, liked her.

Loved her.

He loved her.

As they sped through the city, his stomach twisting on the way to his big career debut, there was no one else Ryan would choose to have by his side. No one else he would want to stand beside. No one else he wanted to hold hands with on the way there, no one else he wanted to go home with when it was done.

He was in love with a badass, sharkish, ambitious, hyper-prepared, cutting, clever, boss of a woman. And he could not wait to stand beside her and watch her, support her, and love her as she took on the world.

The End

Read More

If you enjoyed this story and want to know more about how Ryan and Meredith live their happily ever after, join Ellie's author newsletter! Newsletter subscribers get an exclusive short story that serves as an epilogue to this book. Set a few years after the events of The Date Coach, it gives you a sweet, steamy, fun glimpse at what comes next for these characters.

Join the newsletter at elliefinchauthor.com

Follow

For updates on new releases and deals, follow Ellie on social media and her website.

Website: elliefinchauthor.com

Tumblr: norelationtoatticus.tumblr.com

Twitter: @efinch_writes

Coming Soon

Coming soon from Ellie Finch, a female/female romantic comedy, full of banter and lots of tropes...including forced bed sharing during a snow storm! Available February 2020.

Snowed In

Jayla Jones is a Park Ranger--dedicated, kind, stubborn, and as strong as the mountains she so lovingly protects and calls her home.

Ciara Rigby is a feather-on-the-wind kind of woman. A travel blogger, photographer, and social media influencer, she is constantly moving and looking for her next adventure.

When an unexpected snow storm comes in fast and forces bus cancellations, Ciara gets trapped in Jayla's park with nowhere to hide from the snow. Reluctantly, Jayla drags her along to shelter in a bare-bones cabin.

These two women come from different worlds and are used to very different conditions. Jayla knows she has a job to do, and she is ready to ride out the storm and respond to any emergencies in the park. But she's not sure she can survive Ciara's whining. Ciara complains about everything, from the cold, to the sub-par food, to Jayla's no-nonsense attitude, to the fact that there's only one bed.

But as conditions worsen, they have to rely on each other to survive. They discover they have more in common than they realize, and soon they find plenty more reasons to stay together than just warmth...

About The Author

Ellie Finch is a cat-petting, globe-trotting feminist, fangirl, and author. With a master's degree in International Conflict Resolution, she has a background in youth leadership, community-level peacebuilding, storytelling for social change, and social justice programming that empowers women and girls. As an author, Ellie independently publishes romance novels that celebrate humor in love, equal partnerships, and sexy consent. A proudly queer/bisexual woman, she writes a diversity of stories with some straight couples and some LGBTQIAP+ couples. She lives in Florida with her cinnamon-roll husband, and their snuggly, chunky cat. She is a member of the Romance Writers of America, a devoted introvert, and a fierce Slytherin.

www.ingramcontent.com/pod-product-compliance
Lightning Source LLC
Chambersburg PA
CBHW061940170626
46813CB00006B/2484